Lois Myse

Kiss, Inc.

By Lois Wyse

Fiction

KISS, INC.

THE ROSEMARY TOUCH

Poetry

LOVE POEMS FOR THE VERY MARRIED

ARE YOU SURE YOU LOVE ME?

I LOVE YOU BETTER NOW

A WEEPING EYE CAN NEVER SEE

LOVETALK

WET PAINT AND OTHER SIGNS OF LOVE

Nonfiction

MRS. SUCCESS

LOIS WYSE

Doubleday & Company, Inc., Garden City, New York, 1977

All of the characters in this book are fictitious, and any resemblance to actual persons, living or dead, is purely coincidental.

Library of Congress Cataloging in Publication Data

Wyse, Lois.
Kiss, inc.

I. Title.
PZ4.W99Ki [PS3573.Y74] 813'.5'4
ISBN: 0-385-12083-4
Library of Congress Catalog Card Number 76-42417

PRINTED IN THE UNITED STATES OF AMERICA
FIRST EDITION

For
Betty Prashker, Grace Bechtold, and Phyllis Levy,
who sometimes listened, often advised, and always understood.
With thanks and sincere appreciation.

Kiss, Inc.

Prologue

Chester Masterson walked out of the Fifth Avenue apartment house, mumbled good morning to the doorman, nodded to his limousine driver and settled in the rear seat for the fourteen-block ride to his office. The morning newspapers lay untouched on the seat of the car because Chester's mind was not on the news of the day. Nor was it on the increasing traffic, the worsening weather or the ambulance that came screaming past his car. Chester's mind was where it usually was; Chester's mind was on Kiss, Inc. In just a few days the company's annual sales convention would begin in California. The business sessions had been planned months in advance. Now there was no need to think about them. Instead Chester was thinking about the convention events that would center around him.

It would all begin with the flight out of New York. He would go in the company jet, of course, and he would pick and choose his flying companions among the Kiss executives. Chester liked seeing the expectant looks on their faces. Would they be asked to fly with him this year? Would they be ignored? And what did it mean to their careers? Chester liked to keep the executive group dangling until just a few days prior to their departure. That was Chester's trademark: pressure, pressure and more pressure. Never let them forget who's boss.

Long ago Chester Masterson had promised himself he would always be boss. He meant to keep that promise despite the not so subtle suggestions from Wall Street for more sophisticated management.

Sophisticated management, hah.

The only thing Wall Street bankers knew how to suggest was The Executive Shuffle.

Well, maybe The Executive Shuffle was in the cards for Kiss, Inc., now. Chester laughed inwardly at his own joke. He was at a nice age, young enough to make jokes and old enough to enjoy them. Of course Chester wasn't really old. Nowadays sixty-seven didn't seem old, particularly if you were talking about yourself. But sixty-seven was an age that made Wall Street nervous. As soon as a chief executive reached his late fifties, bankers began nervously looking for a line of succession. They were relieved when Chester brought in younger marketing men and moved them along from windowless office to windowed office to corner office. Now the bankers were recommending that Chester become chairman of the executive committee. Well, maybe he would. But he certainly wouldn't give up the running of the company.

Of course the bankers were not the only ones speculating about the future of Kiss, Inc.

The rumors, according to Chester's barber, were that Henry Burns, the president, would become chairman if Chester stepped up. And the bets were on for president.

The politicking for the presidency would begin in earnest the moment they left for California.

Chester could hardly wait to see what would happen when the maneuvering started.

He opened his eyes, sat upright, and smiled.

Chester was happy for the first time in weeks. He was going to have a ringside seat for the fight of the year. He would be audience and referee. But, most important, he would crown the champion.

Chester loved the taste of power.

Barbara pulled her flannel robe about her and listened, but the phone in the penthouse apartment did not ring. Oh, there were the usual calls. Her fiancé. Someone to tell her she won ten free dancing lessons. And a wrong number. But nothing that mattered. Long ago Barbara Anderson had learned that there is no noise louder than a silent phone. She put a fresh sheet of paper in her typewriter and wrote, "Product Q Market Plan: A Breakthrough in Skin Care." She knew she would find a better opening line for her presentation at the Kiss convention, but she had days to come up with the right words. She was still free to play with ideas. She looked at her watch. 5 A.M. Well, if you didn't have the man you wanted, the safest thing to play with was ideas.

China Edgar looked at the lineup: mink coat, sable jacket, lynx coat, full-length badger cape, and she wept softly.

"Now what are you crying about?" Tim Edgar asked in an exasperated tone.

"I don't know which c-c-coat to take to the Kiss convention. What if I take the wrong one?" China sobbed.

"Don't take any," her husband said with a sweep of his hand. "Who can be impressed by you anyway? Everybody already knows your daddy owns the company."

Jennifer Johnson wakened slowly, rolled over on her back, and looked up. There in the convex mirror on the ceiling above the bed she could see her naked self, sprawled and sensual. She ran her hands down her body and smiled with satisfaction. She turned to her side and suddenly became aware of another body in the bed. She was not startled, just mildly curious. She poked the body gently. "Who's there?" she asked.

"I'm leaving. I'm leaving," came the muffled tones.

She pulled the covers back to see what she might discover, and when she saw the small, lean male body she threw back her head and laughed a deep, throaty laugh. "Wouldn't you know it? Only Henri, the best hairdresser in New York."

"I'm on my way," he said as he sat upright and pulled his legs to the side of the bed.

She reached over and touched him. "Don't leave. You have to do my hair today."

He looked puzzled. "Isn't that why I came here last night?"

"It looks like we never got around to that, and I have to go to a meeting and then to the Kiss convention later today."

"But I must leave," he insisted. "I'm doing the Duchess at ten."

"You are about to put royalty ahead of me," she teased.
He was standing next to the bed.
"You can't go," she said pleadingly. "How would it look if Jennifer Johnson, former great American movie star and now outstanding TV spokeswoman, had messy hair?"
"That's right," sighed the hairdresser, "America can only tolerate messy lives."

Linda Sugarman opened the closet door, removed six of her husband's suits, took her scissors and carefully hacked the legs off all of the pants at the knees. She had sawed the last leg and was surveying her handiwork when Ken Sugarman walked in.
"What are you doing?" he asked in amazement.
"What do you think I'm doing, dummy?" his wife answered. "I told you six times to get some new clothes for the Kiss convention. Now you have no choice. Damn it. Go out today and buy some sports jackets and slacks, and don't go to this convention looking like a 1952 department store mannequin."
"Yes, dear," Ken Sugarman said meekly.

Sharon Kennedy looked at her one piece of scarred canvas luggage. "Is that the pits or is that the pits?" she moaned.
Tom Sales, the writer she loved and lived with, patted her cheek understandingly. "Listen, Sharon," he said philosophically, "you don't always get to go to the White House. Everything you report doesn't lead to big time news."
"But for *Newsweek* to assign me to cover a stinking cosmetics convention. Man, that is the worst."
"Maybe it will give you new insights."
"Into mink coats and lipstick?"
"You don't have to hate people just because they're rich."
"You're wrong. I love rich people. It's being poor that I hate."
"Well, maybe you'll do this story for *Newsweek*, and you'll end up marrying the chairman of Kiss. He gets married a lot, doesn't he?"
Sharon guffawed. "Chester Masterson? Babes, let me tell you something. On my list of desirable men Chester Masterson is lower than King Kong. Rated on a scale of one to seven, Chester Masterson is minus three."

"Shut up, Sharon, and give me one last—"

Her mouth covered his before he could finish the sentence.

In the candlelight Jo Burns's silver hair shone softly.

"That was an excellent dinner, my dear," Henry said.

"Thank you."

"The roast was perfect."

"Yes. Evangeline is the best cook we have ever had."

"I wish we could take her to the Kiss convention and not have to eat the kind of dreary food we will get."

"Oh, we'll survive, Henry. We always do."

"Yes. Indeed. Oh, I have a meeting before we leave for the convention. Why don't you drive to the airport and leave your car? We take off from Westchester."

"Who's on the company plane?"

"The usuals. China and Tim. Linda and Ken. Barbara. Jennifer. Us. And Chester, of course."

"Oh yes, Chester. What would any of us be without Chester?"

"Oh," smiled Henry, "without Chester we'd just be a planeload of happy people. With Chester we're a bunch of bickering, miserable, uptight, scared human beings."

Jo raised her wineglass. "To Chester, the son of a bitch who runs my life."

Henry raised his glass and met her eyes. Silently he pledged, "Not for long."

Chester Masterson is probably the only man in the world who got a divorce without telling his wife he wanted one. When Chester and Gladyce Masterson (the former Gladys O'Grady Shawn, wife of a New York policeman) were married ten years, Chester threw an intimate dinner party in their New York apartment. Thirty-two of their nearest and dearest were invited. Chester gave Gladyce a four-carat diamond drop (the old Gladys didn't know a carat from a carrot), a sable coat, and one share of stock in Kiss, Inc., the family firm founded, run, chaired, supervised, and second-guessed by Chester. Everybody thought it was adorable. Who but Chester would have thought of something so cute as one share of stock? It was particularly cute because Monday morning after Chester had drunk his morning coffee, eaten his doughnut, and gone to work, he had also called his attorneys. At ten o'clock Gladyce was awakened from a sound Seconal sleep. She thought the call was from one of her girlfriends ready to start a heavy week's boutiquing along Madison Avenue. Instead it was Chester's lawyer. He told her to get dressed and come right to his office. Gladyce was so excited she put her pantyhose on backwards. She knew that one share of stock meant that ten thousand were to follow. But when she got to the fancy Wall Street offices, she found that instead of giving her more stock, Chester wanted to buy back her one share. For one million dollars and his freedom. The stock sold for $62.25 that day. She was offered one million dollars. Cash. Gladyce hesitated. But only for a minute. When you have a father living on social security and a mother who still thinks $14.95 is a lot of money to pay for a pair of shoes, you do not pass up any million-dollar opportunities. Even if it means giving up a husband you don't love and a life that you do. Look, the attorney told her, for a million dollars you can still have a nice life. Gladyce didn't see it that way. Besides she had watched a lot of daytime television. She thought she had better cry for the attorney just the way women do on "As the World Turns." On the way out she remembered between sniffles to ask why Chester had never told her he wanted a divorce. The answer was simple. The attorney put his arm around her shoulder. "Gladyce dear, Chester couldn't bear to see you hurt."

Chester Masterson arrived for the meeting in the boardroom exactly twenty-seven minutes late. Why not? That was one of the perquisites of the job. That and the limousine and the yacht, the private dining room off the office, the unlimited expense account, and the decorating of the triplex on Park Avenue. He looked around the table. Well, even though he was faring comfortably, the others were not hurting. No. No matter how you looked at it, Kiss, Inc., and its executives were not hurting.

Chester reached into the small cabinet next to his high back chair and fumbled until he found the right shape . . . aaah, there it was. The Gelusil. He popped two in his mouth. Around the table bodies straightened; all eyes turned toward the chairman because at Kiss, Inc., the sound of two Gelusils being chewed by the chairman meant the same thing as the sound of a gavel. The meeting was now called to order.

Chester stared at Jennifer Johnson. Damned if she didn't remind him of his last wife Gladyce. He wondered if Jennifer had to have a present every day, too. Some little bauble from Cartier or Tiffany to make her smile each night. The thought was enough to make him look for a third Gelusil.

Jennifer squirmed. Oh God. He's looking at me. I better say something. "Chester, are you sure you want me at the convention?"

"Of course," he barked. Dumb ass broad. Just like Gladyce. These women always did better with their backs than with their heads. "Why wouldn't we want the television spokeswoman for

Kiss, Inc., at the convention? Do you think a bunch of horny salesmen want to look at me? Or even handsome Henry?"

Henry Burns, the president of Kiss, Inc., winced. Why did Chester always do that? Did paying a man $250,000 a year plus bonus entitle him to unlimited insults? Damned right it did. So long as the man was Chester Masterson, every employee could expect to be the victim of those little digs. It was part of the deal, like pension plans and annuities.

"Jennifer won't be the only star at the convention, Chester. We have an all-star dinner the last night. . . ."

"Who'd you get?" That was the kind of question that set Chester Masterson apart from many executives. Chester was not a penny-pincher. He never asked, "What did it cost?" His concern was quality. He was that way with his products, too. No skimping ever. If it cost a hundred dollars a pound more to get an ingredient from Switzerland, every executive at Kiss, Inc., knew that Chester would pay the price.

"We've got the number one rock singer, a girl. . . ."

"I hate loud music."

"Don't worry, Chester. She's on the Joni Mitchell side."

"Who's Joni Mitchell?"

"Well, let's say she's like a contemporary Dinah Shore."

Chester nodded. He knew Dinah Shore. Wasn't she that dark-haired girl married to Steve Lawrence?

Henry took a breath and pushed on. "Let me fill you in on a few more details. Tim is setting up seminars . . ."

Chester snorted. "Tim couldn't set up drinks, let alone seminars."

"Sir." Tim stood at his chair. "I think you ought to see what we're doing before you pass judgment." Tim Edgar was the only person in Kiss who addressed Chester as "Sir." That was because Tim was the only person at Kiss who had gone to Choate. He was also the only person who was Chester's son-in-law. The rumor was that Chester would personally have divorced Tim Edgar a long time ago only then he would have had his daughter China on his hands, and he never did know what to do with one woman. Women in groups, the mass market, that was Chester's forte. One woman was always his downfall.

Henry came to Tim's rescue. It was getting to be a habit. "Tim as our marketing director has worked with the district managers, found the topics that will really interest the sales force, and I think we'll get some good give and take in the sessions."

"What's Ken doing?"

Ken Sugarman looked worried at the mention of his name, but he looked even more worried when no one mentioned him. Ken had been at Kiss, Inc., all his business life, all sixteen years, and only last year had been named vice-president in charge of the cosmetics and toiletries division. Until then the division had been called Hair Care, Nail Care, Skin Care, and Body Care, and each had had its own head. Now the company was doing what the Wall Street advisers had recommended. They were initiating twentieth-century management techniques.

"What's Ken doing?" Chester repeated the question.

Ken had assumed Henry would answer, but Henry was quiet. Sure. Henry only came to rescue sons-in-law. "I'll answer that myself, Chester." Ken's voice sounded unnaturally high. Even after sixteen years Chester still scared the hell out of him. "I contacted the Washington people, and I realized that to put another one of those parrots up there who tells you what the labeling law is about and why we need the Food and Drug Administration is too much. Instead I called the three networks and finally decided that it would be best if we got John Kingsley, who's the . . ."

Chester smiled. He knew who John Kingsley was. John Kingsley was the friendly face that gave him the seven-o'clock news. He liked John Kingsley. John Kingsley was accurate and never mush-mouthed like some of the men around this table. "Good going, Ken. That's using your head. Tim, you could learn from Ken. He's got a smart head. All those Jewish boys do."

Ken's face was a mask. So was Henry's. Damn it. The two Jews at the table. Why did Chester always have to finger them?

Ken wondered how to describe this scene to Linda. They both knew that John Kingsley was Chester's favorite newscaster. Come to think of it, it was Linda who reminded him. Linda was the kind of wife who never forgot a birthday, an anniversary, or the favorite commentator of her husband's boss. Linda wouldn't understand how Chester could congratulate you with half a sentence and destroy you with the other half. Even though she had once worked at Kiss, Inc., she never saw Chester in the boardroom. Every time that Linda Sugarman saw Chester Masterson he exuded charm and good will. She'd never believe that the Chester Masterson who apologized for his occasional hell or damn spoken in front of her could break heads in a meeting. Unless you sat in a Kiss meeting you couldn't believe a man like Chester still existed. An individualist in a country of conformists. An independent who bowed only to the will of Wall Street . . . and even then all action was taken as slowly as possible. No, Linda would never believe the Chester Masterson of the marble-paneled boardroom. But who would? Who would believe a company run on the caste system, a company where there was an established pecking order for meetings. To the right of the chairman sat the president. Next to him came vice-presidents in order of importance. The importance varied from week to week. On the chairman's left sat All Others. They included people like Jennifer Johnson and an interchangeable cast of thousands, everyone from advertising agency executives to product specialists, stock analysts, and guest experts. Ken wished that Linda could sit in on one of these meetings. Then maybe she'd understand why it was damned tough to try to become president of this company. Henry was president because he didn't take it too seriously. He could roll with the punches.

Ken tuned back into the meeting. Henry was talking. ". . . and so, Chester, I think we have a stimulating agenda plus the chance to relax and have some informal discussions. One of the big bonuses of a convention is the opportunity to get out of the office, away from the telephones, and just take a walk or have a drink with people you never seem to have the time to see in New York."

"If everybody spent more time working and less time talking, we'd all be better off," Chester snapped.

"Careful, Chester," Henry smiled, "or you'll lose your reputation as Mr. Nice Guy."

Chester managed a faint grimace that could pass for a smile. "What's the girl going to do?"

The girl was Barbara Anderson. She sighed. She was getting used to being The Girl to Chester, but she wished he could get a better fix on her role in the company.

Henry cleared his throat. "Chester, I keep telling you that you have to improve your human relations." When he saw Chester's features stiffen and the cheek muscle twitch, he knew he had gone too far. He quit the joking. "Chester, Barbara is responsible for one of the most significant presentations at the convention. It's great to talk about this year's figures and the ways we will meet them, but since all consumer products businesses live in the future, we are going to introduce the concept for Product Q at the meeting."

"Product Q is a secret, and I don't want anyone knowing about it yet."

"I don't agree, Chester." It was Barbara's voice coming in now. Barbara, cool and contained at thirty-one, spoke briskly. "Part of all selling is the fire you build in advance." She looked at Henry and said firmly, "I want to start fires."

"What good will that do?" Chester asked.

"No, Chester." Now she dug deeper. "What harm will that do?"

"It will give our competitors an advantage."

"No way. It takes two years of lab work just to get the formula. Right, Dr. Schulz?"

Dr. Wilhelm Schulz, who Henry believed was a former camp director at Buchenwald, prepared to give his usual lengthy answer. After six minutes of discourse on hormones and additives and supplements, Chester interrupted:

"For Christ's sake, Schulz, what do you think? Should we tell our sales force or not?"

"Ve should tell." Only the v's and w's remained as proof of Dr. Schulz's previous life. The rest of his speech was as clipped as his straight dyed black hair.

Barbara smiled at Schulz. Good. For once he came to the point when asked. "We'll plan to go ahead with the introduction, then," Barbara said as authoritatively as if she had the power to make the decision.

"I'm still not sure," Chester insisted.

"Well, until you make up your mind, I will have to be ready," Barbara answered. "We'll have the samples, the plan . . . maybe even the advertising. Right, Howard?"

Howard Weston, in his black suit, black tie, and black horn-rimmed glasses, looked like a black-and-white ad for Frank Campbell Funeral Chapel. The only thing missing was the organ music when he spoke. "No. No advertising yet." Even the tone was funereal.

"Why?" Now Henry wanted some answers.

"Because I need package design first."

"You're a lazy goddamned bastard." Now Chester came to life. "If you weren't so busy going out to lunch with space salesmen, you'd have the ads. I want the ads for that convention."

Barbara sat back and relaxed. Easy victory. Just get Chester to hate somebody enough, and you could win your point. Product Q was going to be introduced at . . . what was the name of that place again? Oh yes, The Gates of Paradise. Some name for a convention place in California. The name dripped with ormolu and angels. She hated it already.

"One more thing." Henry could see that Chester's attention was now wandering. "Carol here," he pointed to Carol Morris at the opposite end of the table because, even though Carol had been with Kiss, Inc., for ten years, Chester never remembered women's names, "Carol here now heads the training school for department store salespeople, so she is going to do a beauty clinic for wives."

Chester's eyes narrowed. "Wives? Who the hell said there could be wives at this convention?"

"I did, Chester." Henry was breathing deeply. "I don't want guys whoring around. I don't want marriages breaking up over this meeting."

"If men want to run around, they will anyway."

"You're right, but at least we are not responsible. If a man brings his wife, she loves the company. I've learned that the more a man gets his wife involved in his career, the better he performs."

And what about the man who gets another woman involved in his career? Barbara wondered.

"I'd like it better without wives," Chester grumbled.

"Look," smiled Henry, "you like your life better without women. That doesn't mean the rest of us do." He smiled benignly at Barbara.

"Three wives. Three strikes. I struck out in marriage." It was

Chester's standard answer which had been written for him by Howard Weston after the third divorce, the one from Gladys-Gladyce.

"Just remember one thing," Chester said, closing the cabinet drawer and locking in the Gelusil until the next meeting, "just because you have wives with you doesn't mean we won't work. We will work like hell. Day and night. We'll have meetings whenever I want them, and I don't care what your wives say. This is no vacation. It's not a party. By the way, what do husbands do if they're married to somebody like Barbara?"

Barbara shook her head. Chester never could speak to her directly . . . always through another. Some kind of woman hang-up of his. On second thought he did the same thing with men. Chester has a people hang-up, she decided. Well, no time for thoughts like that. "In my case my husband will not go with me because I am not married. And the man I'm seeing is a doctor involved in cancer research and can't leave his project."

"But his girlfriend can leave him," Chester smiled.

"He understands the pressures of my career, and I respect the demands of his."

"All right. All right." Chester was impatient now. He didn't want to parry with this woman. He was ready to leave, his hand on the twenty-four-carat doorknob. "One more thing. I forgot to tell you. I promised *Newsweek* they could cover the convention. They're doing a cover story on 'The American Convention: How Conventional Is It?' and they asked if we would be the prototype company. I said yes."

The door slammed behind Chester. "How do you have a meeting with the world watching?" asked Howard Weston.

"Don't look at me," said Henry. "He didn't ask my permission. But then, Howard old buddy, when did Chester Masterson ever ask anybody's permission before dropping bombs?"

When Chester Masterson was twenty-three years old, he decided it was time he went into business for himself, so he stole an idea. The year was 1932. Chester was a drug salesman, which was not the most exciting job in the world, but in 1932 there was a Great Depression, and people were very lucky to be anything other than unemployed. Simply having a job, however, was not enough for Chester. Chester wanted to run things. He had entrepreneurial dreams. He also had drive, nerve, daring, and a hell of a lot of larceny in his blood. One day Chester made a sales call at Sam's Kwik Korner Drugs, and after Sam signed the order he invited Chester to stop at the fountain for a Coke. Sam Humphrey loved science, and he had been the smartest boy in his high school class in Albany, New York, in 1926. He went to college to become a doctor, but by the time he was ready for medical school the crash had come. So Sam became a pharmacist because it was cheaper and quicker. However, Sam never gave up playing in his lab. While they sipped their Cokes, Sam and Chester talked about the weather and the WPA and the Blue Eagle and Franklin Delano Roosevelt. And then Sam told Chester about a formula he had developed in his laboratory, a formula for nail color. Chester laughed because he thought nail color was a pretty dumb idea since it didn't really work. But Sam said it worked if you made it right, and he did have a formula and damned if it wasn't going to be the best thing Chester ever saw. Since Chester would not believe him, Sam had to show him. Then when Chester still couldn't believe it, Sam demonstrated the nail color. He put some right on Chester's very own fingernails. But when Chester still didn't believe it, Sam gave him the formula. Chester finally believed. He believed so deeply that he ran home and started making phone calls and finding a lab to duplicate the formula. And the next thing you knew there was this nail color, and it was called Kiss. The reason Chester named it Kiss was that Sam heard Chester had taken his formula, so he called him and said he thought it was a cheap mean rotten thing to do. Chester told him not to worry. And Sam said, "Is this some kind of kiss-off?" And Chester said, "Not a kiss-off, a kiss." And Sam thought Chester said that Kiss was now the name of the product, so he answered, "That's a funny name for nail stuff. Kiss. Ha ha ha." And Chester, who didn't like anyone to laugh at him, not even back in 1932 when there wasn't much to laugh about, said, "There is not a goddamned thing wrong with naming a company Kiss." And about ten years later when the company really started rolling Chester was still sending Sam samples of all the new products. And Sam's Kwik Korner Drugs was never pushed for payment to Kiss. As the credit manager of Kiss, Inc., told Sam one day, "Chester Masterson never forgets his friends."

Sunday

"The Gates of Paradise, a forty-five-minute drive from the San Diego Airport, is as perfect as a capped tooth and just about as real," Sharon Kennedy typed. She looked out the window and shook her head. What an unlikely place for Sharon Kennedy, twenty-five-year-old Girl Idealist, to be. The Gates of Paradise was exactly the kind of place Sharon Kennedy avoided in real life. Now she was here on assignment. The ninety-dollar-a-day room tab was being picked up by her magazine. What the hell, she thought. I might as well relax and enjoy a sybaritic week. No, not week. It was three days, she remembered. Well, it will seem like a week. What can you really learn at a three-day convention for Kiss, Inc., when you believe the greatest cosmetic is loving?

From her chair at the desk in her room Sharon could see people arriving, carts filled with Gucci and Vuitton luggage, an occasional Argentine leather piece. No plastic carry-on luggage here, she thought. What would they think of her beat-up canvas flight bag? Come to think of it, what would they think of her? How would all these people who thrived on making women into something they were not react to Sharon, who did not want to be remade? Come to think of it, in some ways she did want revising. She stood up and walked to the full-length mirror in the bathroom. Sharon was nude because that was the way she worked best. She liked to write without restrictive clothing; she took everything off. She believed that when you stripped your body you opened your mind. Friends who dropped by generally understood, and Tom Sales loved it. He also loved her. They had lived together for six months, on and off really, because they were both involved in magazine assignments.

She had met Tom a year earlier when she was doing a piece on young New York writers. A friend gave her Tom's name, and they met in the garden of the Museum of Modern Art. They spent the whole afternoon talking, and then they went to Chinatown, and then because it seemed silly to separate they went to bed, something they continued to do from that day on. It took six months, however, before they decided to live together. Sharon still didn't know whether she liked the idea. Well, that wasn't something she was going to think about this week. No, this week she was going to think about Kiss, Inc., American conventions, and Sharon.

She looked at herself full view in the bathroom mirror and shuddered slightly. She turned to the side and looked again. It looked worse. It looked about ten pounds worse. She couldn't believe her body. Health foods might be a good head trip, but they certainly didn't do much for your body when all your exercise was confined to typing sixty words a minute. She reached for the robe hanging on the bathroom door. Maybe she would try the steam rooms and massage tables of The Gates of Paradise. It was all part of the story anyway.

Sharon opened the door of her cottage and then closed it. Can I really go out there? she wondered. Can I get a story in this Disneyland for grownups? She opened the door and looked again. The Gates of Paradise was not all tinsel and frou-frou. If one looked beyond the glitter of the buildings in the foreground, there were the mountains on one side and the sea on the other. She would remember that, she promised herself, as she walked across the compound to the Bathhouse. An unlikely name for a fancy place, she thought, but that was one of The Gates' gimmicks: no unpronounceable names. After all, The Gates of Paradise was host to business conventions of many of the five hundred largest corporations in America, and they didn't want a bunch of unpronounceable Spanish names for meeting rooms. It was easier for Midwesterners and Easterners and Southerners to meet in the Living Room, the Bathhouse, the Dining Room, the Exercise Rooms than in all kinds of haciendas. Meeting rooms for conferences were simply "A," "B," "C," through "M." The Gates of Paradise was successful because the center offered more than screens, projectors, and blackboards for meetings. The Gates of Paradise offered all the advantages of a spa: a place to exercise the body while using the mind. There was a golf course, tennis courts, steam and sauna rooms, herbal wraps, massage and exercise facilities. The Gates of Paradise advertised itself as a quasi-vacation. Corporations lined up to book conventions because it offered them a chance to give their employees relaxation at company expense, and since half those expenses were tax deductible, it made good business sense. Without the U. S. Government, there would probably be no Paradise.

Sharon reached in the pocket of her white terry robe and fished for the little piece of paper with the name of the woman who was to be her guide for the week. Barbara Anderson. The advertising manager had called her in New York and told her they would assign someone from public relations. But Sharon knew that would mean a company story she didn't want. "Can't I have someone with corporate responsibility?" she asked. And four phone calls later they gave her Barbara Anderson. A dried-up business prune, Sharon decided in advance. She wondered whether she ought to call her before going to the Bathhouse, the steam-sauna-Jacuzzi pool center. No, she would find her later.

The Bathhouse, a small, round, wooden structure at one end of The Gates of Paradise, was a single large room with a half-wall circling the Jacuzzi pool, the focal point. At the near end of the

Bathhouse were a sauna room, a steam room, and showers. At the sides were dressing alcoves and scales, and across the back a room for herbal wraps.

Sharon tried to take it all in. A white-uniformed female attendant came forward quickly. "What would you like?"

"I would like to be ten pounds thinner." Sharon smiled when she said it.

"What are you willing to do?" Good heavens, was this attendant serious?

"Well, I don't want to murder or steal."

The attendant looked puzzled. Sharon sighed. The attendant, who looked Sharon's age, evidently had no sense of humor. Maybe that's how it was in body places. You forgot about the head.

"Look." Sharon decided to try another approach. "I'd like to relax all my New York tensions. What's the best thing to do?"

Now the attendant looked confident. "Try the Jacuzzi family pool. This is an adaptation of the Japanese style. You will find several other women there. I assume you are with the Kiss convention."

"Not exactly."

"Well, they are, and perhaps you can meet them."

"Are they nice?"

The attendant looked surprised. Editorial comment was not part of her canned speech.

"Come on," urged Sharon, "are they cool or are they the pits?"

"The pits?"

"Forget it." Sharon took off her robe. After all, if you are the pits, how can you recognize the pits?

"What do I do with the robe?"

"Don't you want to use a dressing room?"

"If I'm going to go into a pool with nothing on, what should I start hiding?"

The attendant took the robe. "I'm hanging you here." She pointed to a gold hook.

"I'll bet you're hanging me." Sharon walked behind the half-wall, and there in a crescent-shaped pool about the size of ten big bathtubs were five women. "Good afternoon," Sharon said to the Jacuzzi-ing women. She bowed from the waist and put her palms together in her best fake-Japanese style, then she walked down the four steps into the pool.

The women looked at her, but no one said anything.

"Wow, this is warm."

Still no one said anything.

"Been in here long?"

Finally one woman answered. She looked as if she was Sharon's age. "I came in five minutes ago."

Sharon nodded. Well, so far that was the friendliest thing anyone had said to her. She took another look at the woman who spoke. Even under the water she could see that she was thin and gorgeous. How unfair. She probably had wine and ice cream and pasta every day and went out to lunch with the ladies and complained that she could never gain a pound. Not only did she have a nice body, Sharon decided, she had a glamour face. Not a nice face, but a glamour face. Straight black hair and almond-shaped blue eyes against very white skin.

"My name is Sharon," she said to Gorgeous Body.

"My name is China," Gorgeous Body answered.

"China?" She was incredulous. "You look like china. Bone china."

"My mother was a romantic."

"And your father?"

"Are you kidding?"

"No."

"My father is Chester Masterson."

Sharon thought she was going to sink down to the bottom of the Jacuzzi. She could see the headlines now. Girl Reporter Whirlpools Self to Oblivion. Oh, dumbness. Of course this was China Masterson Edgar, the headline beauty. She looked for the trademark fingernails. Everybody who ever read a tabloid knew about Chester Masterson's daughter and her fabulous fingernails. The nails that extended two inches beyond the fingers were always lacquered in China Red, a color that Kiss changed from season to season, and were square-cut at the ends. No tapering nails for China. Instead her nails were square-cut, just like her diamonds. So this was China Masterson Edgar. Naked yet.

Sharon looked down the waterline to check the other bodies. Arms extended along the ledge, legs thrust forward, and breasts bobbing in the water, it was hard to tell if anybody was Anybody. Well, she might as well tell China who she was and get the introductions settled. "My name is Sharon Kennedy, and I'm with *Newsweek* magazine. I'm here for your convention because I am going to research a piece on the American convention."

"Tim told me."

Tim. Of course Tim. That was the Establishment husband. Sharon had researched him, too. An Ivy League meatball.

At the other end of the pool a voice said, "Sharon, we're supposed to find each other. I'm Barbara Anderson."

"I don't believe it. You're beautiful. I thought Barbara Anderson was going to be a tough old bitch."

"I am," Barbara laughed. "I'm over thirty."

"Thirty-one?"

"Right."

Sharon shook her head in disbelief. Barbara Anderson, a vice-president of this high-powered company, and she looked soft and pretty. Maybe business really didn't rot you all over. Just inside. Barbara's long brown hair was piled on top of her head accenting her high cheekbones and straight nose. There was understanding, maybe even humor, in her gray eyes. And if there was one thing Sharon was going to have to find these three days, it was going to be one person with a sense of humor.

"Are the rest of you from Kiss?" Sharon asked.

Barbara took over. "I'll introduce you, Sharon. On your left in the white hair and blue eyes is the wife of our president, Mrs. Henry Burns, better known as Jo. And to her left is Mrs. Kenneth Sugarman. Linda is married to one of our vice-presidents."

"I am married to a senior vice-president," Linda added, "and I read *Newsweek* every week, and I think it is a wonderful magazine."

Sharon almost swallowed water. "Look, Mrs. Sugarman, I'm not the publisher. I only work there."

"You people must lead such a fascinating life." Linda Sugarman was not to be deterred. "Let's spend some time together this week."

"Absolutely," said Sharon. This was going to shape up as some kind of experience. She looked to her right. An aging sex symbol was stretching her legs right beside her. It was Jennifer Johnson, the not-quite movie star who was now raking it in making commercials for Kiss cosmetics. "I know who you are." There was no mistaking the short, black, curly-haired look, the big round violet eyes. "I've always wanted to ask you something," Sharon said, "and this is my big chance. Are you really six feet tall?"

Jennifer Johnson stood up. Not only was she six feet tall, she had the biggest boobs Sharon had ever seen. Wait until she told Tom. God, how he'd love to be here. She was only a reporter; imagine what a writer could do with a body like Jennifer's. How could breasts that big be no-sag? Almost no fanny and a flat stomach. Jennifer was obviously living proof that sex was good for your body, for Jennifer was evidently well into her forties, and her well-publicized life style was that of a girl of twenty.

Jennifer looked down at five-foot one-inch Sharon. "Any other questions, honey?"

"Not at the moment. I don't have a notebook with me, but I have a lot of things I'd like to ask you."

"What are you trying to do with this story?" Barbara asked.

"I'm not sure. It's up to me to report what I see happening at the convention."

Linda laughed. "Most of what happens you won't see."

"Why?"

"Because everybody knows that behind the cabanas and under the bushes there are lots of secret meetings, and that's where everything happens."

"As the president's wife," Jo said, "I've seen this for a long time. Linda's right. What happens is that people have a pretty good idea of the kinds of changes that have to be made in a company, and then they get together outside the office and get some of the comments outside New York. You know, the West Coast sales manager tells what he thinks, and somebody from the Chicago office begins talking . . . and next thing you know we change vice-presidents."

"And presidents," said Linda.

Only the sound of the Jacuzzi was heard for a few seconds.

"There may be times this will seem like a political convention," Linda said.

"Or a family gathering," added China.

"Like a family," said Jo, "you'll find that we have our differences among ourselves, but to the outside world we try to present a united front. Look, I've been in this 105° water long enough. You know, if you stay in too long it's enervating, and we have a big get-together tonight."

"It's the patio party, isn't it?" Sharon asked.

Jo was already walking up the steps of the pool, and the attendant was handing her an oversize towel. She wrapped herself, and now Sharon could see her as the handsome woman she really was. Such elegance and composure. No wonder she was the president's wife. She wondered if the president came right out of Central Casting, too.

"The patio party is always the most fun for me," Jo Burns said. "It's my chance to say hello to everybody I haven't seen for a year, and the first night no one has had a chance to fall flat in a meeting or catch hell for poor sales performances, so it's kind of sweet and friendly." She waved. "See you all later."

Linda snorted. "Sweet and friendly. Bull. If you are the president's wife, then maybe there is no pressure on you, but even China knows that at Kiss, Inc., the pressure's always on."

"I think that's an act that Jo puts on," China said. "I don't really think she is all that sweet and sugary. I think she kind of masks herself in order to be Henry's wife."

"Well, if she can do that," Barbara said, "it must be great for Henry."

"You sound envious," Sharon said.

"I am," said Barbara quickly. "The only thing I need in order to function better as an executive is a wife."

"Wives aren't what they used to be," Sharon reminded her.

"At Kiss they are," Linda said. "You learn very fast here that if your husband is going to get ahead, you had better help him."

"What do you do?" Sharon was puzzled.

"What are you? Some kind of Mary Poppins character?" Linda asked. "Wives have to befriend wives, and they have to entertain, and they have to send presents and say how interesting it is that your child wrote a report on grapefruit seeds, and yes read it to me again. That's what wives have to do."

"You don't sound as if you thrive on it," Sharon said.

"It's part of the Corporate Gavotte. Three times around the boardroom; it's good for your career."

"Where'd you go to school?" Linda sounded smart. Smart smart. Not kind smart.

"Oh, I'll tell you my story," Linda promised, "but first I follow the leader. When Jo goes out of the pool, as far as I'm concerned it's everybody out of the pool. I'm going to put a few hot rollers in my hair. Jo may not worry about tonight, but my husband is only a vice-president, and I'm worried." Linda floated toward the steps, walked out of the Jacuzzi, and headed toward the row of little gold hooks where her robe was hanging.

"I think the water is shriveling me," said Jennifer.

"Not so anyone could notice," Sharon said. She was still fascinated by the oversize breasts.

Jennifer, either because she heard remarks about her body so often or because she was bored giving the same answers again and again, said nothing. Instead she left the pool. "See you later."

"Jennifer," China called out, "want Tim and me to pick you up at your room before the party?"

"Naw, honey, I can still walk fifty feet alone. But thanks."

"Well, we're down to three," Barbara said, "and since it takes four for bridge, I think I'll leave you ladies. Sharon, why don't I pick you up at your room . . . on second thought, come to my suite . . . it's 6B, and we'll have a drink together at five-thirty before going to the patio party."

"Thanks, Barbara."

China turned to Sharon imploringly. "You won't leave me alone, will you?"

Sharon looked at the frightened girl next to her. Oh no. This beautiful, fragile creature who has nothing but looks and money and power does not want Sharon Klutz to leave. It was too much to believe. "I won't leave you, China, but why don't we get out of this big bathtub and come down to my room where we can put something liquid in us instead of on us?"

"No," said China, "come to our suite. We always get huge suites at Kiss conventions. That's how Father remembers who I am . . . by the size of the suite."

Chester Masterson married the first nonprostitute he ever took to bed. To Chester there were two kinds of women: the kind you paid for and the kind you married. He filled his needs when he recognized them, paid for all services rendered. Afterwards he would go back to his job and she to hers. Chester was a one-dimensional young man with his eyes on the pot of gold. After he started Kiss, Inc., he found that his sexual appetites decreased in direct relationship to his business success. At the beginning company assets consisted of Chester's selling ability and his used Essex. Later it included a small plant in New Jersey and two people who filled bottles plus a part-time chemist. Chester kept the books. He kept them not because he cared so much, but because he cared so little, about the books. To Chester the product was the most important thing. He knew you couldn't resell a bad nail enamel. And you couldn't sell anything in an expanded line of products if your customers didn't like what you made in the first place. So Chester, although he didn't know the words in those days, was very careful about quality control. The books were another matter. So what if an entry wasn't absolutely accurate? Chester didn't give a damn for bankers or for money. He wanted only power and position, and the way to buy them was with money. Therefore, money was important. One day Chester went into a drugstore to sell nail enamel to the owner. He wasn't there, but his golden-haired twenty-year-old daughter came out from the desk where she was keeping her father's books to tell Chester to come back later. Instead Chester told her to leave her books and come with him. She did. She went to work for Chester balancing his books. She also kept Chester off-balance. Chester fell in love. Chester was so in love he almost forgot about the nail business. He didn't think about anything except how good it was to be inside her. Chester would drop into the office unannounced at any time—morning, lunchtime, 5 P.M.—lock the door, and undress her quickly because he could not wait for her body. One day she told him she was pregnant. Chester married her the next week. Two days later she said she had a miscarriage. Four weeks later Chester found her in bed with the boy from the grocery store. He never mentioned her name again. He could not even remember it. Chester threw her out, announced to the world that all women were whores, and he'd get them yet. Chester mated many times and married twice afterwards, but he never again touched a woman who worked for him. As the personnel director of Kiss once said, "Mr. Masterson never dips his pen in the company inkwell."

Sharon Kennedy looked around China's palatial suite. It certainly was different from her room. Hers was done in Latter Day Motel, simple but satisfactory. This room had golden angels holding back a canopy over a king-size bed.

"China, this place is like a princess's room."

"Is it?" China was standing at the bar in the living room, about forty feet from the entrance to the bedroom, where Sharon stood.

"Come on. The place I have is the pits compared to this."

"The what?"

Sharon shrugged. Nobody understood her patter. Maybe she'd better change it. "I said the place I'm in looks like lace curtain Irish compared to this."

China nodded. Sharon still had not gotten through.

"Why do you need that whole big bar in here?" Sharon asked.

"In case we want to entertain."

"Do you?"

"Of course not. I'm the boss's daughter."

"That must be terrific."

"Were you ever the boss's daughter?"

"Me? Hardly. My father has a civil service job with the city of Chicago."

"Civil service?"

"Forget it, China. It won't do a thing for my *Newsweek* story."

"I think it's unbelievable that you would have a job on *Newsweek*. You must be really smart."

"Smart in some ways, dumb in others. But then we all are. What ways are you smart, China?"

"Everybody talks about the ways I'm dumb. I'm really dumb, you know."

"Come on. You're beautiful, and you have to be smart to know how to look like that."

"No, you don't. I could show you in a minute."

Sharon sucked in her stomach. Well, even if she got rid of the unwanted bumps and bulges she couldn't look like China. Come to think of it, she didn't want to look like China. China looked like a young woman who made a career out of her face and body. Sharon was trying to make a career out of her head. "No. I'm hopeless. Outside of looking sensational, what's your biggest talent, China?"

China's eyes opened wide, and she searched her mind. Finally she answered. "Needlepoint."

"That's very good. I admire people who can do needlepoint. I can't even sew a hem." That reminded her that her blue jeans needed a new patch, and her one long skirt brought for the banquet was held together with a safety pin.

"I'm not too good. But I did do two pillows for Father's office."

"What are they like?"

"One is my right hand, and one is my left hand."

"I don't understand."

"We had my hands drawn." She extended her hands to remind Sharon. Yes, there they were. The signature hands. The nails that extended inches beyond the fingers. The nails cut in squares and polished in this season's China Red. "We had them drawn, and I needlepointed them. My father is very proud of my hands."

Bully for Daddy. Sharon tried to imagine what her own father, William Patrick Kennedy, would think of a daughter with nails like that.

"How do people in the company treat you when you're the boss's daughter?" Sharon asked.

"Most of them treat me like a little girl. Lots of these people have been here for ten years or more, and they remember when I was young and in school."

"Where did you go to school?"

"Why don't you ask where I didn't go to school. I went to every private school in New York City."

"How did that happen?"

"Oh, I'll tell you, but first I want to get out from behind the bar. What do you want to drink?"

"A Coke."

China looked at her quizzically. "I thought reporters were big drinkers."

"Some of them are, I guess."

China giggled, a little girl giggle that did not go with her big girl looks. "Well, I drink a lot."

"What do you drink?"

"Bourbon mainly. But I also like wine. And I drink scotch if that's what's around."

Sharon had the feeling she was on the edge of a story. It might not fit the story she was trying to do, but then again it might. "Have you been drinking long?"

"I really learned to drink in boarding school."

"Where did you go to boarding school?"

"You're not listening to me. I told you I went to a lot of schools."

"You're not listening to yourself. You said they were in New York. Now you're talking about boarding schools."

China splashed some ginger ale into her tall Bourbon glass, added one ice cube, and went to sit on the oversize stuffed sofa across from the bar. She kicked off her shoes and wrapped her robe tighter around her. "Hey, this may take a while." She walked back to the bar, brought the bottle of Bourbon to the coffee table in front of the sofa. "Now we can talk."

Sharon poured herself a Coke. Evidently China was so excited about her Bourbon she couldn't remember her guest's Coke. What's more, China still did not realize she had forgotten. She was drinking the Bourbon and ginger ale as quickly as if it were water. Sharon thought she ought to try to slow China down. She walked to the sofa, took the glass from China's hand, and said, "Hey, wait for me." Was China's hand trembling or did she just imagine it?

"Come on. Tell the poor girl from Chicago about the rich girl from New York."

"I'm Chester Masterson's daughter. Every psychiatrist thinks he knows the answer to that setup. And I've heard every one of them try to analyze me. I've heard everything. Honest, Sharon. Everything. I've heard my father can't relate to women. And I've heard that he regards me as a company asset. And I've heard that he never wanted kids because he hated his first wife . . ."

"Was that your mother?"

"No. I don't know much about the first wife. I don't even know much about my mother, but I'll tell you what I know about him. What I know about him is that he never loved me, still doesn't, and the only thing he can discuss with me is my nails. My father hates me, Sharon, but he loves my nails."

"You're probably dramatizing a little."

She shook her head. "I told you I went to every private school you ever heard about. I couldn't last. I'm really dumb. I can't read."

"Of course you can read."

"A little bit, but not much. I'm like some ghetto kid. I look at the pictures in *Vogue,* and I can get the easy words, but I can't read a book."

Sharon didn't know what to say. She poked the ice cube in her Coke with her finger. "Well, what did you learn at all those schools?"

"Nobody would keep me very long. I was too dumb. What I learned was not to talk much so nobody would know how dumb I am. When I was about thirteen I started to drink. I was home for Christmas holidays. Father was married to Gladyce then. Gladyce was his third wife. Anyway, I was home, and nobody even noticed. Gladyce's two kids were there, so she didn't talk to me, and my father just went to the office at ten o'clock every morning, then met Gladyce for dinner someplace around eight or nine, and they'd get home about two in the morning. So I didn't have anybody to talk to. I went to the bar one night; it was in the library where I watched television. I decided to mix a drink. There was a bottle of Bourbon out, so I took it, and it tasted terrible. I liked ginger ale, so I poured a lot of ginger ale in it. That night I went to bed and didn't cry. Do you know how good it felt to go to bed and not cry?"

Sharon's eyes were wet. Oh no, she wasn't being taken in by some poor little rich girl story, was she? Yes, she was. "And you've been drinking all these years?"

"I never really stayed in one school long enough to make friends. Two schools kicked me out for my drinking, and that's when my father started to send me to shrinks. The minute they said he had some responsibility for what I was doing, we'd quit the shrink and go to another."

"Where was your mother all this time?"

"Mostly getting married and unmarried. She's had some really strange marriages."

Sharon nodded, and China continued. "My mother came from a fancy family. You see, Father had this ghastly first marriage nobody talks about, and then he met Mother, who came from a *Mayflower* family. Her family had everything but money, and Father had lots of money by then so it should have worked. But I don't think my parents ever liked each other. I guess Mother really did marry him for the money because when I was two she took off with somebody else. She didn't even get much money from Father because he wouldn't give her me. He kept me, not because he wanted me, but because he didn't want her to have anything of his. At least that's what one psychiatrist told me. I guess that doctor was trying to make me feel good about myself." She poured a little more Bourbon into the glass. The ice cube had long since melted.

"How do you feel about yourself?"

"Terrible. I'm a thing. I'm not even a person."

"Well, I'm sure Tim loves you."

She shook her head. "Tim is my mother all over again. Fancy family and no money."

Sharon decided to forget her questions about Tim and ask about China's early life instead. "Where did your mother go after she left you and your father?"

"She married a movie actor and went to California for a couple of years. Then she went on location with him in the Middle East, and she met an Egyptian. She divorced the actor and married the Egyptian."

"What happened then?"

"It's all sort of weird. She never had any kids with the actor, but she had another daughter with the Egyptian. The daughter's name is Mary Ahmet. Did you ever hear of her?"

Sharon went through her mental name file. "No."

"She's a long-distance swimmer."

"That's not exactly my biggest sport."

"I mean she's one of the greatest long-distance swimmers in the world. She swims the English Channel and other places like that."

Sharon didn't know any other places like that, but look, everybody couldn't march for clean air. Maybe some of them had to swim for it. "So how come she's a swimmer?"

"Well, I don't know if this will make a lot of sense to you, but one of my psychiatrists explained it to me."

Sharon was beginning to think that if China had spent as much time on her present as she did understanding her past, she'd probably be in a lot better shape.

"The Egyptians are long-distance swimmers. Well, anyway, the Egyptian, Mr. Ahmet, deserted my mother and this girl. And this Mary has been swimming ever since looking for her father."

"Outrageous."

"It sounds logical to me." China drifted into a small reverie.

"China, isn't that someone at your door? Maybe your husband is coming back."

She smiled. "My husband doesn't knock. He just takes what he wants."

Sharon got up and opened the door. Barbara Anderson . . . it was Barbara fully clothed, wasn't it? "Barbara?"

She smiled. "Yes. Me Barbara. You Sharon. But you about to be Late Sharon if you do not dress for patio party. You were supposed to meet me, but you never showed, so I came looking for you."

"Want a drink, Barbara?" China called from the sofa.

"Thanks, but I'll wait until we get to the party. Come on,

Sharon, I'll walk you back to your room and answer some of your questions so you won't need a program to identify the players tonight."

"I'm telling her about me," China called.

Barbara's lips tightened. If there was one thing Kiss, Inc., didn't need, it was a confession from the chairman's daughter. Who knew what that little dum-dum would say? "That's nice." Barbara tried to keep the irritation out of her voice. Money certainly didn't care who had it, she thought. Here was this bubblehead chattering about her stupid life when Kiss had the opportunity to score some points, make the stock go up, and look good in the eyes of the business world. Of course it was strange that she had to deal with someone like Sharon Kennedy, a younger-than-Barbara post-hippie. Probably hated business, too. It would have been easier if they had sent a young MBA. Oh well, there were ways to get to the Sharon Kennedys of the world. "Come on, Sharon, you have to get your Kiss cosmetics on your face and some clothes on your back. You have to face our world."

Sharon put her hand on China's. She had been right. China's hand did tremble. "We'll talk some more this week."

China smiled. "I am a case, huh? I told you you could write about me. Everyone wants to."

Sharon shook her head. "I don't want to write about you. I want to help you."

"I think," said China, "you are about ten years too late."

Sharon sighed, put down her Coke, and walked out the door with Barbara. "See you later, China."

Sharon blinked walking into the sunlight. "I didn't realize the sun was still shining," she said.

"We start our parties in sunshine, and sometimes we end them that way, too."

"Is that some kind of symbolism, Barbara?"

"No. That's just my way of covering up that I'm nervous about what China may have said to you."

"Don't get pissed . . ."

Barbara winced.

"What China said is stuff I'd never use. But it does help me understand the company, and maybe I'll know why all of you people are the way you are."

"All companies are in the image of the people who run them, so I guess Chester Masterson's personality is stamped on all of us in some ways."

"Hey, Barbara, come off it." They were walking across the brick courtyard now. The courtyard was done in imitation country French. Even the bricks weren't real.

"You're only a few years younger than I am, Sharon, but there is a bigger difference between you and me than there is between Chester Masterson and me, and he's thirty-five years older than I am."

"You think that's good or bad?"

"Look, let's not get into my personal life. You've had enough of that from China. One True Confession is enough for any day."

"I don't mean to sound antagonistic. I guess I just come off that way. Deep down I hate big business because I don't trust it."

"Well, I don't trust professional radicals and young people who are continually looking for themselves in the glove compartments of used Volkswagens, and I don't trust phony liberals."

Sharon smiled. "I gave up marching, and I don't have any car . . . not even a used Volkswagen . . . and I think I'm a real liberal, not a phony. So let's be friends."

"I'd like it better that way," Barbara promised.

"Now tell me about Kiss," Sharon said insistently.

"I assume you know the early history, and I don't have to tell you how the company was founded and that Chester Masterson drove from drugstore to drugstore to get his new nail enamel displayed. And he kind of revolutionized things because it was a time when Lana Turner in a sweater was the accepted sex symbol . . ."

"Sure," Sharon interrupted, "it was titty time in America."

Barbara smiled. I will accept the language, she said to herself. I will accept the language. "Yes, it was titty time in America, and Chester Masterson changed it to nail time. He made long nails a sex symbol."

Sharon thought about her half-bitten nails. Hell, you couldn't type with long nails anyway.

"Here's your room," said Barbara. "I know because I came

here looking for you to see if you were ready, and then I decided you must be with China, so I went there."

"Come in while I get dressed, and we can talk some more." Sharon looked at Barbara and wondered what to wear so that their clothes would be similar. Sharon smiled. There was nothing she could wear to match Barbara's beige silk pants and shirt. Around Barbara's neck were slender gold chains, the tiniest of which had a small gold heart. Sharon pointed to the heart. "That's pretty. Does it mean something?"

Barbara nodded. "It means I have his heart."

"And he's . . ."

"He's my fiancé. A cancer researcher."

"Tell me about him."

"For a reporter covering a convention you seem to be worrying a lot about everybody's life. First let's go through the lineup of people whom you will meet."

"You manage to make it sound boring. Or is it just that I expect everything about business to be boring?"

"Stop making up your mind in advance. You may like us."

"Okay. Who are the characters?"

"Well, we've explained the chairman. The president is Henry Burns. Remember his wife, Jo? She was the pretty one with the white hair in the Bathhouse."

Sharon nodded.

"Henry is a supersalesman. That makes him a good foil for Chester. Chester is our personality, and Henry is our contact person with stores. Chester gets the headlines, but Henry doesn't resent that. After all, Chester did start the business, and that is always worth points."

Sharon started to poke through the three things she brought to wear. "Well, the women on the Best Dressed List can breathe easy, Barbara. I am not going to take over even tenth place with my outfit tonight. Do you think I can wear jeans?"

"Forty-dollar jeans or Army-Navy store jeans?"

"Barbara, the only thing I have to wear that cost forty dollars is a winter coat."

Barbara laughed. "Wear your jeans, and if they don't like it . . . up theirs."

"You're improving. Now back to Henry."

"Henry's getting restless. He's tired of being president."

"What does he want to be? A secretary?"

"He wants to be chairman. He wants Chester to get out of the business and let him run it."

"How can Henry expect Chester to do that? After all, you just said that Chester started the business. Why should he just turn it over to Henry?"

A small smile played on Barbara's mouth. She had been saying the very same thing to Henry, but then she had been inside the company. Here was Sharon, an outsider, understanding with just one sentence of explanation.

"Let me explain Henry a little," Barbara said. "Henry wants the company to expand throughout the world. Chester has concentrated on expansion in the United States, but he won't move into Europe and Japan the way Henry wants to."

"Why?"

"You seem to understand people pretty well, so I'll tell you my theory. I think that with all his money and all his power, Chester is conscious of his inability to speak any language but English. He can be rough and tough here, but he doesn't want to bite off more than he can chew in his native tongue."

"Why does Henry want that expansion so much?"

"Because," said Barbara with the zeal of a convert, "Henry knows it's right for us to be strong throughout the world. Henry is a brilliant man who is tired of having his hands tied. He doesn't want to play second fiddle to Revlon and Factor and Lauder in the world markets. Chester just won't accept the marketing facts."

"Why doesn't Chester retire?"

"What would he retire to? He doesn't have a wife. For the love he gives China he might as well not have a child. He doesn't even look at her children."

"I didn't know China had children."

"There are days she forgets, too. But she has two. The girl is Abigail Adams Edgar, and the boy is Chester Masterson Edgar."

"Natch."

"Grandfather couldn't care less."

"Is the business his whole life?"

"Not only this life, but the next one as well. I think he has his will set up so he controls us from the grave."

Sharon put on her clean jeans. Well, they were almost clean. There was a little chocolate ice cream stain on one leg, but she could wash that off. "Do you think Henry will get the chairmanship?"

"Eventually, yes, but that isn't what the conflict is all about."

"Conflict? What conflict?"

"It was going on back in the Bathhouse, but I guess you couldn't tell. The big question is going to be: who gets the presidency?"

"Assuming," interrupted Sharon, "that Henry first gets the chairmanship."

"Right. We have two big contenders, Tim Edgar . . ."

"Not the son-in-law who doesn't know what is happening to his wife?"

"The very same. In the other corner in the blue tights we have Ken Sugarman, husband of Linda."

"She's very smart."

"She is so smart that Ken just may become president."

"Who's going to make the decision?"

"Chester, of course. Henry will take anyone as president because he truly wants to be chairman. If Tim gets it, then Henry will just make Ken executive vice-president and give him all the responsibilities. If Ken gets it, I'd guess it would be a good team."

"You know just what Henry is thinking, don't you?"

"Yes. It's an awesome thing to watch him work, though. He is so smart" she said with a touch of pride in her voice.

"You're evidently a part of his major decisions."

"We're a team. We all are," she added.

"Will the management change affect you?"

"Not really. Chester has already given the company its personality, and these men won't change it. I'll get to do the things I like."

"What are those things?"

"Mainly new products. I really like product development. It's sort of like having a baby."

"Do you have any real babies?"

"I'm not married, remember? Where I come from, we get married first. I did raise my brother and sister though after my mother died, so I know that feeling of having your ego tied up in something outside your own body."

"What are some of your new products?"

Now Barbara's eyes were shining. Sharon wondered why anyone would be so turned on by product development. "Tuesday morning," Barbara announced, "I am going to introduce Product Q."

"What is it?"

"I can't tell anyone."

"The only people I could tell wouldn't care."

"*Newsweek* will be interested in this," Barbara said.

"Oh, I wouldn't tell them."

"But you work for them," Barbara said in surprise.

"I don't tell them my secrets. Now what's your secret?"

"I cannot tell you now," Barbara said in tones that Sharon was sure she had used in explaining things to her little sister. "You have to come to the meeting," Barbara added dutifully. "I think we have created something that can totally change our business. Nobody knows about it except Dr. Schulz and me."

"Who's Dr. Schulz? Sounds like some mad scientist."

"You're close. When we introduce Product Q we're going to change a lot of women's lives. They'll think we have some real geniuses at Kiss—scientists, marketing people."

Sharon felt embarrassed by Barbara's corporate ecstasy. She threw a faded blue jeans top over her pants. Good. It covered the chocolate ice cream stain. "Just one more question before we go, Barbara. Who are you really rooting for? Who ought to be president?"

"Well, he ought not to be president, but from a human point of view, I'd like Tim Edgar to get it."

"I would have thought you'd say Ken Sugarman."

"Ken's a good person, very smart, hard worker, but he doesn't have flair. He won't really understand that showmanship is a part of this business. Tim may be an ass in some ways, but he does know his way around the demitasse spoons."

"In other words you'd settle for a plastic president."
"I never thought of it just that way, but I guess the answer is yes."
Sharon shook her head. "Business is the pits."
"What did you say?" Barbara asked.

Chester Masterson catapulted to success on the grave of his brother. Prince Masterson was six years older than Chester. Prince was one of the sweethearts of the world. When Chester and Prince were younger their mother used to wonder how one son could be so sweet and the other so tough. Prince was the kind of child who would give not only the shirt off his back but the shoes off his feet. And during the Depression, when no one had much, Prince still managed to give a part of what he had. After Chester started Kiss, he persuaded Prince to come out and help him bottle nail enamel at the small plant he had leased in New Jersey. Prince would leave his young wife and two children at 6 P.M. after working all day in the post office, go to New Jersey, work half the night, and go back home to Queens to sleep for three hours before reporting back to the post office. "Someday," Chester would promise, "we'll have money, and I'll be able to pay you a salary." Prince never reminded Chester that he wasn't paying so much as his train fare to New Jersey. Chester did not even offer Prince a ride in his then new secondhand Buick. "Look, Chester," Prince used to say to his kid brother, "I'm glad to help you. After all, blood is thicker than nail polish." Chester would wince. "Call it nail enamel. It sounds classier." The details of Prince's death were never made clear. The police could not understand how a plant like Kiss's could have had such a devastating explosion, but Chester explained that they were working with new, secret ingredients and probably did not realize just how volatile the stuff was. Those were the days before precise scientific analysis. The insurance company conducted its own investigation, but in the end they paid Chester the two million dollars insurance he had on Prince's life. It seemed sort of odd that Prince's life would be insured for two million dollars by Chester, and only a post office pension would go to his wife, but Chester gave his widowed sister-in-law ten thousand dollars plus five thousand dollars for the children's education. And the two million? Well, Chester put that into advertising (remember the famous "Hot Rocks" campaign, the one that compared nail color to precious jewels?). That was one of the first campaigns that pushed Kiss to the top. As Chester Masterson once said to a class at the Harvard Business School, "No matter what you have to do in order to advertise, make sure you do advertise your product."

Jennifer Johnson stood on her tiptoes in front of the full-length mirror in her suite. She was naked. It had been a few months since she last checked her body carefully, but this was convention time, and the chances for body checks were very good this week. She squinted and looked closer. The famous big tits were beginning to sag. She cupped them and turned sideways. Then she put her hands down. They were. Yes, they were moving downwards. She pulled her shoulders back. There. Now they looked better. She'd have to remember to keep her shoulders back. She walked to the dresser, opened the drawer. Aaaah. There they were. Convention panties. Black lace with an embroidered opening big enough for any man. The matching bra had matching embroidered openings to let the nipples come through. Jennifer knew that at a convention she had to be ready for action. She started for the door when she realized she forgot one thing: the clinging red jersey sheath that went over the underwear.

As Jennifer crossed the compound to the patio area she heard someone call her name. She turned around. He was tall, maybe six foot four, and when he came next to her she felt like a little girl. Not too many men made Jennifer feel like a little girl. "Hi, Jennifer. I'm Sid Fisher from South Bend, and I always wanted to meet you. I used to see you in the movies when I was a kid." Her heart sank, another big Dumbo in her life.

"Look, honey, you probably have me mixed up with somebody else. I'm not Shirley Temple."

"Gosh, I'm sorry. That was a dumb thing to say."

He looked so pained that she felt sorry for him. "Oh," she said, putting one hand on his arm and turning just so the hard nipple on the right breast was fully outlined by the red jersey, "I'm sure you didn't mean anything nasty."

He smiled. "Just to show you my heart's in the right place . . ."

"Your what is where?" Good. Now she'd tease him.

"Hey, let me buy you a drink after old Henry makes his speeches. Okay?"

"Okay." Definitely okay. The panties and bra would be put to good use. She leaned against him slightly. Better remind him what was under that red jersey just in case he got the idea that some other one of those twenty-five-year-old Kiss women brand managers might be willing to take him. "Okay, Sid honey, it's you and me."

Sid felt his mouth go dry. Who would ever dream Jennifer Johnson would come on with him? He decided to drink ginger ale. Wait till the guys in his Sunday morning golf game in South Bend heard about this one. And to think he had been sorry when his wife, Ellen, decided to visit her mother this week.

The sounds of a seven-piece quasi-rock group filled the compound. Chester Masterson hated the music he heard. What ever happened to Lawrence Welk? Why couldn't they ever hire that kind of musician? He closed the windows, drew the draperies to shut out the view of the towering mountains, turned on the air conditioning and the television. There. Now it was better. It was like home, and he could forget he was at some son-of-a-bitch convention.

Across the patio and facing the band stood Henry and Jo. Henry Burns wore gray slacks, a red turtleneck sweater, and a Cardin blazer. His black hair gleamed almost blue-black under the lanterns. His year-round suntan looked deeper tonight because he had been sitting at the pool earlier in the day. In a patio filled with people, Henry stood out. He looked like the perfect president: sleek, well fed, untroubled. No one, not even Jo, knew that he was weighing the decision of his lifetime.

Jo turned to greet Jack and Connie Burton. Jack was Kiss's West Coast sales head. Not only did he represent the second most important sales area, he was the host salesman. Jo, however, was superhost next to the Burtons. She did her Gracious Lady Convention Greeting.

"Hello, Connie dear." A small kiss in the air as the two women clutched each other. "And hello, Jack." This time he kissed her soundly on the cheek. "How are the children, Connie?"

"Little Jack just started school, and little Connie is still in nursery school." Damned thoughtful of the Burtons to name their children after themselves. She wished everyone else would. Ooops, where were the name tags? "Excuse me, Jack, but did you forget my name tag?"

"Oh, Jo," he laughed, "everybody knows who you are."

"Yes, but sometimes I forget." All right. Everybody laugh. The boss's wife made a joke.

"All kidding aside, Jo, you think we need name tags?"

"All kidding aside, Jack, we need name tags."

"We thought it was sort of California and friendly not to have them."

"We can be just as California and a lot friendlier with them."

Jo never knew where the name tags came from, but minutes later everyone was dutifully writing his or her name and affixing it on everything from sports shirt pockets to décoletté dress fronts. Jack was dumb. Didn't he understand that in order to be a gracious lady you had to know names, and she couldn't remember names from one meeting to the next.

Barbara sidled up to Jo. "I hear you got the name tags for us."

"Good news travels fast."

"Just wanted to thank you, Jo. I can't remember people's names. It's so embarrassing." Jo looked at Barbara. Why did she stop to say that? She could not ever remember Barbara speaking to her without Henry present.

"It's especially hard when you're the president's wife," Jo said.

Barbara shrugged her shoulders. "I wouldn't know about that."

A high-pitched singsong voice interrupted them. "Hi, Jo. I'm Shirley Winters, and my husband . . ."

"Oh, my dear," Jo hugged her tight, "of course I know you. You're Jerry Winters' . . ."

"Jimmy Winters . . ."

"Of course, Jimmy Winters' wife. How are the children?"

"We don't have children, but we did adopt a Vietnamese orphan."

"That's what I was talking about." Whew. That was a close call.

"Oh, Jo, you're so wonderful to remember. Well, our daughter is having a very interesting time. I'd like to show you her picture."

"Tomorrow at the pool?"

"Tomorrow at the pool." Shirley's eyes were shining.

"It's a date," said Jo as she did the President's Wife's Turn to greet still another couple.

"Oh, that Jo Burns must be the finest woman I have ever met," Shirley said soberly to Barbara.

Barbara nodded. Where were these people's heads? Couldn't they tell that Jo was role-playing? No, thought Barbara, the tough jobs aren't executive wives. The tough job is being a woman executive when your co-workers have their wives around.

Barbara walked toward the bar. "Hey, Barbie doll."

Damn. It must be that idiot Rick McCormack from marketing. "Hi, Rick."

"You didn't even turn around to say hi."

"Didn't have to."

"Sure you do. You didn't see who's with me."

"Karen? What are you doing here, Karen?"

"Rick's wife couldn't come so I did," said Karen.

"But we just don't bring secretaries to conventions," Barbara said sharply. "Rick, get Karen out of here before both of you are embarrassed."

"What are you, Barbara," he asked, "some kind of queen of the convent? Karen is my secretary, and she is here for business reasons, and I think you have one hell of a dirty mind." Now his face was getting red. What did she need this for? Rick didn't work for her. His affair with Karen was none of her business. Did he think she was taking her anger out on Rick because she hadn't brought someone for her bedroom? Maybe. She clenched her fists. Maybe she ought to see how Sharon Kennedy was doing with her story. Maybe she needed to be with another no-man-tonight woman. She spotted Sharon at the bar. Jeff Garfield from p.r. was talking to her. He was wearing white Levis, a black shirt, and a few hunks of hardware around his neck. At the Kiss convention, the boys were definitely prettier than the girls.

Sharon spotted Barbara and pulled away from Jeff. "Hi, Barbara, when do they feed us?"

"After they think we are semiloaded."

"Anybody ever get tanked at these things?"

"Not at this hour."

"Well, what's the balling and boozing hour?"

"Sixty seconds after Henry finishes speaking."

"And when does he make his foam rubber speech?"

"After we eat."

"So, like I said in the first place, when do they feed us?"

Barbara looked at the Cartier watch on her wrist. It was the first present Paul Thurston had given her after they decided to get married. "In about ten minutes."

"Well, I can cruise another ten. Then I'll eat with you."

"What do you think so far, Sharon?"

"It's like an Elks convention in Illinois, only the Elks have their name tags typed."

Barbara grinned. "I don't care if you get a lousy story. You just may help me keep my sanity this crazy week."

"Good. And you can keep me in line. I've already had three offers from guys who are willing to help me avoid dandruff and menstrual cramps by laying me regularly beginning tonight. I think I want to stay faithful to my boyfriend, so keep an eye on me, will you?"

"I promise," Barbara said solemnly.

Sharon turned and ran squarely into China. "Oh, China," she sighed, "you are the most exotic woman here. When I look at you, I feel I should be taking in laundry."

"Oh, get off it, Sharon. Come here, though. Want to meet Tim?"

Old Ivyhead himself.

"Tim," called China, "here's Sharon."

He walked toward the women, hand extended, teeth shining, eyes crinkling at the corners. Sharon knew he would have perfect manners, and he did. He complimented Sharon on *Newsweek,* offered to freshen everyone's drink, and then he went back to talking business with the group he left in order to meet Sharon.

"China," she whispered, "what are you drinking?"

"Don't worry," China patted her arm. "I only drink alone."

Sharon shuddered and turned to walk away.

"Where are you going? Don't leave me, Sharon," China pleaded.

Sharon stopped. She remembered what Tom Sales had told her once. "No good deed goes unpunished." Her good deed was to listen to China's story, and for that she was about to be saddled with China for the entire convention.

"Look, China," she said, "I'm really trying to do some work, and I have to meet with Barbara and have dinner with her. You know, Kiss set it all up. There must be someone who'll be happy to have you."

"Okay." China understood. Rebuffs were second nature.

Sharon did not like herself as she turned to look for Barbara.

"Hi, Sharon."

Sharon cocked her head to one side. She did not know who this good-looking blond woman was. "Have we met?"

"Yes, but never with our clothes on. I'm Linda Sugarman."

"I know. The Jacuzzi. You certainly are attractive. All you Kiss women are."

"Oh?"

"I'm not bullshitting you."

Linda flinched.

"Honestly. No b.s. You happen to look very good when you're all dressed up." Suddenly Sharon realized that if she didn't talk to Kiss women about their clothes she had nothing to say to them. "Great-looking pants."

"They're by Kasper. Mostly I wear his clothes or Calvin Klein. That's because my husband is a vice-president, and one of the things you learn is that you never outdress the president's wife.

Of course we can't dress better than Jo. She wears superchic stuff. You know, Galanos and St. Laurent and that kind of designer."

"I don't know St. Laurent from St. Francis," Sharon said. "I'm not into clothes, but I think the men at Kiss really are. Are all businessmen? Or is it just these men because they're sort of in the fashion business?"

"Mmmm, I think Kiss, Inc., probably overdoes it as far as the men are concerned. The pants are always a little too tight. Of course, Ken is kind of the company conservative."

"Ken's your husband, right?"

"Right. I want you to meet him. He's very intelligent, but it takes a lot of pushing to make a *mensh* of Ken."

"A *mensh*?"

"*Mensh* . . . a man. It's a Yiddish word. I always think people in the media know those words."

"I never heard that one. I'm from the shlep-klutz school."

"Doesn't matter. All I can say is that Ken's job takes a lot out of me. It was really easier when he was just in marketing."

"Why is it all so tough on you?"

"He brings reports home, and I have to go over them . . ."

"You *have* to?"

"Oh, I suppose it isn't mandatory, but when I don't go over every paper myself there are mistakes, and next thing you know we're sending Minnesota's advertising schedule to Alaska."

"You mean Ken really couldn't do all this without you?"

"That's a tough one to answer. I think he could do it, but now we're at the point where he isn't sure he could do it."

"This is called helping your husband?" Sharon was incredulous.

Linda smiled modestly. "Well, we each do what we can in our own way."

"Right. You're a definition of working wife I have never met before."

"There's an army of us, Sharon."

"I'll bet. Linda, can we talk some more this week?"

"How about now?"

"I told Barbara I'd have dinner with her, and I want to spend some time talking to her because you know she has that big presentation Tuesday morning, and I need plenty of background for it."

"What big presentation?"

"Oh, I'm sure you know. It's the Product Q thing."

"What's Product Q?"

"The new revolutionary something or other."

Linda eyed her thoughtfully. She decided to bluff her way through Product Q. "Of course I know all about Product Q, but it's so top secret I didn't want to seem as if I knew."

Sharon decided to let her play her game. "I knew you did. Maybe we can have coffee tomorrow morning."

"To be perfectly honest I always try to nab Jo on the first morning of meetings because she and I don't go to the business session, and then it gives me a chance to be with her. You know wives are really important in a lot of executive decisions, and when Henry recommends the new president, I want to make sure Jo gets her two cents into it."

"Sure, Linda." She knew she must be dreaming. Women were not really like this, were they?

"See you around." Linda moved away. There was bigger game on the other side of the bar.

As they stood in the buffet line Barbara explained convention food. "Sunday night, the first night, is supposed to be an extension of Sunday night supper at home. Nothing fancy, just sort of pleasant and easy to fix. You'll find cold chicken and salads and cold cuts. That's it."

"Is it a Kiss, Inc., convention special?" Sharon asked.

"Honey, it's the world's convention special."

"You mean all conventions feed their guests the same thing?"

"Basically yes. Mass feeding is always run on philosophies. And the basic philosophy is that the crowd has been traveling all day, doesn't want heavy, rich food, and so everybody gives them something simple."

Sharon took her plate of basic convention food to a round table with five others including Barbara. Also at the table were Jennifer and someone from Indiana, Rick Something or Other, and Karen No Last Name. It was dull conversation, about two stages past high school. Sharon made a mental note to avoid these people. Barbara was interesting, but the rest were a bore.

As soon as she felt she could make a gracious getaway Sharon pleaded the need to return to her notes and went to her room. "Oh, Tom Sales," she said to herself as she closed the door behind her, "I need you now." Her phone rang. It was Barbara. "Hey, you forgot something. You went away so fast you forgot the president's welcoming speech. He'll start in a couple of minutes. I do have an advance copy with me, though. Want me to give it to you?"

"You're a good kid Barbara. No, I'll come back." She took a deep breath, opened the door, and went back to Henry in Conventionland.

Henry patted his pocket. Touching the speech gave him a sense of security. Not that he would read the speech. No. That was insulting to an audience. Besides it made everyone think that you couldn't say your own words. When you talked without notes, they believed you. And that was part of the act. Belief followed by Loyalty. The old one-two President's Soft Shoe. This convention Henry was going to give his best performance yet. Catch me, Chester Old Boy. I am going to be an impossible act to follow.

Henry strode to the microphone, all smiles and style. He opened with a joke that was appropriately inoffensive, swung to a welcome to all, and delivered his real message at the end. . . . "So I want to say in closing that this is the time for all of us to put aside petty grievances and everyday problems. This is a time for each one of us to rededicate himself or herself, to become more effective individuals, more effective parts of the team. For we are a team, a cohesive, proud team. And this week we think we will show you things that will make you prouder than ever of your company. Every year we have a theme at our meeting. This year our theme is 'Kiss the world.' We're about to become a global company. We have the talent. We have the products. And you'll hear more this week. Ladies and gentlemen, Kiss the world, and the world will thank you."

Jo was flushing through her fine Palm Beach tan. The proud corporate wife, Sharon decided. The other wives and employees were applauding dutifully. The men seemed to respond on a more personal level to Henry than the women. So good-looking and not even a ladies' man? That's odd, Sharon thought. "Does Henry make it with any of these women?" Sharon whispered to Barbara.

"There's an old company expression that reminds us, 'Never dip your pen in the company inkwell,'" Barbara said. "Henry takes it seriously."

"Bully for him," said Sharon. Barbara had not answered her question.

Sid Fisher drank the last of his coffee slowly. This was the time to make the big play for Jennifer. She wasn't going to turn him down. He could tell that already. He felt a little nervous. What if he couldn't . . . ? No, no thoughts like that.

Twenty minutes later he lay in her bed. It had been easy, so easy. He hadn't expected that at all. What did he think she would be, a blushing virgin? No. But he didn't expect the sexually aggressive woman he found. Now she was lying quietly in his arms. "You're all right, Sid," she said.

"So are you." What do you say to a woman who overwhelms you that way? And the bra and panties. She was like a porno movie come to life, every sex fantasy rolled into one. "I've never known a woman like you."

"You think I'm sexy?"

She must be kidding. He laughed.

"Don't laugh at me."

"Hey, are those tears in your eyes?"

"I said don't laugh at me."

"Look, Jennifer, I'm not laughing at you. I'm laughing at me."

"Why? You came."

"Yeah, but with a woman like you. I'm laughing because I can't believe I could be so lucky."

"You mean it?"

"Sure."

"Tell me more."

"You're beautiful, and . . . well, it's like a dream."

"Do you love me?"

"Hey, Jennifer, I'm married."

"But do you love me?"

"Come on, does every guy you go to bed with have to love you?"

"I think so."

"What do you mean you think so?"

"I think I have to be loved a lot right now."

"You? Come on. The whole world loves you."

"All I want is one man."

"I told you, Jennifer, I'm married."

"Well, I'll tell you something, Sid. It's a big handicap to have a body every man wants."

"At Kiss I learned it's a bigger sin to be ugly."

"I'm not joking."

"You're married, aren't you? I read something about your husband."

"Do you have all night, Sid?"

"What do you mean?"

"Are you staying with me all night?"

He got out of the bed and looked down at her. The famous body was still in good shape, but there were lines around the eyes. The make-up was smeared. He guessed Jennifer was pushing fifty now, and he sensed she needed him. Every instinct told him to go back to his room and get out of the way of this oversexed, maybe sick broad. He poked around the floor, found his trousers, pulled out a pack of cigarettes, folded the trousers neatly, put them over the back of a chair, settled back into bed, lit a cigarette, and said, "I'm staying, Jennifer."

"I love to sleep with a man. And I promise I'll let you get some sleep."

"Do I have to make the same promise?" he asked.

"You're a nice man, Sid. Your wife is lucky."

"It's too bad I can't tell her she has your endorsement."

"My endorsement isn't such hot stuff, and it isn't enough to keep a man I want."

He killed the cigarette, slid down on the sheets, and held Jennifer close. "Any man would be proud to have you."

"I couldn't hold Lou."

"Is that your boyfriend or your husband?"

"My husband. Didn't you ever hear of Lou Burke?"

"Guess not."

"I forget you're not a Hollywood person. Lou Burke," she said with emphasis on each word, "is the most important agent in the whole world."

Sid dredged his memory. "Does that mean talent agent?"

"Agent means . . . oh hell, Sid, agent means agent. He's a big shot. Do you understand that?"

He was miffed. Sure, be nice to Jennifer, and two seconds later she has you feeling like you belong in a split-level house in Indiana.

"Hey, Sid, it doesn't matter if you heard of Lou or not. In the one-horse town in Texas where I grew up no one ever heard of Lou Burke either. You know, I look around at all the money being spent here and the big way these people live. When I grew up, we were lucky if we had turnips for dinner. Hell, I've eaten turnips more ways than you've eaten hamburger. But I knew I'd find my way out. When I was eleven these started to happen." She fingered her big breasts. "I knew they'd buy me out of Texas."

"Did you win a beauty contest?"

"No. You have me mixed up with some other old stars. I became a country singer with a little band. We traveled, and I married one of the guys in the group. He loved me when he was sober, and he beat the hell out of me when he wasn't. Between the fucking and the beating it's a wonder there's anything left."

"How'd you get out?"

"Lou Burke was my passport. Lou was a small-time agent, heard the group and told me I could be a real singer. I left the band in the middle of the night and ran away with Lou. You know the rest. Lou turned me into a big blues singer . . ."

Sid knew she hadn't been a big blues singer. A blues singer maybe. But big? No. She had always been on the fringe of the big time.

"Lou got me all the good jobs around. I played everything from TV shows to state fairs. We traveled together, and we had a lot of fun in those days. I always wore these low-cut dresses, and guys would come up and make remarks. Sometimes Lou would get jealous, but it was always pretty good between us. I didn't screw around. I was strictly his girl."

"But you were married to another man."

"Of course I was married. Aren't we all?"

He laughed. "Okay. I get the point."

"Somewhere along the way Lou figured how we could get a divorce for me, and we got the divorce and married each other the same day. It was in Reno, and it was very romantic."

"Sounds like it should have worked."

"It always did for me. What I didn't know is that Lou was always involved with a lot of girls, even before we were married. Agents can get every piece of ass in town. All they do is pick up the phone, promise an audition, and the hot little bodies leave the Beverly Hills Hotel pool and go running to their offices."

"What did you do when you found out?"

"Got uptight just like your wife would. I threw things, and I made scenes, and I screamed and yelled."

"What happened?"

"Nothing."

"What do you mean nothing?"

"I mean finally he could get it up for every two-bit whore in Hollywood . . . but not for me, his wife."

Sid felt himself getting hard again.

"He could do it with every twenty-one-year-old nothing, but he couldn't make it with his own wife. The goddamned son of a bitch." Now the tears started flooding her face.

She was older than he thought. She was frightened. He gathered her in his arms. "Don't cry, honey. Sid will take care of you."

Jo Burns sat in front of the dressing table counting her brush strokes. One hundred times through the white hair. Keep it shining. Keep up the looks. Make sure everyone knows you are the president's wife. "Your speech was good, Henry."

"Really think so?" He walked out of the bathroom, where he was brushing his teeth.

Henry stood and looked at his wife. He had once wanted her every time he saw her. What had become of that early lust? Did it fade with her dark hair? No, long before then he had stopped feeling that ache, that overwhelming surge of emotion when she walked into a room. In those days it had been so easy to talk to her about everything. Yes, everything that happened was spilled in full detail to Jo. When did he stop telling her? When the surge of emotion stopped? Or when her talk of babies and crab grass interrupted his of profit and loss? Or was it when he first got involved with his little secretary, Pamela . . . Pamela . . . oh, Pamela Whatever. At this point she probably couldn't remember his name either. He wondered where she was now. Every man in the office was after her. So sexy-looking. Good figure, but she wore falsies. It was sort of sad. Pretty face, good body, and she wore falsies. He never could figure out why.

"Yes, Henry," Jo was saying . . . good old Jo . . . "it's nice to have you really settled at Kiss. You know, when we go to meetings now, we know everybody, and it's comfortable and easy . . ."

What was this? Didn't she know how Chester ate at his insides? Didn't she realize Henry's blood was spilled for each of these meetings? Pamela would have known. So would Barbara. Women like Pamela and Barbara wouldn't seem so . . . smug. Yes, that's what Jo was. Smug. Hell. He'd blast her out of her little Galanos coma.

"Jo, I'm thinking of leaving Kiss."

She didn't think she heard right. This man with a toothbrush in his hand and a towel wrapped around his waist was thinking of leaving his job as president of the biggest cosmetics company in the world, and he chose to tell his wife as if he were asking for room service. She thought her stomach was going to drop away. She felt the tips of her fingers grow cold. "What's this about, Henry?"

He smiled. He had reached the smug center. "I've had an unbelievable offer."

"Oh," she said in her knowing tone. "Another from Revlon? Or is it Factor this time?"

"Neither."

She waited, and the silence hung between them, thick as morning fog. "Who, then?" she asked, irritated.

Now he was feeling a little drunk. What did it? Toothpaste or upsetting a complacent wife? "This is one you would not guess, my dear. Oxxon, the Swiss conglomerate, wants me to head their cosmetics operations. We have a choice. We can live either in Basel or New York. I'm sure we could really live anywhere I want to set up executive headquarters. We'd have all the kinds of money we have now. The only new perk would be the use of a jet."

She felt relieved. He wasn't going to take it. He was just aggravating her. That was a thing husbands did. When they were locked into marriage, they compensated by giving their wives moments of unhappiness. Along with the girlfriends, they picked up guilt, and men got rid of the guilt by finding reasons to get annoyed with their wives. She understood this. Henry had been fooling around with young office girls for years. Nothing serious, of course. And she was smart enough never to let him know what she knew. And as long as it wasn't one woman, she was safe . . . wasn't she? She smiled benignly. "Then if the job doesn't mean anything more than your own plane, why do you want it?" As soon as the words were out, she felt the first stirrings of panic. He was so controlled he must want it very much.

"I want to get out from under Chester."

"But he loves you."

"Get off it, Jo. Chester is insanely in love with Chester, or maybe Chester is just plain insane. I don't even know anymore."

"Henry, you're too old to make radical changes in your life."

"I'm too old not to. Don't you see? If I don't take this opportunity, where's the next one? I'm forty-nine now, just the right age for a move like this."

"I don't agree. You can't take it. You're too old for change. You experiment in the thirties, settle down in the forties . . ."

". . . and rot in the fifties? Is that your brilliant formula, Jo? Or are you really saying that you're too old?" Ouch. That was hitting below the birthday cake.

"All right, so I'm fifty-one. I'm fifty-one and contented. I love my life. I like being Mrs. Henry Burns, and I kind of like my perks. I like the house and the maid and the driver when I want to go into the city. And I like the children's schools . . ."

"Do you also like the fact that your husband plays the role of Number One Son while Chester Masterson plays God?"

Now Jo tried to be light. "Number One Son isn't such a bad role."

"It is if you want to be God."

"What do you really know about Oxxon, Henry?"

"Oh, Jo, it's a great company. Wonderful people. They already are a multinational, and you know how I believe in that."

"Henry, all companies look good from the outside."

"Some must look better than Kiss on the inside."

"Henry," now her voice fell, "I can't let you take this job."

"Jo, the job is for me. It isn't yours. I want your approval, but I want the job."

"Henry, it will kill me."

"Cut the dramatics," he said sharply.

"Henry, it will mean all new people, and they are going to hear about me, and I'll have to live it all over again. I can't."

Henry gripped the back of a chair. "What are you trying to do? Make that the focal point of our lives? You can't relive that day, nor can I. Stop making me live in the past."

Tears filled Jo's eyes, and she was startled when the phone rang. "The children?" she asked anxiously.

Henry reached for the phone. "Yes, Chester. Your room? And you want me to get Barbara, Ken and Tim. Immediately. Yes, sir. See you." He hung the phone back on the receiver. He laughed out loud. "And Jo, my dear and darling, perfect and beloved wife, this is how you want me to spend the rest of my life?"

To Chester Masterson there was only one thing better than an original original. That was a new, improved original.

By the late 1950s Kiss was making great strides, thanks in part to an advertising campaign, "Put a little Kiss on your lips," created by Irving Penfield. Irving was a supersalesman, a hot idea man who moved easily between show business and real business. One day Irving received a call from a TV program packager who suggested that Irving's client, Kiss, take the old radio quiz show idea and give it added zip: Big Money. Irving ran to Chester Masterson's office with the idea for "Kiss for the Money." The producer knew it would take Irving's special brand of salesmanship to sell the show to Masterson. From the moment Chester heard the idea, he loved it. His only regret was that he had not thought of it. He knew women would be intrigued by the promise of wealth. Hadn't his first and second wives married him for his money? In those days Chester had yet to meet Gladys-Gladyce, who would marry him for power and position, the only things money can buy. This day, it was May 13, 1954, Chester knew what the promise of money could make women do. He bought the show, put it on the air, and within two weeks changed the viewing habits of America. Nobody went to the bathroom from 8 to 8:30 P.M. Thursday nights; that was proven by the flush-o-meter or water pressure tests in every city. Nobody went out; that was proven by the lowered restaurant and theater receipts. Everyone was transfixed in front of a TV set. The gimmick was the climb to the Biggest Kiss in the World.

Contestants were experts in categories, and the more unlikely the category, the more fascinating the contest. Ratings went beyond anyone's wildest dreams the week Donna Smithfield appeared. Donna looked like something out of an Easter basket, all fluffy hair and bubbly giggles. Her category was Eastern philosophy. Week after week she twirled her feather-cut hair around her finger as she puzzled the answers. Her gesture replaced Churchill's V as the hand motion of the decade. And when she came up with the right answers America collectively breathed a sigh of relief—and went to the bathroom. They also went to the drug and department stores and literally bought out Kiss. Donna was the all-American dream girl. One week alone she had more fan mail than Elizabeth Taylor, John Wayne, and Frank Sinatra combined. Men proposed. Women copied her walk and the barely inaudible sigh she heaved before coming up with her always correct answers. Donna was good, too good to be true. After the quiz scandals broke, Donna was burned at the stake professionally. She couldn't even get her old job as a masseuse. How did honest Donna find herself cheating? Who gave her the answers in advance? The producers confessed. Who was the motivating force, the person who screamed at the producers each week for higher ratings? Certainly not benign, benevolent Chester Masterson, who denounced cheating, fraud, chicanery, and deceit as he canceled the show. By then who needed it? Business had doubled; the stock was skyrocketing. As Chester said to Irving, "The secret of doing business is always to get out on the top floor."

"I told you this wasn't going to be a vacation," Chester promised the assembled group. It was 11 P.M., and they had been sitting in Chester's garishly furnished suite for only a few minutes. "What were you doing when I called, Henry?" As he asked the question, he leered.

Henry sucked his breath. Oh no, not another one of the late night raunchy meetings. "Not that, Chester. Not that. I was brushing my teeth. See my smile?" He bared his teeth.

"What were you doing, Ken?" Damn. He wanted the satisfaction of pulling one of them out of his wife's bed.

"I was in bed with my wife," Ken replied dutifully.

Chester leaned back and smiled. Triumph at last.

Ken was going to say, "We were talking," but he had learned to read Chester's smiles and frowns. Chester was smiling. Why push his luck and tell them that Linda had indeed been in bed with him, giving him the third degree on Product Q?

Chester turned to his son-in-law. "Where were you, Tim?"

"In the bar, sir."

"Is that where you usually make your sales?"

"As a matter of fact, sir, I was learning something interesting. There was a beautiful young woman there named Ginger Mallory . . ."

"Does she work for us?"

"No . . . she . . ."

Chester's interest was piqued. Beautiful, on the premises, and not a Kiss employee. "What does she do?"

"I'm not certain, sir, but she is obviously a prime prospect for us."

"Why us, Tim? I may be an old man, but I can handle things alone."

"I am referring, sir," Tim continued as if the interruption were both useful and intelligent, "to the fact that she is in the twenty-five- to thirty-five-year-old category, believes in cosmetics to judge by her appearance, and is not some natural foods and natural beauty aficionado."

"A what?"

"She likes to be pretty. None of that stringy hair and no make-up look. The point is that she was talking about our advertising . . ."

"Tim, for a son-in-law, sometimes you're all right. I called you all here to talk about advertising. While you were out drinking and laying your wives . . . oh, excuse me, Barbara . . . I was here working. I was watching television, and I want to tell you that of the four major cosmetics companies we are number one in sales and as far as I'm concerned we're number seven in advertising."

"But, sir," interrupted Tim, "there are only four companies on TV."

"It was too much to expect you to be smart twice in a row,

wasn't it? I used seven as an exaggeration, to make a point," said Chester contemptuously.

Tim flushed. It was a well-bred, civilized flush.

Barbara thought that if she liked Tim more she would probably feel sorry for him.

"Chester," Henry interrupted, "if we are going to discuss advertising, why isn't Howard Weston here? After all, Howard is head of our communications, and the advertising department reports to him."

"You know what I like about you, Henry?" Chester asked softly. "You are logical," and now his voice began to grow louder, "but I don't give a good damn for logic. Howard is a dumbbell. He was stupid when we hired him, and he gets dumber every year. Did he ever come up with a replacement for 'Kiss for the Money'? The only reason I keep him is that I still hope that one day he is going to present just one good idea and make this whole thing worthwhile. Howard isn't here, Henry, because I don't want Howard here."

Barbara yawned. This was not a stellar performance. Chester could really do better. This was just Chester putting the old knife into everyone, reminding them that he could rouse them out of their beds because he put them there. For Barbara it was the price demanded and the price she was willing to pay to run a new products department and make a lot of money. Or was it make a lot of money and run a new products department? She didn't always know, but she kept doing it. Suddenly she heard the words, "new product." And Chester was speaking them.

"Well, look who's come to life. The little lady. I'm talking about commercials that make new products look and sound revolutionary. I want to make sure that when we introduce Product Q to the convention here we say 'revolutionary.' Is that clear, everyone?"

"Chester." Barbara now was going to make her stand. "Revolutionary went out of style a long time ago. The use of those kinds of words, all that hyperbole . . ."

"Hype what?" he asked.

"Exaggeration is in bad taste."

"Oh, Miss Smart Girl, and you think bad taste can't sell?"

"Bad taste does sell, but how do we know that good taste would not sell better? Please don't make us exaggerate. The product itself is so remarkable that we don't want to have to say old-fashioned things about it. Let us keep the advertising fresh and new. Let's make our honest claim. For God's sake, Chester, this is the first time a cosmetics company has ever been able to make this claim. We have the dream product. Now let's not treat it like a detergent in a new-size box."

"She's right," Henry said, coming to her defense quickly. "Let us put the creativity into the product and just plain honest sell into the ads."

"Plain honest sell never sold anything," Chester reminded him.

"It sold me on coming with this company," Ken said.

"Then you were misled," Chester argued. "We can't underplay the best thing we ever had. It's like sending the Olympic ski team on the slopes in nothing but their jockstraps. Oh, excuse me, Barbara."

"Sir," now Tim was entering the debate, "if we expect the finest stores in America to sell this product exclusively . . . that is, if we expect it to be a franchise product sold not in drugstores but only the best department stores, then we cannot be indistinguishable. We have to look . . . oh, let's say we have to look like a classic. We need to look a hundred years old and sound a hundred years young."

Barbara was amazed. Tim had never expressed himself so well.

"For once I understood you," Chester said. "All right. Let's try it with class."

Barbara breathed a sigh of relief. The ads prepared by the agency were in her room. They had been delivered only hours earlier. They were low-key and strong, yet romantic. She loved them. Whole hunks of her product rationale as well as her emotional and intellectual input were in the ads.

"Thank you, Chester," she said with feeling.

Henry cleared his throat and spoke brusquely. "It's after midnight, and I want to be fresh for tomorrow's meeting. May we end this now?"

Ken looked in stunned silence. He had never before heard Henry ask to end a meeting. No one ever asked Chester to bring a meeting to an end. Chester ended meetings by getting up and leaving the table. No good-bys. No thank-yous. Just out the door.

Chester seemed nonplused by the request. He sighed wearily. "Good night. Yes, go. All of you go. Tim, one minute, though. I'd like to see you."

The group dutifully filed out. Tim beamed his best son-in-law smile at Chester. Was this the time Chester was finally going to confide in him and tell him that he was about to become president of Kiss?

"Tim, about that girl in the bar . . ."

Tim frowned. What girl? What bar? Oh yes. Ginger Mallory. He smiled again. "Yes?"

"Can you get her for me?"

"I don't think she's really looking for a job. I don't think you quite understand just what kind of young woman Ginger is . . ."

"I don't think you quite understand just what kind of old man this is," Chester interrupted. "I want that girl in my room tomorrow night. When everybody is at some damned fool party, make sure she's here. I am not going to watch this goddamned television two nights in a row."

"Yes, sir." Procurer was not the new job he had in mind.

Barbara crossed the courtyard with Henry and Ken. "I don't like you walking around here at night alone, Barbara," Henry said.

"Let's walk her back to her room," Ken offered.

A look of annoyance crossed Henry's face. "You don't have to, Ken."

"I want to. It's all right."

Barbara smiled. For a minute she wished Ken were not so sweet-natured.

"Well, we're all getting to bed earlier than I expected," she said. "Henry, you must really be letting this California sunshine go to your head. I never heard you end the meeting before this."

"I'm feeling uppity, Miss Scarlett," he grinned. Wait till she heard the reason.

"Did somebody leave you a million dollars?"

"Maybe."

"What does that mean?"

"You'll know when I want you to know."

Ken bit his lip. Linda would certainly want to hear that Henry was up to something. "When will we find out?" Ken asked.

"No more questions," Henry said. Then, as if he were reading Ken's mind he added, "But I promise you will hear before Linda."

Ken breathed an audible sigh of relief.

Barbara looked at Ken with compassion. If she married Paul, would he be like that? Or were women the only ones who lived through others? No, she knew that Paul had his own life, but maybe she ought to call him and make sure. She thought about good, solid Paul Thurston, and then she knew she must have missed some kind of conversational exchange between Henry and Ken. They seemed to be looking at her, waiting for her to say something. She looked at the door. It was her room. She gave a small, embarrassed laugh. "Thanks for walking me home. I'm bushed. I didn't even realize we were here. I guess I have just enough time to take off this face and put on my next one."

Henry kissed her quickly on the cheek. "The old face is a nice one, and I like the old brain that goes with it."

She closed the door behind her. It was hard to see Henry go back to his room to sleep with his wife. 1:45 A.M. That meant 4:45 A.M. in New York. Paul was probably asleep by now. And why should she wake him just to say she needed to be wanted?

Barbara lay awake and watched the luminous hand on the luminous dial move toward the morning meeting. Now it was 4 A.M. Good. That meant it was 7 A.M. in New York. She could call Paul now. She dialed his New York apartment and let the phone ring. Busy. There was a busy signal. Why was his phone busy at 7 A.M.? What kind of research was this? What other person had lain awake until 7 A.M. New York time in order to call Dr. Thurston? She felt the start of long-buried tears. Who but a doctor answered the needs of everyone but the people he supposedly loved?

But she should have guessed. What man had ever been there when she needed him? When you came right down to it, who ever answered your needs but yourself? She put the phone back on the receiver and reached for the pad of paper and pencil on the night stand. There was her security: her own ability. Security was not another man who wasn't there when she reached for him. No. Men did not give women security. Men were neither the problem nor the solution in a woman's life. The problem was security; the solution was self. Barbara had learned that when her mother died. She shut her eyes and squeezed back tears. Fifteen years later, and still she could cry for her long-dead mother. She pulled the long hair back, fastened it with a rubber band, and brought herself back to the Kiss convention. She started to write, "When Chester Masterson came up with the idea for Product Q, that was our cue to some up with the kind of innovative positioning, packaging, naming and advertising that would make this the greatest launch since Cape Canaveral." Now the pencil moved faster. She was swinging into her presentation for the meeting. The guts of the presentation were ready; she always waited until the one or two days before the big meeting to write the introduction. Introductions could be killed by headlines, changes in management, and changes in viewpoint. It was too late to change the product or the advertising, the things she would present. She wrote faster and faster. Forget the man who wasn't there. Forget the men who did not answer—ever. There was more security in a moving pencil than in all the men in the world. Including Chester Masterson.

Chester Masterson needed a vehicle to take him from the financial pages to the society pages. Marriage did not do it, for even though he married a woman listed in the Social Register he had no status of his own. Mary Jones Masterson would have been perfectly willing to be the proper corporate wife. Chester, however, never wanted a corporate wife. Like so many people who marry, they each wanted what the other had, but neither liked what each had to offer. Mary Jones hated the meaningless society life. Chester hated the grubby business life. The end of their marriage was predictable, and after the divorce Chester was even more anxious to make a name for himself in society. He hired a society columnist, and from time to time his name was dropped discreetly into her column. But that fooled no one. Her column sold for more money than a page of advertising in her newspaper. Chester was aware of no more avenues into the social pages until he hired Ike Powers, the corporate p.r. genius of the '60s. "Look, Chester," said Ike, "you should have named the company after yourself. You know, like Arden and Lauder." "So how does Masterson fit on a little nail enamel bottle?" Chester snapped. Ike Powers did not make $250,000 a year and live like a maharajah by just saying, "You should have—" Ike's real money was made because he prefaced all ideas with, "You will—" One day Ike went to visit Chester in his oak-paneled office off the hallway called Fifth Avenue (all Kiss hallways were named for the fashion avenues of America; there was Michigan, Wilshire Boulevard, Lincoln Road). Chester, of course, took Fifth Avenue as the gateway to his domain.

"Chet," Ike said, "you will—you will be on the society pages of every newspaper in the country." A smile hovered on the corners of Chester's mouth. He wet his lips. "How?" he asked. "Buy yourself a charity," advised Ike. "Jerry Lewis has one, and Danny Thomas has one. Bob Hope goes to entertain troops, and they all get on the front page. You can make the newspapers, too, but you'll be on the society pages. First thing we do is create the Masterson Foundation." Chester was pleased. It sounded as if he would become not only a personality but a philanthropist. Could dinner at the White House be far behind? "Hey, Ike, what disease will we get?" Ike frowned for a minute. All the good stuff was taken. He needed to fend for time, so to divert Chester he said, "Here's how we'll do it. It really doesn't make any difference what disease we pick. We'll have a Masterson Charity Ball; it will make you socially. You take a bunch of society broads who want their pictures in the New York *Times* and you name them to your committee. Then you hire the best decorators in New York, have food flown in from Maxim's, get the prettiest people in town to attend. That's all there is to it." The telephone on Chester's side table rang. That meant a personal call. He picked it up. "Who? Oh yes, the head mistress at China's school. Put her on . . . Hello, Mrs. Holmes, how's China? . . . What do you mean, she's—disturbed? . . . Too disturbed to learn? You don't know what you're talking about. She's a normal, healthy little girl. You're the one who's disturbed." He slammed the telephone. Ike looked up. "It will be the talk of New York, the greatest ball in the city for the Masterson Foundation for Disturbed Children." Chester stood and shook Ike's hand. That damned Powers was worth every cent he got.

Monday

"Exactly what happened last night, Ken?"

"Exactly what happens every time Chester Masterson calls in the night people. Nothing."

Linda Sugarman looked carefully in the mirror. Damn. The black roots were showing again. Well, nobody except another wife would ever notice a thing like that. "Don't tell me nothing happened. Don't you understand that when you repeat a conversation I can hear things in it that you don't?"

"Oh, come on, Linda," Ken said, a note of irritation creeping into his voice, "I don't like these interrogations."

"For God's sake, these are not some no-brainer interrogations. I am only doing this for you." She slammed the hairbrush on the dressing table.

"Don't get emotional, honey. I really didn't mean to upset you. It's just that I have a hard time concentrating when Chester talks."

"You have a hard time concentrating." She parroted his tone. "I'll bet little old Tim Son-in-Law hangs on every word."

"Matter of fact, Tim didn't do so well last night."

"Tell me."

"I can't remember exactly. You should have asked me last night."

"How could I? I was out getting votes for you."

"What do you mean, getting votes?"

"I was at the bar with Jack and Connie Burton."

"I don't think Jack is going to have much voice in picking the next president."

"You never know. Corporations change executives faster than men change mistresses."

"That's a funny thing for you to say."

"Well, if you hang around the Paradise bar long enough you see that's the only thing on men's minds."

"Anybody try to pick you up?"

"They know better. I look like a wife."

He looked at her closely. It was the first time he had looked that carefully in years. She was right. She was dark at the roots, the first sign of a wife. He decided to change the subject. "Are you meeting anybody for breakfast?"

She smiled. "Is the Pope Catholic?"

"I hate that kind of answer."

"Look, Sir Lancelot, I'm tired of answering the easy ones. Of course I am meeting someone for breakfast. And knowing me you ought to realize it would be the only someone worth meeting, Jo Burns."

"Just one more question from your first husband, Ken Schlemiel," he said softly, "does she know you are her breakfast date?"

"Come on over here, Linda," Jennifer called. "I'm the best you can do. Jo didn't show."

Linda flushed. Damn that seven-dollar whore. What made her think she knew what Linda was trying to do? Linda walked slowly to the table. The dining room of The Gates of Paradise was a kind of open air "21." There were toy airplanes and boats hanging from the ceiling. The sides of the room were open to admit the sunlight and air, and when the smog subsided both did manage to come in. All in all, it was a New Yorker's idea of California. Never mind what Midwesterners thought. Everybody knew the conventions were booked out of the Big Apple. Everybody else took what was bought. "Some day, huh?" Jennifer asked with the triumph born of more than six months of California residence.

Linda squinted. "It's okay."

"Face it, honey," Jennifer said matter-of-factly, "you're bugged because Jo isn't here. Everybody knows you kiss around her in order to make your husband the next president. But she has about as much influence as I do so you might as well have breakfast with me."

Linda smiled. "You're not serving poison cookies, are you? Why wouldn't I want to have breakfast with you?"

"Linda, you don't want to have breakfast with me any more than I want to have breakfast with you."

Linda ignored the remark. She patted her Calvin Klein pants and sat down slowly.

"What are you doing there? By the time you sit down they'll be serving lunch."

"Look, Jennifer, I do not like smiling pants."

"Smiling pants? Your pants should only have something to smile about."

"Smiling pants," Linda said in a supercilious tone, "are wrinkles around the crotch."

Jennifer put her hand on her forehead. "Linda, no man ever refuses to make love because you have wrinkles around the crotch when you're dressed."

"But I don't dress just for men."

"Well, relax, I'll tell you now. Jo is not interested in your unpressed crotch."

Linda was not going to discuss Jo with Jennifer Jump-in-Bed. "Can you catch a waiter's eye? I want some coffee."

"A waiter's eye is about all you can catch here."

"What are you trying for? Syphilis?"

"You must have had all B's in college. You talk like an almost-smart woman. Don't mess with me, Linda. Just take yourself over to the breakfast buffet. You'll love it. Mass-produced cold scrambled eggs, underdone bacon, greasy sausage, and canned orange juice. It's the regular convention breakfast. Doesn't matter if you're at La Costa, the Doral or the New York Hilton; it's all the same. I think they ship it from hotel to hotel."

Linda looked at Jennifer. Maybe she wasn't so dumb. "We could at least get fresh orange juice in California," Linda said, joining the new conversation with enthusiasm.

Jennifer sighed. "No. All California is canned. We start everything out here . . . health foods, unmarried motherhood, casual screwing, and then we can it and ship it East."

"You'd screw whether you lived in California or New York, so why blame the sunshine?" Damn. Linda had blown it again. Jennifer made her feel like a dummy housewife. She hated her for it.

Jennifer sipped her coffee. Linda was a bitch. Now she'd play with her. After all, Jennifer had not had speaking parts in Grade B movies for nothing. "Sex is no different in Hollywood than it is in New Jersey. That's what people say, but you and I both know that it is different. There's more money and more sunshine out here, so people react differently. You take somebody like me, a country singer, and give me some pretty clothes, change my name, cap my teeth, add a little eye make-up and right away I'm a made-to-order sex symbol. So a guy from the Midwest comes along and has big ideas about what making love to me must be like. He figures I have to be a hell of a lot better than whatever it is he ever had. And the truth is that I'm probably not as good because, you see, the woman he loves back home in Indiana and he have something going between them, and even if he doesn't do all the latest stuff from the how-to books, they've got feelings and tenderness, and that's better."

"Jennifer, you're a liar."

"Only with women like you, Linda. You bring out the worst in me."

"Who brings out the best? Midwest hicks and Hollywood jocks?"

"Hollywood jocks? Don't make me laugh. Most of them are acey-deucy. There's hardly a straight guy around."

"But there is a lot of bisexuality, isn't there?"

"Bisexual? Ha. Do you know what bisexual means?"

Linda shook her head.

"Bisexual means he went to bed with a woman once—and hated it.

"Look, Linda, let's forget about sexual activity for a minute. Let me ask you something. How come you're such a pushy wife? Why do you campaign for your husband's career all over these meetings? Why aren't you just a plain liberated woman? Why don't you open a needlepoint shop or take in laundry? How come you put all that talent and energy into a slow-moving guy like Ken?"

Linda waited until the little stabs of anger passed, then took a breath. "Ken would be terrific whether he married me or not. But I do think it is my job to be a part of his life. I care what happens to him."

"You're slobbering all over his career."

"He seems satisfied."

"You call a nervous tic satisfaction? I go to meetings with Ken. I see him twitch."

Linda's eyes narrowed. "He never said you went to meetings with him."

"Cool it, baby. I said we went to meetings, not to bed. Ken is incredibly uptight in those meetings, and I think you're the reason. He's more afraid of you than he is of Chester Masterson. You ask so many questions. You kind of bore in on a person. I feel naked when I talk to you."

"You feel naked when you talk to anyone."

Jennifer ignored the remark. "You want your husband to be

president? Then don't let it show. China doesn't let it show . . ."

Linda snorted. "China? Does she know that Tim may become president? China is such a total zero that she has no idea what goes on in Tim's world. I think Chester has to send her a letter on her birthday each year to remind her she's his daughter."

"China isn't educated, but she isn't dumb."

Linda was not going to dive deeper into the Tim/Chester/China trap. So Jennifer went to those meetings. In that case she needed Jennifer for an ally. She needed anybody who ever went to a Kiss meeting with Ken and Chester and Henry in the same room. "You're probably right, Jennifer. I worry a lot about Ken. He is so talented, but he won't blow his own horn. I just want him to get everything that's coming to him, and I want the people who work with him to understand just how great he is, and I want everyone to know how much his family is behind him . . ."

"His family?" she asked with a sarcastic laugh. "You mean his father in the drugstore is behind him?"

"How do you know his father has a drugstore?"

"You think I thought he was Henry Ford's grandson? I know Ken Sugarman's father has a drugstore because in meetings he talks about knowing the drug trade and how to reach them. Don't sweat, Linda. It's not so bad to have a father who owns a drugstore if it makes you more knowledgeable."

"I want to help Ken. I really do."

"Then don't be so obvious, Linda. I like Ken, too. Now look, I am not a great actress, but I have been around long enough to know that you can be clever about the ways you get what you want. You can get him the presidency the same way women get men—or men get women. Be imaginative."

Linda licked her lips. "Give me a for instance, Jennifer."

"A story about the way a man or woman sold themselves? Let me think a minute. Hey, did you ever hear the story about Annie Sweet and T. D. Rock?"

"You mean Annie Sweet, the singer?"

"Yes. She's the one who married the banker, T. D. Rock."

"I didn't even know she was married."

"Honey, she was married six months before she realized she was. It's a great story. From the minute T.D. saw Annie, he knew he was going to marry her. Never mind that she already had a husband. He couldn't care less. T.D. was powerful like Chester Masterson, but under it all he was a softhearted sweetheart."

"Not exactly the way you'd describe our Chester."

"Hardly. Well, T.D. was dating Annie because she was on the way out of her marriage anyway, and he was getting about as far as the living-room sofa. Even these days he couldn't make it to the bedroom with her. And I know you can't believe that about any singer, but it's true. Finally one night he knew he'd have to do something really . . . well, imaginative . . . to get her into bed. One night she and T.D. were going out to dinner, and he got to her house early. She called from upstairs and told him to make himself a drink, so he went into the kitchen. As he stood at the sink and looked out the window, an idea came to him. He reached for a kitchen knife and cut a hole in the window screen."

"Why?"

"You'll see. He and Annie went out to dinner, and when they came back she invited him in for a nightcap. He walked past the kitchen on the way into the house . . . they were going in through the back door, and suddenly he said to Annie, 'Don't panic, but I think someone just broke into your house. Look, the screen is cut.' Well, Annie started to shake all over, and Chester said she should just go back into the car, and he'd check out the house. He walked into the kitchen, made himself a drink, and when it seemed like a reasonable amount of time he waltzed back to the car and told Annie that they must have arrived just in time because the burglars had left. Then he asked Annie if she were afraid to stay alone in a house where burglars had been just a few minutes before . . . and might come again."

"Why didn't Annie ask him to call the police?"

"Linda, you think too straight. Of course she told him to call the police, but T.D. thinks shrewd. He said that calling the police was dangerous because it just alerted them to the fact that there were valuables in the house. And Annie, in her hysteria, agreed not to call the police. Then T.D. made his big pitch. 'Baby,' he said, 'why don't you come to my house and sleep in Alice Jean's room?' Alice Jean is T.D.'s grown daughter. Well, needless to say she went to T.D.'s, and that was the last time she ever slept in Alice Jean's room."

"And the moral of that story is cut the screen."

"Right. Stop pushing Ken; start shaping events."

"Will you help me, Jennifer?"

"Of course not."

Linda was startled. "But it's your idea."

"With you, Linda, nothing is anybody else's idea. All I'm doing is planting seeds. And I can hardly wait to see what comes up."

"Jennifer, excuse me, will you? I think I want to get some air."

"You're in an open air restaurant right now."

"Okay then, I want to move around. I want to think."

"It's about time, Linda. Do something interesting. I want to be part of the audience."

Linda threw her napkin down on the table and got up a lot faster than she had sat down. "Oh, you will be part of the audience, Jennifer. This will be one Kiss convention where the best action won't be confined to your bedroom."

"First mistake," said Jennifer. "Don't waste your bullets. Stop firing at me."

Linda walked outside. Of course Jennifer was right. Disorganized pushing of her husband with Jo wouldn't get him the presidency. Nor would insulting, pseudo-smart remarks. It would take something sharper. Bitchier. It would still take another person's help. Preferably an outsider. She smiled. The perfect outsider had been dropped in her lap. The *Newsweek* writer. Okay, Linda, she said to herself, the first thing we do is cultivate Ms. Sharon Kennedy. For Ken's sake and maybe even Linda's.

Chester called room service. "What do you mean you don't have Milky Ways? It's 8 A.M. You have until 6 P.M. to get me one dozen. And no excuses, do you hear?"

Barbara had three choices. She could do her isometric exercises, go to breakfast in order to clue in one more district manager on the Tuesday presentation, or she could stay in her room and rehearse her role in the meeting. She shook her head. Why couldn't she ever offer herself delicious choices? What was the matter with her? Why couldn't she come up with good stuff for herself the way she did for everybody else in her life? Why were Barbara's options for Barbara always confined to advancing her body or her career? How about some fun and games for little Barbara? Look at that Sharon Kennedy. She looked as if she always had a good time. Why couldn't Barbara be more like Sharon? She smiled. Somehow she couldn't picture herself dragging around in faded blue jeans saying everything was the pits. It wasn't in character. She would just have to accept the fact that she was a purposeful woman who couldn't stand life when she was not performing in the center ring. No way that Barbara could be a wisecracking fun-loving carefree young woman like Sharon.

"Person-to-person, Tom Sales," Sharon said cheerfully to the operator, and she was ecstatic when Tom answered. She didn't even let the operator ask for him. She attacked the voice as surely as she did the man. "Tom, I called you person-to-person, and it isn't even collect," she said proudly.

"How the fuck did you do that?"

"I'm at such a big deal convention that they buy me food and massages and saunas, so I figured they might as well pick up my phone bills, too."

"That's even better than ripping off the phone company."

"I knew you'd love it."

"So what's big business like?"

"I think it's the pits."

"Bad people?"

"No. Just bad vibes from sort of nice people. There's a girl here who's drinking herself to the end of her life. And there's a woman who's a little older than I am who thinks she's Rosalind Russell in a 1940s movie. And another who is a perfect wife. And one who, I think, is a perfect bitch. It's one wild story. Oh, and Tom, the best is Jennifer Johnson. Biggest tits in the world."

"Bigger than yours?"

"You still remember?"

"Yes."

"Does it make you want me?"

Silence. Big silence. Sharon giggled, something she usually

avoided doing. Still silence. "Hey, I just asked if you miss my tits."

"Sharon, I want to say something."

Oh no. He was moving out.

"Sharon, I think maybe I need to be alone for a while. You know, really alone. No obligations. No responsibilities. I still care, but—"

Damn. Women always knew the bad stuff in advance. Even when it was seconds in advance.

"Sure, Tom." How could two words get stuck in her throat?

"So here's what we'll do." Now he sounded sure of himself, strong.

"I have an assignment in California, Northern California, and I think I'll stay for a while."

"How long?" She was going to be sick.

"I'm not really sure."

"And?" One word was all she could manage.

Deep breath. Sigh. "And I think, Sharon, that we ought to be relaxed about everything. I really feel totally asexual now, and I want you just to go out and have a good time."

With what, she wondered, some junior executive who sells lipstick for a living?

After she hung up, Sharon sat for a few minutes. What I need, she thought, is to be contained and composed like Barbara Anderson. She wouldn't go to pieces like this. She'd just pick up her briefcase and run to the next meeting.

Barbara picked up her briefcase.

Amazing.

Really amazing.

Chester Masterson calling her to come this minute for a meeting in his suite. How was she to know that he had first called Henry, Tim, and Ken only to find they were all out? She put on brown pants, a voluminous beige shirt, cinched her waist to twenty-two inches with a big leather belt, and strode across the courtyard to Chester's. She had never seen Chester so early in the day. He usually arrived at the office around eleven. Why was he awake so early? Probably the three-hour difference, she reminded herself. She hoped she would get out in time for the opening session at nine. Chester didn't give a damn if anybody showed up or not. Everyone knew he wouldn't be there. Chester hated meetings. He only liked confrontations. Well, she was ready for this one.

Chester sat in a silk dressing gown at a breakfast table. Before him were three glasses of orange juice, two orders of eggs, bacon (well crisped, not the soggy variety offered at the breakfast buffet), toast, and two pots of coffee. Enough food to serve breakfast for two. Or even three.

When Chester heard the knock, he snapped, "Come on in." At the sound of his voice the confidence went oozing out of her body. She opened the door. Chester did not look up from the Los Angeles *Times*. He buttered a slice of toast, one whole slice at a time, stuffed it into his mouth. "Sit down." He pointed to a side chair at the opposite end of the room. He still did not look up. He did not speak. She cleared her throat and realized that she had been invited to his suite to watch him eat breakfast. Evidently he thought he was the "Today" show live. Unshaven and in his horn-rimmed glasses, he looked like some small-time hood. And he was performing for his audience. Butter the toast. Spread the jam. Put it in the mouth.

She watched the performance. She was fascinated by the way Chester choreographed his breakfast. This was the man Kiss people respected and feared in equal parts. Barbara had never really felt safe with Chester. She had no idea what would happen this morning. It was exciting to live on the edge of unpredictability.

He was still chewing. He did not look up. He wiped his mouth with a napkin. "So what's all this about Product Q?"

She jumped, startled by his question. Ah, so that's why he had asked her here. Well, she had the answers right in her hot little briefcase. "Chester," she sighed, "we've gone over this in New York, but if you want it again, I'll trot it all out."

"You don't want to?" For the first time he looked up.

"Not really. I think we already agree on the key parts."

"Like what?"

"Product concept, testing period, national introduction, marketing and advertising strategies."

"I just decided. We're not going to test the Product Q at all. We will just go ahead with it."

She smiled. "You have guts."

"I didn't think girls said things like that."

"Nowadays, Chester, they say even worse things. But I'll rephrase it. I think you have a great deal of daring. But I happen to agree. We don't have to test the product. In fact, if we do, we only alert the rest of the cosmetics world to what we are doing and give them a chance to run to their laboratories and come up with competitive products. I think the formula may get out fast."

Chester had had no intention of killing the test market. How had he been trapped into saying it? Oh, that's right. He had wanted an audience, and she was the only audience in town. Then he wanted a fight, and so he said the most outrageous thing he could. And she agreed. The breakfast was not following the script. She was not going to get off so easy. "Let me see the ads."

"I only have rough versions with me, but I have all the copy."

"Who's the model?"

"You won't see a face," she said triumphantly.

"Won't see a face? What kind of dumb ass . . . oh, excuse me, Barbara, what kind of silly idea is that?"

"It isn't silly. The idea is that every woman can then identify with the woman in the ad. Every woman can feel she is the one to get the benefits."

"Let me tell you something. You may know something about writing a market plan, but you don't know anything about advertising. Doesn't being a woman let you know that women *identify* with beautiful women? Show a woman another woman who's fantastic, and she immediately thinks that's who she is. Don't you understand why women walk like movie stars or toss their hair the way they do or try to smile like them?"

Barbara listened. He really was smart. He really did know how women think and why they buy the things they do.

"Now let me see the copy," he said.

She reached in her briefcase. She wondered how fast a creative team could reshoot and get photos to her. She looked at her watch. It was 11:30 A.M. in New York. If she split by noon, she could call the agency and get them to find a photographer, arrange a sitting today, develop tonight. She would get a company plane . . . she thought again. She had still another idea. But she'd have to get out of Chester's suite fast.

"Let me see the copy." He was repeating himself. She must be too slow.

"I'll read it to you," she said.

"No, you won't." He got up from behind the table and took the copy from her hand. She pulled back in surprise. In the office, copy was always read to Chester. She looked at him again. Now she knew why copy was read to him. He needed glasses. He was alone today—or had been—so he wore glasses to read the newspaper. She was amused by Chester's vanity. Now that he had his glasses, he was not going to trust her with the precious words for Product Q.

"That copy stinks."

"I didn't write it, Chester."

"You approved it."

"So did you." Damn. She wasn't going to take the rap for his decisions as well as hers.

"Where was Mr. Genius, our president, when this was approved?"

"He was in the room telling you he hated the copy."

"Then why was it done this way, Barbara?"

"Because you made us rewrite it right there in the boardroom. Remember? We had the agency people there, and you sweated with us over every word."

"It's no good."

"Then why don't you write it yourself?"

"Because you can get it rewritten. Call New York, and get what you want."

"Chester, we won't get what I want. We'll get what you want. Now tell me what you want."

"The headline has too much love in it."

"Don't you think women put things on their face to make men love them?"

He snorted. "Love? What kind of goddamn nonsense is that?" He was so incensed he forgot to apologize for his profanity.

"Chester," she said softly, "I think women respond strongest to love."

He shook his finger. "You have a lot to learn, Barbara. Self-love maybe. But storybook love? Never."

"Why?" She wasn't going to let him give her maxims without reason.

"Oh, love is all right," Chester said, "but it takes too much time. Take out the love."

Barbara shrugged. "Okay. Kill the love."

"And give me a good headline."

"You have a good headline," she said sharply.

"Oh no, we don't. And you don't even know why the headline is no good."

"All right. Why is it bad?"

"Because it doesn't startle anybody."

"We had love in it."

"What's so startling about love?"

"All right," she said in exasperation, "you want revolutionary in the headline, right?"

"That headline cries for revolutionary," Chester said slowly as if he were speaking to a dim-witted child. "Don't you know that people react to headlines, not articles? Nobody knows what Reston and Wicker write. They don't quote anything but the headline when they tell you about somebody's story. Nobody reads articles. Nobody reads copy."

"Nobody?" she asked sarcastically.

"Nobody," he answered firmly.

"Chester," she said, "you would make a great dictator. You are so absolutely sure of everything."

"Barbara, I am a great dictator."

"Is that what it takes to run a successful business?"

"That or a father-in-law who started the business."

"I want to talk to you a minute about the headline," she said in her softest, sincerest tone. "I don't want to be cornball."

His eyes flashed. "And you think I do? What do you know about me, Miss Vassar or wherever? You were studying your ABC's when I was making my nail enamel for your mother. But that doesn't have anything to do with it either. Everybody has experience. Experience doesn't mean anything. All that matters is something new. I'm going to tell you something, Barbara, and when I finish telling you, you'll change the copy."

"What is it?"

"The only reason that people do not do things is not that they can't. It's just that they don't think of them."

She nodded.

"Now go back to your room. Forget the meeting where they all look at each other and Henry makes some asinine statement about owning the world. We still have a lot of the United States to sell. You just go back to your room, and you think of the one thing that none of that bunch of martini drinkers we call an agency thought of. Who knows better than you what the copy should say? Why do you trust people who aren't as smart as you and don't care as much as you?"

Barbara listened carefully. She understood what he was saying. He was telling her not to depend on anyone else. She was her own security. She was her own solution. Of course. She had known that ever since she had dialed Paul Thurston hours earlier. She stood up and gathered her papers. "I hear you, Chester," she said evenly, "I hear you."

Then she left the spacious suite. She forgot the time. She forgot the place. She forgot that Chester had never even offered her breakfast.

She could remember only that she had to call Los Angeles, and she had a headline to rewrite.

Chester Masterson turned Randy Partridge from a nice up-and-coming junior executive into the werewolf of the West. Of course, Chester didn't plan it. It just happened that way. Randy got his MBA at Wharton, then headed straight for New York with his eye on the big dollar in the Big Apple. It was said by one of Randy's professors that "this student has the potential for great good or great evil, and his first job will make the difference." Randy's first job was with Kiss in the accounting department. Within months Randy had leapfrogged over men with more talent and more seniority. What was it Randy had? "Balls," announced Chester Masterson as he made Randy assistant treasurer. During the money crunch of the early 1970s Randy made his big play. He speculated in Swiss currency. He asked no one's advice. He invested $2.2 million in Swiss banks, and within six months he had made over $5 million for Kiss, Inc. He went to see Chester Masterson and told him what he had done. "You speculated?" Masterson asked, rubbing his hands together. Randy was practically foaming at the mouth. "Yes. Yes." "Good," said Chester proudly, "it's against corporate policy to speculate, but keep it up, kid." The kid kept it up. He kept it up so long that three years later he had lost $7 million for Kiss, Inc. One day the auditors came in to discuss the books with Chester. "The kid's been speculating," one of them told Chester. "Fire the dummy," Chester said, reaching for three Gelusils. Randy's boss had the job of telling the kid he was through. Randy was boiling. "I am going to the board of directors and tell them that Big Chet gave me permission to speculate even though it was against company policy." When Chester Masterson found out . . . because Chester Masterson always found out . . . that Randy was planning to go the the board of directors, Chester sent a special delivery letter to every board member informing him (there were no women board members, of course) that Randy was in personal financial difficulty, had therefore speculated with company funds, and was being dismissed without benefit of annuities, pensions, or other fringe benefits. The directors were shocked. So was Randy. Because not only did the board refuse to see him, so did every other major American company. Randy moved to California and set up his own consulting firm. In the beginning only fringe companies dealt with Randy, but as his raiding of companies became legendary, the biggies clamored for him. *Fortune* called him "the werewolf of the West," but when anyone asked Chester Masterson to comment on Randy Partridge, Chester would shake his head sadly and say, "You just can't trust an MBA."

Jo Burns watched the Kiss conventioneers filing into Convention Room A. They looked to her like a sartorial smorgasbord. The people from package design and communications wore jeans and T-shirts that said everything from "Genuine" to "Two for the Money" on the front. Sales and marketing executives wore Ralph Lauren pants and polo shirts, but the easiest ones to identify were the men from production. Production came to the meeting at the lush, informal Gates of Paradise dressed in business suits and ties.

As they walked past Jo, she felt proud. These were the people who worked for her husband. He controlled their destinies, and she was his wife. She had a subtle power over their lives, and at the sales convention she recognized it. This was her once-a-year time. The rest of the year she was humble about her position. The other months she pooh-poohed the advantages of being Mrs. Henry Burns because the rest of the year she was caught up in the disadvantages: the separations, the decisions to be made alone. But now, for a week, she was Mrs. Henry Burns, and she tried not to let anyone, especially Jo Burns, forget it.

Henry stood on the small stage in front of the group. He

smiled. Why not? It was the last time he would ever do The First Morning Speech. Unlike the informal remarks of the preceding evening, this speech was meant to look prepared. It was the heavy executive number. Henry reached inside the pocket of his navy blazer and took out his glasses. He did not really need the glasses to read, but they insulated him, gave him the privacy he needed to face his audience. Looking at three hundred people, all of whom expected Henry to know their names and secret desires, made Henry feel uneasy. The glasses somehow protected him from all those impractical dreamers who thought he was talking just to them. He cleared his throat and looked for familiar faces. Was that really Jo sitting there looking at him in that adoring way? Yes. Well, it was something to see how the limelight could turn on the lovelight. He never saw that same look in the secretness of their bedroom. He fumbled for the prepared papers and then thought better of it. If seeing him there could turn Jo on like that, what was it doing to the rest of the audience? He took his glasses off, forgot about reaching for the prepared speech, and almost immediately felt relaxed. Ah, said Henry to himself as he looked about the room, I certainly am going to leave gorgeous traditions when I depart for Oxxon. Who will be able to follow this?

He took the prepared speech, ripped it in two, flashed a big smile, and said, "Who needs to read a speech to friends?"

The applause was loud and long.

Henry raised his hands to stop the ovations. "Wait," he said, "you ain't heard nothin' yet. Now just in case you don't know, I am not Chester Masterson. The company is getting so big I thought I better reintroduce myself." Small ripple of laughter, but it was enough to let Henry know he still had his audience. He went smoothly onward, talking about the year that was and the year that was to be. He promised them all bigger, brighter futures, and he assured them they'd find the way to the future in the present. It was an informal talk, but it had currents of power. A good example of a presidential speech.

Barbara slipped into the last row just after Henry began his talk. She made a small circle with her thumb and forefinger to signal that she approved of what he said. She knew he was right; this was their year to howl. Kiss, Inc., was on the way. Judging from her morning, it was going to be some year. She opened the plastic notebook on her lap, the notebook with Kiss, Inc., emblazoned on it, the same kind of plastic notebook that every corporation from IBM to the plumbers' union gives to convention delegates. She opened it, found the regulation ball-point pen and pad of yellow lined paper, and she began writing notes to assure herself that she had remembered everything from her confrontation with Chester. She jotted "airplane" . . . that meant the company plane would be waiting at 3 P.M. at the airfield down the road and would fly her to Los Angeles. Then she wrote "agency" . . . which reminded her the agency creative team would be on hand to reshoot the ad at 4 P.M. The last word was "layouts" . . . and that was her code word for the meeting she had scheduled in her room for midnight, the time when the agency people would fly in from Los Angeles, and after holding typesetters and stat people on overtime, they would bring her the revised layouts for approval. The whole operation was geared to make Barbara's absence unnoticed. She would be at the morning meeting, slip away at 2:45, return at 7, attend the evening dinner, and who would know? No one except Henry Burns, who authorized the use of the plane.

Henry spotted Barbara. He had missed the gesture of encouragement. All he noticed was Barbara writing. Taking notes on what he was saying? he wondered. Well, he'd soon find out. "Our big reason for being bullish on next year is something called Product Q," Henry said. Barbara lifted her head and gasped. Was Henry going to steal her thunder? Henry smiled at her. Good. She was listening. He was only testing. She'd have to understand that was presidential prerogative. Presidents were allowed to scare the ranks. Besides Henry knew that fear kept more people in line than respect. Or love.

Monday had been scheduled as "Quality Day" in the convention doings, so the spotlight was on research, development, and production. That was all right with Barbara because it all provided good lead-in stuff for her presentation on Tuesday. It was solid and informative material, but she knew it was as boring as hell. The twitching in chairs began shortly after Henry introduced Dr. Wilhelm Schulz for research and development, and massive boredom set in when Carol Morris took everyone through a slide presentation detailing the training school procedures for department store salespeople. By the time they broke for coffee at 10:15 the group was wishing it had broken for the day.

Barbara went over to Henry. "Thanks for the nice intro on Product Q. I was afraid for a minute that you might tell everything."

"If you sit in meetings and write notes instead of listen to the teacher, then you won't always be certain."

She smiled. "Okay. I'll pay attention."

"So will I." It was a female voice. Barbara turned. Sure enough. There was the ubiquitous Linda Sugarman. "Are we going to have our annual tennis game, Henry?" she asked.

Henry nodded. Then he decided to tease Barbara. That was both a personal and professional prerogative. "Of course, Linda, you are the best woman player here. Nobody can beat a California girl on the tennis courts."

Barbara bristled. Had she been the junior champ in Westchester County for nothing? "I think I'd like to play in that game. How about doubles?"

"Of course," Henry said gleefully. He liked nothing better than a good fight or a good match. "Since Linda is my partner, who will you get?"

"I'll get Tim," she said fiercely, "and then we'll see if Linda really can beat Tim at his game."

"It's a tennis game; that's all," said Linda with a laugh.

Barbara turned and walked quickly back to her room. She was angry at herself now. What was it about pushy Linda that really bothered her? Why did she let Linda annoy her?

The telephone was ringing as Barbara turned the key.

"Hi, honey."

It was Paul Thurston. The cool, clear doctor voice of her fiancé.

"Hi, honey," she responded.

"How's it going?" The slight solicitous tone she hated was creeping into his voice. The save-a-life-a-day researcher versus the moneygrubber.

"I haven't isolated any viruses lately," she said briskly.

"Nor have I," he sighed. Why was Barbara always so defensive?

"Then what *are* you doing?" Now he'd see what it was like when she asked the questions.

"I'm winding up a week's work in two days," he said in an effort to sound unruffled.

"Why?" she asked suspiciously. Paul never acted without motivation.

"I'd like to spend a couple of days with you."

"Me?"

"What's so strange about that?"

"It's strange," she said crisply, "because it's damned impractical. You're in New York, and I'm in California."

"Planes fly every hour."

"And—?"

"And I'd like to be on one tomorrow."

"But I'm in the middle of the most important convention of my life—"

"Hey, relax," he said quickly, "I thought you'd like it."

Waves of guilt flooded her. Of course she should like it. What woman wouldn't welcome some unexpected time with her husband-to-be?

"Of course I like it." Now her tone was lighter.

"Then suppose I come out in a few hours. Today."

"Paul," she spoke tenderly now, "listen a minute. I'll be honest. I am going to Los Angeles in the afternoon, but I can stay only a couple of hours. I have my big presentation tomorrow morning. Why don't you come to The Gates of Paradise and go to the closing dinner with me tomorrow night?"

He hesitated. He knew her dilemma. He also knew his. "No," he said, matching the tenderness in her voice. "Don't you see? If we meet there, I have to see you in a business role again. And this is one time I don't want to see the lady who has to smile at the boss. I want to see the lady who wants to smile at me."

She smiled unconsciously as he spoke. "Like the first time?" she asked hopefully.

"Like the first time," he promised. He hoped he sounded convincing.

"But this isn't Puerto Rico," she said.

"Let's be crazy anyway. Let's make it like Puerto Rico."

"But not at The Gates of Paradise?"

"No, Barb. Definitely not at The Gates of Paradise. I want neutral territory. I'll meet you anywhere in Los Angeles. Go to your meeting, and then tell me where to be. And I'll be waiting for you."

Barbara was torn. She wanted to be with Paul. She wanted again the scent of the flowers and the rhythm of the love that first time in Puerto Rico. But people were depending on her. She couldn't just walk away. "How about a compromise?" she asked.

"Like what?"

"Paul," she said eagerly, "there's a motel about twenty miles down the road from The Gates of Paradise. Why don't we meet there tomorrow night? Then I can come back for the closing session."

"You're sure you don't want moonlight and roses in Los Angeles?" he asked.

"Of course I want it. But it just wouldn't be right tomorrow. And I do want to see you." As she said the words, she knew they were true. She did want to see him. But on her own terms.

He sensed her vulnerability. "And we'll set a wedding date?"

The old panic came over her. Commitments. People always wanted commitments. Paul had been so safe because he was a man who had avoided commitments all his forty-one years. Why did he suddenly want them with her?

He laughed as if he read her thoughts. "Funny, isn't it? Paul Thurston, the perennial bachelor, begging a woman to marry him."

"Hey," she laughed, "what's so funny about that?"

"I love you," he said with the shyness of a man who seldom says the words.

"Thank you," she answered. "I'll get the reservations and let you know where and when. I'll call the lab and leave word there in case you're busy."

"Thank you," he answered. Such a polite love, he thought. Nothing like the first time.

Barbara sat for a long while after her conversation with Paul ended. If only tomorrow night turned out to be like Puerto Rico, it would give her life real meaning, wouldn't it? If she could have a night of wild, abandoned love-making, wouldn't that be proof that they were right to want to be together forever?

She undressed slowly. She hoped her body would give her the answers her mind could not.

It was not the center court at Forest Hills, but Linda knew she would play as if it were. She stood at mid-court and gripped her racket tightly. Tim was serving to Henry, her partner. She focused on Tim. She wanted the first game. She wanted every game. Tim tossed the ball, moved his body forward, and blasted the first serve to Henry's backhand corner. Henry swung seconds after the ball passed him. He had never seen a better serve.

"Foot fault," came Linda's firm voice. Henry reddened. Oh no. It was going to be that kind of game. Henry was nervous. He did not want to humiliate anyone, but the first serve told him Linda and Tim were fighting for the presidency; he and Barbara were only their partners.

Did Linda really think that if she won Ken would be made president?

Did Tim honestly believe that this kind of decision would be made on the tennis court?

Henry had been both a tennis player and a company president long enough to know there was indeed a correlation between people's characters and the way they played tennis. Slow, deliberate businessmen took their shots the same way . . . with caution. They avoided unnecessary chances, waited for someone else's mistakes. That would not be Tim or Linda, he knew. No, Tim would be looking for opportunities to dazzle the gallery with tricky, tantalizing shots. Linda would be out to prove she could win, and she would do it any way that she could. Yes, that was Linda's style. Now he felt less embarrassed by her call.

Linda was only playing the game her way, her tough and relentless way. But for Henry the game was over. He wasn't really playing; he was watching. He was out of the game. He had stopped trying to win at Kiss. All he wanted were a few accolades when he left. So this tennis game was not Henry's usual fight-to-win tennis; this was his new let's-remember-what-a-nice-guy-Henry-was game. It would be his responsibility to keep the game as clean as possible. Linda would make that difficult. She was like the salesmen who gave advertising allowances that customers did not earn and then had everyone covering up for them. Yes, Linda's ambition was even more ferocious than her forehand. Suddenly Henry felt sorry for Linda.

Tim felt only rage. "That was a foot fault?" he asked sharply. "Well, if that was a foot fault, I guess we're playing Wimbledon rules."

"I always do," Linda snapped.

From the time the match was planned Linda had been mindful of her strategy. She would play to Barbara's backhand, and since she could count on Barbara to lose points that way, Tim would poach. She knew that Tim shared her philosophy: win. Win at any cost. As Tim poached, Barbara would become protective, play harder and with less caution. Careless mistakes would follow. That was Linda's game plan: upset the balance. Throw the other team off. Let them make mistakes.

Tim's second serve was square in the court. Henry fielded it weakly. Was it really too hot to handle or was he making up for his partner's embarrassing call? Tim wet his lips. Henry was trying to out-gentleman him. He didn't like it. It smacked of patronage. He was not going to patronize anybody. He served to Linda. The ball caught her backhand, flipped over the net, and Barbara bubbled it back. Henry reached, but not fast enough. The score was thirty–love.

Tim knew he was the most powerful person in the foursome. He was six feet four inches tall and weighed one hundred ninety-two pounds. His muscles were developed on the squash court, and from the time he learned to shake hands with a racket, he excelled in every racket sport. Despite his bigness, Tim was fast. He covered a lot of court, and he covered it with ease. He had a fighter's instincts. He squinted at Linda. The bitch would not get to him.

Tim's serve to Henry caught the corner, but Henry was ready. He returned as hard as Tim served. Tim stepped to his left and lobbed to the back of the court. He needed time to make the killer shot. Henry raced back. He was puffing slightly. Linda shivered. The third point, and her partner was already out of condition. Henry, slightly off balance, returned the shot. Tim, with a grace worthy of Nureyev, pirouetted and returned the ball hard and fast. Henry watched it go by. "Good shot," he called. The gallery applauded.

Tim's serve took the fourth point, and the first game. The four walked to the net to exchange courts. Tim wiped his face on a towel hanging at the net. Barbara kept on walking. So they won the first game, and she had done nothing except walk from one side of the court to the other. Great team player she was. "Nice game," Tim said to her. She smiled weakly, then remembered she had been responsible for one point. A dink shot. Now she knew. Tim was out to be a one-man show. It was Tim Time at Tennis. They were all patsys for him.

All Barbara's life had been set up for other people. She was always the supporting player. Her strength was her consistency. No particular brilliance, just steadiness. The gallery would never applaud her. She stood at the net and thought how hot the sun was now. The temperature must be in the nineties, and along the courtside the gallery was beginning to order cold drinks. Carol Morris, the training school head, was sitting with Dr. Schulz. Barbara smiled. Conventions certainly made for unconventional pairings. There was a smattering of salesmen, and Rick McCormack of marketing was now standing with his arm around Karen, his secretary. Rick was so open he must be ready to quit, she thought. Then she came to attention. It was Henry's serve.

Barbara watched him take his practice serves. He was working on accuracy, holding back steam. Who in all of Kiss could match Tim's serve? Barbara knew the answer to that one. Henry.

The gallery gasped when Henry's serve came in with the same ferocity as Tim's. But Tim handled the serve with a return that went a million miles down the middle. Linda reached, but she was nowhere near the shot. Henry missed the ball by a beat; he had expected Linda to return it. She had failed. She felt miserable. Barbara moved back to receive the next serve.

Henry looked at Barbara cross-court. He felt sorry for her. He knew she would not return the ball with the killer instincts of Tim Edgar. Who at Kiss had those same instincts? Chester Masterson of course. Henry felt a slight chill. Was Tim trying to wear the robe here and now? Henry tossed the ball. He was intent on the game again, but only the game. He felt good. He knew who he was. He was the cool and cagey head of Kiss, and leaders always make the troops look good. He wanted to be remembered at Kiss as Henry Burns, the man who never won at the expense of his people. No, he would not flatten Barbara. He'd serve solid, but clean. No topspin. No zingers. Barbara dug her feet into the court. She wondered how Henry would play her. Probably through clever placement, not force. When the serve came in short, she was ready. She ran forward and returned the shot. Linda moved in and fired a fast ball to Barbara at net. But Barbara's mind was still on the last shot. Her racket was too low to meet the ball in time. Henry's next serve to Tim was non-returnable. The score was now one-all.

Only at conventions can this kind of tennis game happen. It is born of convenience, bred of insecurity, and the results are felt long after the courts are relined. Barbara remembered the tennis game two years before when Carlo Santori, the marketing director for pharmaceuticals, had won the singles tournament against Henry and proudly proclaimed at the final banquet that on the tennis court one met the real winners in life. Carlo Santori never knew what he did wrong, but two months later he was working for a soap company. All Henry ever said was, "Carlo made a few mistakes in new products costs that he thought we wouldn't find."

To qualify for the game this day, the participants spent a total of twenty years in college and fifty years at work. In Tim's case it also took a family tree. Tim was descended from Henry Adams of Somersetshire, England, who arrived in Massachusetts in 1640 with a grant for land originally occupied by Indians around Braintree. Barbara's roots may have been as deep; she had never bothered to find out.

In business they nicknamed her Barbara Cool; she never showed her emotions. Sometimes they called her Barbara Cold. She wondered if she would live up to her name as she geared herself for the next game. It was her turn to serve. She wondered if all the people who thought her self-contained would be surprised to know that she was perspiring as much because of fear as heat.

Barbara looked up. She had the sun behind her, and she meant to take advantage of it. She threw the ball up high and followed through with a perfect serve. Linda returned it sharply, and Barbara lobbed into the sun. Henry, playing without sunglasses, lost the ball as it arched, and bounced behind him. Barbara smiled. If you can't smash 'em, blind 'em, she thought. Between the first and second points Henry put on sunglasses. So her strategy would work for only one point. Well, one point was better than nothing. Three long volleys followed, and the score went to deuce. I have to get this game, Barbara thought. Tim and I must get ahead. If we miss this game, then we're behind. That puts too much pressure on us. She pulled back and served. Linda picked up the ball and fired it cross-court to Barbara. She dove and moved up. The ball teetered on the net, then fell to the other side. Her point. She smiled wanly. Imperfect point. But then what in life was perfect? Certainly not her life. If her life were as controlled as everyone thought, why was she standing here frightened about a tennis game when her relationship with Paul was crumbling like three-day-old birthday cake? She did not know just when she realized the Paul-Barbara romance was less than perfect. It should have been right. Wasn't it true that she needed a father, and Paul Thurston was the perfect father figure? So if she needed a father, why did she demand a lover?

Barbara double-faulted to Henry. Then Linda returned Barbara's serve to her backhand, and Barbara, still stinging from the humiliation of a double fault hit weakly into the net. Henry powdered her serve past Tim. Barbara and Tim's serve was broken. They moved to change sides, and Tim said sharply, "I hope you're better in that meeting tomorrow than you are today or I'll sell my stock."

Finky son-in-law. Out of the corner of her eye she spied Sharon Kennedy standing with the gallery. I bet she knows better words to describe Tim, she thought.

It is doubtful whether a more competitive tennis player than Linda Sugarman ever stood on a court. What she lacked in skill she made up in aggressiveness. Not a steady player, Linda was tough and strong. Her serve was potent, and she made some shots that would make a pro smile. Yet at other times she missed the easy ones. "You're not consistent," Ken would say to her. "You're not even good," she would fire in return.

Linda took no practice serves. She couldn't wait to get to the game. They were winning two-to-one. Now was her chance to make it three-to-one. Ah, she thought, it is Linda Star Time on the tennis court. She could hear the applause she was certain would follow her serve. Linda tossed the ball, addressed it to Barbara's backhand, and to Linda's surprise Barbara smashed her return. Henry sent the ball back with ease. It came directly to Barbara, and her arm went back. As she stepped forward to hit the ball, Tim dove in front of her. He poached. She felt a hot flush begin behind her ears. It had nothing to do with the heat of the day. Tim shot the ball back, and it dropped dead at Linda's feet. The gallery stood. It was a brilliant shot. It was an unbelievable get. Barbara didn't know he put that spin on the ball. She didn't even know how he found the ball. Tim was a good player; she had to admit it. But she hated him for taking the shot that was rightfully hers. She smiled. "Great shot." "Beautiful," Henry called. Linda bent down and picked up the ball. "Let's get some new balls," she said. "Obviously if the ball dies, there's something wrong with these." Tim gritted his teeth. Only six generations of careful breeding kept him from speaking the words on his mind.

Linda served carefully and won the second point. Now her confidence was back. Then, on flukes that happen only in tennis, she lost the next three points. Score: two-all. Maybe she wasn't a winner. She clenched her teeth. She hadn't ever tried harder to win anything.

Tim bounced the ball twice. It was his serve again. He liked to get the feel of new balls before he served them. He looked at the gallery. Yes, there was China. China with her long red square-cut nails was sitting by herself on the grass, sitting alone as if she were a nobody. He felt the waves of rage wash over him. Did he really hate China or was it her father he despised? Which of them held the key to his social prison? He looked to see if China had a drink in her hand. Not that he cared if she drank; it did not matter to him. He rather liked to see her drink. It was proof positive of her weakness, her inability to cope.

Tim had a sardonic view of himself. He wanted to win and knew that he could with ease if only he practiced more. That was true of all his talents. He used everything he had without effort.

Deep down he knew he was a lazy bastard. But at least, he told himself, I am a lazy bastard with good reflexes.

Now he was about to use those good reflexes.

Henry Burns's mind was wandering. That was most un-Henry-like. Henry never let his mind wander. Tim sensed that Henry was not with the match; he knew that meant opportunity for him and Barbara. Tim ran his tongue around his lips. He could taste the win now. Henry was off someplace in his head. Tim might be lazy, but he was there. Tim lifted the ball and hit to Henry's forehand. Henry was thinking . . . and next year at this time I'll be playing in the Oxxon game. The ball whistled past him. "Henry," Linda said sharply, "are you in this game?" He smiled benignly. Poor Linda. She was still in this game; he was on his way out. "Sort of," he said. Then he was sorry. It mattered to Linda, and he had no right to let her down. He bent over with his racket low. There. Now he looked like a tennis player.

Tim said to Barbara, "I am going to serve to Linda. Watch it because I won't smash. When it comes back, you play close to the net and smash mid-court. Henry's asleep so we'll get the point." Barbara nodded. She followed instructions, and they took the second point. The next two points were won in exactly the same way as the first two. Four straight points. Games stood at three for Tim and Barbara, two for Henry and Linda.

Linda called time as they changed courts. She wanted some water. She looked to see if Ken was anywhere near. No, of course not. Damn him. He was always in the wrong place at these conventions. Probably sitting with some nobody salesman while she sweated her dimples trying to make him president.

She watched Henry walk slowly to the service court. She shook her head. Not only could she pick the losers in life, she could even pick a loser on the tennis court.

For Henry the walk to the service court at The Gates of Paradise tennis courts was a long walk from the apartment in Brooklyn. But despite his occasional grousing he had enjoyed it. He knew he had pandered to Chester, but Henry felt he had done it with style. Like the time he walked into the boardroom twenty minutes after a marketing meeting started. It had been all right to be late that day because Chester had wanted him to interview a new ad manager. Henry walked in, slid into his usual seat at

Chester's right, then pounded the table and smilingly said, "I don't know what has happened so far, but I agree with Chester." Everyone laughed. That was how Henry demonstrated his aplomb. Making jokes of all the things that were not jokes.

In the game today Henry knew he was not displaying his best form, for he was master of the kind of subtle shots one did not unleash in this kind of boy-girl game. Today, however, he felt no need to perform. For the first time in his eighteen years at Kiss, Henry Burns was totally relaxed. He knew that he was relaxed because the pressure to be chairman of Kiss, Inc., had finally ended. Now he could taste the newness of Oxxon. He had found his way without Chester. It was the most liberating feeling he had ever known. Henry waved to Jennifer Johnson before he began serving. The gallery looked at one another knowingly. This was not the old Henry. They had never seen such absence of concentration in Henry before.

Henry began his service by double-faulting. Linda walked over to him. She was angry. "What's that about?"

"You afraid I'm losing my grip?" he asked casually.

"You're making me look rotten, and I don't like it," she said sharply.

Henry lost the next two points. The score was forty–love. Tim was beginning to like what he saw. Then Tim overdrove the next ball. Forty–fifteen. Barbara's backhand flopped into the net. Forty–thirty. It was Tim's chance. He was not going to muff it. He returned Henry's serve to Linda who popped it back to Tim. He sent the ball sailing over Henry's head. Henry ran back but not fast enough. It was now four–two, favor of Tim and Barbara.

"Now let's see how you work under pressure," Tim said as he tossed the balls to Barbara.

So Tim wanted to see. Well, she'd show him what made her new products head. She'd show him so that in case he became the next president he wouldn't take her little kingdom from her. Barbara threw the ball into the air, and her serve curved in with all the heat she could put on it. She knew from that service that she had never been better. Now she was going to keep her mind on the game. It had been a tough route to be the first woman head of new products. She wasn't going to lose it on the tennis court. Now Tim would find out why she had the respect of everyone at Kiss, why Henry always went to bat for her. She was cool and tough and powerful. She could not be scared out of winning. Barbara served to Henry. He missed the shot. The gallery gasped. "Good serve, Barb," Henry called. Tim grinned. Linda looked around. She was not about to be a loser. She had to do something, and she had to do it fast.

Linda returned Barbara's serve. When the ball was returned in Henry's court, Linda flew from her position, reached and dove as Tim would have done—and fell on the court. Henry ran to her. "Are you hurt?" She nodded, rubbing her ankle. "I think so." She hobbled off the court, and Sharon Kennedy came forward.

"I can tell if it's a sprain," Sharon said. "That's one thing you learn in a big family."

"I come from a small family," Linda said quickly, "and it's a sprain."

"You mean the game's over?" Tim asked.

"I guess it is for you," Linda answered.

"We give you the set then," Henry said to Tim and Barbara. "We have to forfeit, but I think you would have won anyway. You were on. Both of you. Nice playing."

Linda stood up forgetting her twisted ankle. "They didn't win," she shouted. "They didn't win. We had to stop playing. They didn't win."

"Oh yes, we did, Miss Wimbledon," Tim answered.

"Come on," Henry said, "I'll buy you all a drink."

"Forget it," Tim snapped. "I can buy my own drinks."

"I'm going to my room," Linda said. Her eyes were angry.

Barbara looked quickly at Henry. Henry shrugged. "Okay, if that's the way you want it. Come on, Barbara."

As soon as they were out of earshot Henry turned to Barbara. "Everything still the same?"

She nodded.

"Nothing changed?"

She nodded again.

"You still love me?"

She nodded once more and started to speak, but before she could say a word Henry quickly added, "I wish we could tell the world, but you can't let anyone here know."

She looked at him with all the love she felt. "Have I ever told anyone anything?"

"No," he sighed. "I know you haven't, and maybe that integrity is one of the things I love about you."

"Integrity is a peculiar word to use between us."

"Wrong again, Miss Clean White Sox. Integrity may be the best word to use between us."

Chester Masterson built his company with products he created, but it was not until he acquired Brown Pharmaceutical that Kiss, Inc., was included among the five hundred largest American corporations. Kiss, Inc., was already listed on the New York Stock Exchange when their popular television show was at the height of its success, and the general interest in Kiss at that time caused a flurry of action in the market. The stock, supported by good earnings, rose. As a result Chester was able to take over Brown Pharmaceutical in what some wags called the happiest headache in the world.

What made Chester, the king of cosmetics, decide to acquire a pharmaceutical company? For one thing, both Brown and Kiss sold to drugstores, and secondly, Chester was a hypochondriac, and owning his own pharmaceutical company was as good as growing up to own the candy store. But more interesting than the acquisition itself was the way it all happened. On Wall Street they still shake their heads and take two more Brown pills to make it all digestible.

The acquisition was underway in March of 1964, when Kiss, Inc., purchased one and a half million shares of Brown common stock on the fourteenth of the month. The next day, March 15, the stock split three for two. A million shares, or 18 per cent, of Brown president George Gordon's outstanding shares, were purchased by Kiss prior to the split at $40 a share. The purchase price, after the split, was $26.16 a share. For the Kiss shares bought prior to the split, George Gordon and related parties received about $37 million, which was paid in cash.

Where did Kiss get that kind of cash? They borrowed $30 million from a number of commercial banks against unsecured promissory notes which matured December 31 of that year. The loans were repaid in part by a $17 million insurance company loan.

In April 1964, Kiss, Inc., purchased on the New York Stock Exchange another million shares of Brown common stock at an average price per share of $27.50.

By May 1, 1964, Kiss, Inc., held approximately 31.6 per cent of the outstanding shares of Brown common stock.

In a prospectus dated August 17, 1964, Kiss, Inc., offered the remaining shareholders of Brown a deal that was so complicated most of them accepted because it was too embarrassing to say they did not understand. As a result another five and a half million shares were acquired by Kiss for roughly $23 million. Kiss had now gobbled up 88 per cent of the stock.

And Kiss, Inc., had acquired Brown at a savings of about $20 million through stock manipulation. It was all legal and pure and quite wonderful. As Chester said, "I always buy wholesale when I can. And I did it without screwing the owner of the company."

Nobody ever pointed out that the only ones he screwed were the stockholders.

Barbara threw her tennis dress in a corner and turned on the shower. She laid out the clothes she would wear for her quick trip to Los Angeles, before she stepped under the steaming spray. Ah, now she was in her small, private world. How she loved her private world. Yet from the way her life had begun, no one could ever have foreseen anything but the open world of a comfortable, suburban life style. Barbara grew up doing all the things little girls who grew up in the affluent postwar society of the 1940s did. She took riding lessons and played tennis on the country club courts in Westchester. She was a good but not outstanding student, and she had a lot of friends. She had a mother she loved very much and a father who was handsome and charming, so handsome and charming that he was seldom home. It seemed everyone in New York also wanted to be with her charming and handsome daddy. There were two other Anderson children: Barbara's sister, Kippy, who was four years her junior, and a brother, Greg, ten years younger than she. The four of them . . . Barbara, Kip, Greg, and their pretty mother . . . had fun together. And then one day Mommy was driving Greg to a friend's house to play, and there was an accident. The police came to tell Mr. Anderson, but he was in New York, and no one seemed able to find him, so fourteen-year-old Barbara accepted the news for the family. Mommy was dead, and Greg was hurt but would be all right. Two days later Daddy came home. By then Barbara had taken charge. She had made the funeral arrangements with the help of their minister and Mommy's friends, and she had also made an important decision. She would be the mommy for Kip and Greg, and she would be as good a mommy as her mother would have been. They would never know what they had missed. Barbara learned that little children have temper tantrums and bad dreams when they are aware, consciously or unconsciously, that somebody in charge is frightened. So Barbara learned to hide her fears. She wanted Kip and Greg to be happy. She was not sure what happy meant, but she was positive that they did. Daddy did not get married again, but after Mommy died he took an apartment in the city because he hated the drive back and forth to Westchester, and more and more he stayed in town. Barbara hired a good housekeeper, ran the household, and supervised the children. Her mother's old friends found that their eyes filled with tears whenever they thought about the Andersons. Barbara would see their blinking eyes and wonder if the tears were for her and her brother and sister, or were Mommy's friends really all choked up because someday they would die and maybe their children would not take such good care of one another and disgrace, not honor, their memory?

During Barbara's senior year in high school, she made another important decision. She would not leave her little family; she would not go away to school. She would commute to Columbia, and she would not take a liberal arts course. No, she would learn how to do something that would permit her to be self-supporting. Barbara decided to be a business major. She didn't know much about business, but if a playboy like Daddy could make money at it, how tough could it be? Every day she took the train to the city, went to class, and took the train home. She participated in no extracurricular activities. She did not even enjoy the museums and galleries and theater of New York. She came to the city for an education, and with her single-minded determination that was what she would get. One thing she did to prepare her for her later life was to investigate companies where she might work. Representatives from all the large corporations came to Columbia, and Barbara met with them. She decided to eschew the burgeoning electronics industry in favor of consumer goods. She had a feeling for the housewife (after all, hadn't she been one for years?) and she knew the needs of mothers. Her senior year she went to work part-time for Kiss. The job was in the personnel department, but Barbara knew she would never stay in personnel. She wanted to be on the firing line. She was used to making decisions, to running things. She didn't want to pick the people for the jobs. She wanted to be one of the people.

From personnel Barbara moved to assistant product managership, then a product manager's job, and finally she came to her position as head of new products. It was tough and grueling and took all of Barbara's energy and thought—it left her no time for contemplation.

Barbara had never believed in love until she met Henry. She had been at Kiss about thee months when Henry called her into his office to help him find a new secretary. Barbara was in personnel in those days, and even now she could remember how she felt when she walked into his office and saw the black-haired man behind the desk. There was a power that came from him in sharp, electric surges, and Barbara was quick to plug into that kind of charged personality. For her it was love at first sight. For Henry it took longer, about ten minutes longer. Barbara had read the poetry of Edna St. Vincent Millay and she had wept in all the right places in *Wuthering Heights,* but as a teen-ager she had been forced into a mother role, and she had squeezed her burgeoning sensuality into a pleated skirt, low-heeled oxford attitude toward love. Now, with one look, long-accumulated tenderness came rushing out. She couldn't believe herself. Solid, sensible Barbara actually going weak in the knees over a man. It was really too silly. But it got sillier because Henry was attracted to Barbara, too.

At first Henry had not believed that Barbara loved him. It was easy to believe that a secretary who never even dreamed that the boss would take her to lunch might be overwhelmed by going to bed with the president. But for Barbara? For a golden girl with taste and education and breeding and a future?

Barbara was amused by Henry's insecurity. "It's all a part of the liberated life," she explained. "Men are now allowed to fall in love with their equals. They don't have to scout the typing pool. They can screw an executive who just may turn out to be the girl next door."

Henry hated that lack of romanticism in Barbara. Why did she have to use words like screw?

Barbara had never been happier. She had never worked harder. She had never felt better. She knew Henry was married, but she did not think about it. Nor did Henry let it interfere with their relationship. His marriage was simply a thing apart from them. It had nothing to do with their love or their life. Barbara sensed early that for Henry the Number One Turn-on was business. What occupied and preoccupied most of Henry's waking thoughts were Kiss and Chester Masterson. Or Chester Masterson and Kiss. Barbara found that the better she was in business the better Henry was in bed with her. Sex with Henry moved in direct ratio to business performance. When Barbara did well in a meeting, Henry's five o'clock love-making was particularly ardent. If she did something in a meeting he did not like, he found a reason to stay in the office and not meet her that evening. Barbara started to find little ways to get better and better at her job so that after a few months Henry and Barbara fell into a regular Monday-Wednesday-Thursday pattern of afterhours love. On Tuesday nights his wife met him in the city, and on Friday the children were home for the weekend, and Henry's family gathered in the suburbs. It was all right with Barbara. For the first time in her life she had real love, and just because it was not ending in happily-ever-after, it was still appealing. Henry could not believe that there were no young men in Barbara's life, but this was pre-Paul Thurston, and there had been nothing more than the usual succession of young attorneys and stockbrokers and refugees from parties who called for an occasional date and were turned off when Barbara explained she was interested only in dinner, not a long-lasting relationship. She already had a meaningful relationship with a man. Who needed these boys? At the end of a year, however, Barbara began to assess herself and her life. She was moving fast in her job, a fact that by then was more attributable to her business acumen than to Henry's interest, for Henry, in an effort to seem fair and uninvolved, chose to remain silent every time a possibility for Barbara's advancement arose. Two of Barbara's Kiss friends had told her to try to be more friendly toward Henry because he seemed indifferent to her talents. They should only know, she thought. She smiled to herself, but only on Mondays and Wednesdays and Thursdays. On Tuesdays and Fridays and those terrible Saturday nights and lonely Sundays she did not smile so much. Henry adored her, of course, but he was out in the suburbs arranging weekend tennis games and admiring Jo's rose garden.

Barbara resented weekends; they upset the balance of her life. Then she met Paul Thurston. When she told Henry she was dating Paul on weekends, Henry shrugged. How could a man like Paul Thurston compete with him? He met Paul in the office one Tuesday evening when he came to pick up Barbara. Henry was unimpressed. Paul was of medium build, had sandy-colored hair, and tortoise-shell glasses that he constantly pushed up on his nose. Henry could tell that Paul was the kind of man who reached in the closet and wore the first thing he found. No sense of style. None of Henry's innate good taste. And that, Henry smiled, was supposed to be his competition. But there was no competition when it came to weekends. Only Paul was there for Barbara. And because Paul was kind to her and filled her time alone with things she liked to do, she decided to show her gratitude and accept his invitation to go to Puerto Rico for a weekend. She never expected the magic love-making. She was totally unprepared for Paul's full commitment to her. On the plane going back to New York, Paul proposed. And Barbara accepted. As the plane circled New York she withdrew her hand from his. Paul sensed that something had happened when New York came into view. "We won't set a date just yet," Barbara said. And then

Paul knew. There was still something she had to finish in New York. A man or a job. But there was unfinished business.

On Barbara's return she plunged into the everyday world of Kiss, Inc. Henry did not seem to notice any change in her at first, but when a few weeks later she told him of her decision to marry Paul Thurston, he nodded. Her apathetic love-making in recent weeks had told him something had changed. But he could not believe that it was Paul Thurston, a boring man with a face the color of tortoise-shell glass frames, who had caused the change.

How could she go from the glamour of their relationship to Paul? Then she told him about the love-making, that it had been totally unlike anything in their lives. It was the strongest single response she had ever had in her life. Doesn't that mean something? she asked Henry. Sure, he told her. It meant she had not had the attention and devotion from him that she deserved. From that time on, Henry's attitude toward Barbara changed. He was now in a competition, and a fight made Henry strong. This was the Puerto Rico Challenge. The first thing Henry did was take an apartment in the city. "I don't want Paul walking in on us at your place," he said. The new apartment was "theirs" instead of his. She knew she was the only woman who stayed there. As Henry's attentiveness increased, Barbara's feelings toward Paul diminished. She knew that her relationship with Henry hurt her relationship with Paul. But Paul didn't come forward and aggressively seek the answer to the post-Puerto Rico depression. Like a researcher, he preferred to retire to the laboratory and study before coming to wild and dangerous conclusions. Henry, on the other hand, told Barbara that if it were not for her he would be unable to stand his home life. Barbara said nothing. If she made him feel so good, why did she feel so bad?

In the last six months, however, Paul had evidently decided to make some demands. For Paul, however, the demands came out sounding somewhat petulant and not authoritative. Where were you last night? he would ask. She would shrug and tell him she was at the office late. So was I, he would say, and then Paul would do what he had never done before in his life with a woman. He would open up and talk about his work. He asked about her work, too, but Barbara didn't feel like making office talk with Paul. Next to his, her job seemed insignificant. Did he look down on her work? Or did she just lay that guilt at his doorstep rather than hers? Anyway, Barbara already had a business confidant who was also her bed partner, and now Henry's role as bed partner was good once again. Henry had bested the challenger from Puerto Rico. Barbara's needs for Paul were really confined to weekends, when she wanted an escort but not another business adviser or lover.

Barbara stepped out of the shower. She dried herself slowly with the big fluffy towel. Life wasn't ever easy, was it?

"How did the tennis game go?" Jo called when she heard the door to the suite open.

"Rotten," Henry answered.

"I thought you liked tennis." Jo walked into the living room. She looked cool and imperturbable. Henry was hot and irritated. He hated her for looking so composed at this minute. He wanted to be in Barbara's room. He wanted to be with sweaty, smart Barbara and not with this cool lady who was pouring ginger ale as if it were Dom Perignon.

"Was Tim insufferable?"

He shrugged.

"You're not exactly what I'd call communicative."

"I don't feel like talking," he snapped, and was instantly sorry for the anger he had displayed. Was the anger his resentment toward Jo? He wished he could go to Jo and hold her close, but it was not the fear of displeasing her with his overheated self that kept him away. It was the fear of pleasing her. He was out of the love habit with Jo, and he knew he did not want to get back into it. The little feels, the touches, the pats were no longer part of their life. He walked to the bar and poured himself ginger ale. Then he threw it out and mixed a vodka and tonic.

"Are you drinking just to make me angry?" she asked.

"Probably." Damn her. Why did she have to read him like the morning paper?

Inscrutability had always been his long suit in business.

In college it had been versatility, for he had been president of everything that elected a president. Ohio State had been the perfect school for Henry. It was big and political. He loved it. It was at Ohio State that Henry changed his name from Bernstein to Burns. His father said, "What's the matter? Bernstein's not good enough for the fancy college boy?" And Henry had just shrugged his shoulders and said, "So, Pa, where did your father get the name Bernstein? From the immigration officer at Ellis Island." The family name, an unpronounceable Russian name, had been "Americanized" and "still kept Jewish" by the greatest name changers the world has ever known. At Ohio State, Henry met Jo McGonagle, the most popular girl in Coshocton, Ohio. She was two years ahead of Henry, and he thought she was like the fairy princesses he used to see in the books during school library reading hour back in the third grade. She had coal black hair and huge blue eyes. She was president of her sorority, and Henry met her at a dance. He was glad he had changed his name before he met her. He hoped she wouldn't notice he came from a Jewish fraternity until he had a chance to get her to love him. As it turned out, it made no difference. Jo McGonagle would have loved Henry Burns if he had been deep purple with blue spots and a member of a Far East sect. She fell head over heels in love with Henry. Even her parents loved Henry. One day when her father and mother came to visit, her father asked to take a walk with Henry. This is it, Henry thought. He's going to tell me about his little princess, and I better not touch. Instead Mr. McGonagle said, "Son, we are so proud that our daughter fell in love with a Jew. You are God's chosen people." At that moment Henry thought he was. But he knew not many people in the world were going to agree with Mr. McGonagle. The next week Henry joined the Unitarian Church. The first time Henry's parents came to visit him at Ohio State after he had met Jo, he told them her name was Jo Goldman. Jo thought it was sweet that he did not want to hurt them; she did not know he had already joined the Unitarian Church. "Why do you call me Goldman?" Jo asked. "I mean why that particular name." "Emma Goldman," he explained, "was a family heroine. My parents and their parents were all radicals, anarchists, and they loved anybody who wanted to overthrow the government. So I figured that since I'm giving you a name, I might as well give you one with positive overtones." "What about you?" Jo asked. "Are you a radical, too?" "Definitely not," Henry assured her. "I want to belong. I want good grades, a good job, and I don't have any of those ideas about owning my company. All I want to do is run something big." "Sort of like Ohio State?" Jo asked. "Exactly like Ohio State," Henry promised. "I want to be a big man in a big place."

Henry's first job after school was with a big drug company. Jo had taken a job in the alumni office at Ohio State, so they were together all the time he went to school. The year after his graduation when he was twenty-one and she was twenty-three they were married. After a year with a drug company in the Midwest, Henry said to Jo, "The big opportunities are in cosmetics. I have to go to New York." Jo nodded. "Whatever you say." "You'll be happy in New York," Henry promised. Jo shrugged. "Do you think the people will like me?" Henry was indignant. "How can you even ask such a question?" "But, Henry," she reminded him, "I'm only a small town girl. I'm from Coshocton, Ohio, and all the fancy people you'll meet went to Radcliffe and Vassar." "Don't be silly," he said. "They'll love you." Of course they did not love her, but Henry was too busy to notice. Kiss, Inc., was like a super Ohio State. There were dances and parties and lots of exams, only you couldn't tell the exams from the games. It was at Kiss, Inc., that Henry developed his tense mannerisms. He became a finger tapper and a lip biter. Nobody knew precisely what it meant, but it managed to distract everybody during meetings.

Jo was pouring her second glass of ginger ale. Had they been talking the last few minutes, or had he just been standing there sullenly?

"Henry, you're always tense, but why are you nasty? What is bothering you?"

There was good old Jo interpreting him once again. He'd give the only answer he could. "I'm bothered by Kiss. This miserable setup. These phony tennis games." Yes, he was beginning to feel better now. It was good to get mad about something.

"Is Kiss worse than usual?"

"Worse is usual at Kiss. Don't you know that? Don't you understand that Chester Masterson is a monster in a dark blue suit with ice water instead of human kindness?"

"Oh, there have been times you've liked Chester."

"No, there haven't." Now he was getting madder. God, it felt good. It was a catharsis. He was beginning to feel clean. Anger was a wonderful thing to get out of your body. Pent-up anger made you ache all over. Release made tense muscles feel strong, not overworked. "I'm going to do something about Masterson," he said quickly.

"Sure you are." She sounded cynical.

He hated the sound of her. "I'm leaving Kiss."

"No, you're not, Henry." Her voice had become strangely tight.

"Yes, I am." Oh, he was feeling a lot better now. He was scaring the hell out of her. Good. That was what he meant to do.

"I refuse to allow it." Her voice rose one octave.

"You refuse?" He downed the drink in one gulp. "Who are you to refuse to allow me anything? You're a little farm girl. Stop playing fancy lady."

She carefully drew a manicured finger around the rim of her glass. No, she would not answer that. He was attacking the most vulnerable part of her. There must be a reason for it. She would wait him out. That had been her Henry strategy since she had changed her life.

"What do you think you will do?" she asked slowly.

"Ha. You're wrong. It's not what I think I will do."

"Are you giving me a choice?" she asked.

"No." He did not know he could be this tough with her. Was this what he was doing to punish her for staying with him? "I have made up my mind. I am going to Oxxon."

"Henry, that means Europe and a different way of life."

"Take French lessons."

"That's not it. You know it." Now her face was flushed. She could not control the pain and sadness. "I can't do it."

"You damn well can if you expect to be my wife."

So that was it. It was down to Henry and The Job or being alone. Henry wouldn't divorce her. She knew that. Henry simply couldn't go through the messiness of divorce. She folded her hands and looked down at them. Now what? Another round of Henry and his little amours? More of Henry's excuses about missing dinner parties and working late while he pored over the bodies of little Swiss secretaries and product managers? I can't keep up with the romantic opportunities of his world, Jo thought. The age and brain gap will get bigger as the years go on, and I'll go back to . . . no, she thought. No. I won't go back. But is he pushing me back?

"Well, Jo, I thought you were going to do a lot of talking. You're just sitting there."

"Right, Henry. I'm just sitting here. I'm wondering what kind of miserable monster you really are. I'm wondering what happened to the nice, ambitious boy from Ohio State. I wonder where your love went."

"It went out with the empties from the liquor store."

"You really are cruel, Henry."

"I didn't mean that," he said quickly.

"Sure you did. More truth is spoken in anger than in kindness. You still hate me from the drinking days. You still hate the story that ended all my drinking. Most of all, Henry, you feel guilty because my drinking was going on heavily just at the time your little series of office romances was going on heavily. You always wondered whether I knew. Well, I did know. But that isn't why I drank. I used to want you to think that was the reason, but now I don't want you to have the satisfaction of thinking that what you do can change my life that radically. No, I didn't drink because of you. I drank because of me. And you can take your job at Oxxon. You can take it and shove it—" Now her emotions were leaving her. She was sliding downhill. She knew it. She had to get away from Henry. Jo did what she had done on a long-ago night. She ran to the table, picked up the keys to the car, and ran out the door.

She found the rented Mercedes in the parking lot, put the key in the ignition, and then sat there. Where should she go? What should she do? She bit her lip. She'd drive into town. She remembered the road. There was a drugstore and a bar. Well, at least she'd have a choice.

China jumped slightly when she heard Tim's knock at the door. She wasn't really expecting him just now. What time was it anyway? She scrambled from the sofa, turned off the TV soap opera she was watching, and dumped her drink in a vase of flowers. Then she opened the door.

"What are you doing?" he asked sarcastically.

"Just sitting around reading."

He laughed. "Then why is the television set still warm, and why isn't there a book in sight? Book. You remember book, China. B-o-o-k. Book. The thing in libraries."

China's eyes filled with tears. "I know I'm dumb."

"Yes, my dear," he replied, kissing her lightly on the cheek, "but you are rich. And that is helpful."

"Not to me," she sighed.

"By the way," he said as he started peeling his tennis clothes from his lean body. "Where did you get rid of your drink? Is it under the sofa like the last time? Or did you put it in the medicine cabinet? I always thought that was very clever of you, China. For a dumb woman you sometimes do surprisingly bright things, but I guess that's true of most alcoholics."

"I'm not an alcoholic."

He laughed. "You're not?" Tim reappeared from the bedroom. He was naked. He walked over to China and put his hand under her dress. "I have to take a shower anyway so we might as well go to bed first," he said.

China shivered slightly. "No," she said. It was the first time she had ever said no to Tim. He pulled her by the arm, but she twisted and caught him off-balance. He fell against the sofa.

"What the hell do you think you're doing, China?"

"I d-d-d-don't know." That was the truth. She did not know why she had said that. She had never felt so frightened.

"Did you say no to me?"

She nodded.

"Then you'll pay for it, you bitch." He walked to the liquor cabinet, opened the doors and pulled out the bottles, opened each, and poured the contents down the drain of the bar sink. When he finished his face was crimson. Then he walked back into the bedroom and threw the car keys on the floor of the living room. "Take the car, and go into town and find yourself a bar where you can drink alone, China. Take plenty of time because while you're away I'll be busy, and I don't want you interrupting me and the girl who's coming here."

"Who's coming here?" she whispered.

"You don't know her, but I do, and she goes to bed whenever I tell her to."

"What should I do?" China asked numbly.

"Get the hell out of here. Fast."

The tears were running down China's face now. Sooner or later every person in her life left her. Her mother. Her father. Now her husband. They'd all be better off if she were dead. China picked up the keys from the floor and walked toward the door.

"Move a little faster," her husband said.

China ran to the parking lot and got behind the wheel of the Cadillac. She was not sure which road went into town, but she knew she had the rest of her life to find it.

Jo parked in front of the Long Lounge, the one bar in town. She folded her arms over the wheel of the car and put her head down. The Gates of Paradise was a long way from Ohio. Why couldn't she have married the boy next door or a postman or plumber? Why did she have to marry the first complicated person she met? But who was to say boys next door and postmen and plumbers were not complicated? Funny, but you did not see all the faults of the world when you drank. Nowadays she missed drinking only at cocktail hours, but at this moment she missed drinking not because of the ambiance but because of the comfort it gave her. She longed for the foggy, don't-give-a-damn feeling. She wanted to cloud the world, erase the vision of Henry as president of still another company, obliterate the thought of new people and new places and new things to live down.

Her mouth felt as if it were stuffed with cotton. That was odd. She was getting the effects of alcohol without even drinking. She lifted her head. If she were going to have a hangover, she might as well have a drink. She tried to open the car door, but the Cadillac next to her had parked so widely that she was wedged in on the driver's side. She was about to crawl over the passenger side when something made her look at the Cadillac again. Was that China huddled in the corner of the back seat? And what was wrong with the poor child?

Jo scrambled over the seat, opened the door, and ran over to the other car. She tried the back door, and China came tumbling out of the car on to the ground. Jo bent over her. "China. China. Speak to me."

China opened her eyes. "I'm all right."

China had not really fallen out of the car; she had literally spilled herself on the parking area. Jo put an arm under China's head. China coughed, and Jo recognized the smell of her breath. "Are you drunk?" Jo asked.

China shrugged. "I don't know. I can't tell when I am."

Jo squeezed her eyes shut. She knew how China felt. Old pain filled her body, but she did not have time to think about herself. Jo knew what she had to do next. "Are you able to move, China?"

She nodded weakly.

"I am going to take you for a walk around the block. I'll put my arm under yours. Don't try to talk. We'll just walk, and then I am going to take you for a ride in the country."

"Why?"

"Because," Jo said firmly, "it's about time somebody did."

They did not speak for an hour. China, like a dutiful child, permitted Jo to lead her in a circle around the town, put her in the front seat of the Mercedes, and set off on a drive that had no beginning or end. Finally Jo said, "How long have you been drinking?"

"Since this morning."

"And you just continued from last night?"

China nodded.

"You don't have to tell me why you drink, but I'll tell you why I did."

China sat upright. Jo, perfect Jo, a drinker?

"Don't look so surprised, China. You mean you never heard? I'm sure Tim knows, and I'm positive that your father does. Everybody in Kiss, Inc., heard about my drinking."

"I didn't."

"That's because you are a nice person."

"I am?"

"Of course. You're not a gossip. You don't thrive on the misfortunes of others."

China nodded. "That's true. I like everybody to be happy. Do you ever watch 'Search for Tomorrow' or 'As the World Turns' or any of the other stories on television?"

"No."

"Oh, you should. Those people are like my family. I love them. I want them to be happy just the way I want my children and Tim . . ." Now her voice broke.

Jo pulled the car into a roadside rest area. "What about Tim?"

"He's so nasty, Jo."

"Does he love you?"

"He loves my father's money."

"But that's your money. You could leave Tim any time you want."

"Would you leave Henry?"

"Henry didn't marry me for my money."

"No," said China thoughtfully, "but are you sure he loves you? You know, just for yourself, not because you're a mother."

"You mean if he doesn't love you for yourself you shouldn't stay with a man?"

"I don't know," China said. "I am staying with a man who doesn't love me for myself. I guess others do that, too."

"You are very aware of people, aren't you?"

"Everybody talks about how dumb I am."

"Well, maybe you are when it comes to the stock market and James Joyce. But you have a heart full of wisdom."

"Do you think so?" China asked innocently.

"I think so. But I'm afraid you're not using it enough."

"I'm so frightened. Nobody wants me around."

"You know, China, the worst feeling in the world is the feeling that you are worthless."

"How would you know? You're always so perfect."

"I'm so perfect that my husband has a carload of girlfriends."

China registered no shock or surprise. Instead she felt a great sadness and sympathy for Jo, who always looked magazine-perfect to her. "It must be hard for you to talk about," China said softly.

"It is. Look, I used to drink, and I don't anymore. That does not mean my problems ended when I stopped drinking. All it means is that I can now deal with them."

"Why did you drink, Jo? You said you'd tell me."

"Can you stand another soap opera?"

China nodded.

"This one is called Small Town Princess. I won't go into all the details of my growing up and going to Ohio State and meeting Henry. I'll just tell you that this little girl from Ohio had never met anyone like this New York Jewish boy. He was good-looking and smart and ambitious, and I had never dealt with anything like it. Even though we were small town Ohio, my parents were always liberal thinkers, and they not only permitted me to marry Henry, they welcomed him with open arms. You'd think that with such a beginning everything would be sort of storybook for us."

"Wasn't it?"

"Well, maybe it was the first year or so. I loved being married to Henry, and I liked playing house in our tiny apartment. But everything changed when we moved to New York. Henry had an ambition that was bigger than anything I had ever imagined."

"What did you do?"

"Well, for a while I just continued to play housewife. I had worked in the alumni office at Ohio State, and so I thought I'd get a job in New York. But that didn't fit Henry's idea of his wife. He wanted someone who would be able to run a grand establishment because Henry knew he was on his way to heading a kingdom of some kind."

"Is Kiss a kingdom?"

"Of course it is. I suppose when you have had it all your life you don't really understand, but Kiss is a very large company, China, and running it means the responsibility for thousands of people working for you. And then there are the millions of women you influence with your products and your advertising. Sure it's a responsibility. Well, I knew that Henry was destined for some kind of corporate stardom, and I suppose I should have started taking cooking lessons at Cordon Bleu and having my clothes selected by someone who does such things. But I was a little girl from Ohio, and all that seemed phony and pretentious to me. Anyway Henry kept moving up and up. First he was a product manager and then a marketing director. Finally he was made Eastern regional manager, and he started the big round of entertaining, and that included me. I was scared. I knew which fork to use, but I couldn't read the menu, and I couldn't bear to stay home. I was so frightened that I would go to dinner and never say a word."

China smiled. "I know the feeling."

"One night we went to '21' for dinner. We had a corner table. Even I knew that meant we were important. Cary Grant was at the next table, and a Rockefeller was on the other side. And we, Mr. and Mrs. Henry Burns, had the best table. I was awed. That was the first I really understood how important Henry was becoming.

"Now that also gives you some idea of how much he was telling me. The only way I could figure what was happening to him in business was by the kinds of tables headwaiters gave us. That night we were entertaining the president of a department store in Los Angeles. Everybody was talking about chic things, and I couldn't follow the conversation. For the first time I was more than scared. I felt helpless. So I drank. I don't remember how we got home, but nobody seemed to notice.

"From that time on whenever we went someplace for dinner, I kept quiet and drank. I don't know whether Henry realized just how much I drank, but he never spoke to me about it. So maybe he didn't know. Or, if he did, he chose not to mention it because if he did, he would have had to do something about it.

"So we went on like that for—oh, maybe six or seven years. Then one night we were dressing for dinner. I knew I'd never make it to the restaurant unless I had a drink, so I went downstairs and opened the liquor cabinet, but it was bare. I didn't remember drinking it dry, but I suppose I had. I needed a drink. I was shaking. I had to have a drink to get through that night. So I called upstairs to Henry and said I needed lipstick. Imagine. The wife of the president of Kiss, Inc., going out to the drugstore for lipstick. Well, if Henry thought it peculiar, he didn't say so. I went out to my car. Of course I had been drinking all day, but by then no one could tell. I held my liquor so that only I knew the levels of my intoxication, and even I wasn't sure.

"Parts of my life flash in and out, and I don't remember much of that night except a lot of police cars and sirens. I remember wishing I had killed myself, but I hadn't. Instead I had plowed into another car and killed the son of Senator Jefferson Morrow."

China gasped. "Now I remember. But I thought it was an accident. You know what I mean . . . not because of drinking."

"Well, the rest of the world knew, and they never let me forget. I don't know quite how they did it, but your father and Henry got me out of the mess without my having to go to jail. One thing I did have to do, however. I had to promise the court that I would seek psychiatric help and go to Alcoholics Anonymous. There was another thing I had to do, too. I had to live with that memory every day for the rest of my life."

"Do you drink now?"

"I did not have a drink today, and that is how I live my life, China. I understand that alcoholism is a disease, and I can only get by one day at a time. I didn't drink today, and I will try not to drink tomorrow. But I have more strength now than I did then, and while I cannot bring the Morrow boy back to life, I can bring life back to me."

"And to me?" China asked hopefully.

"Do you want to try?"

"Would you help me?"

"Yes."

"I'm frightened, Jo. Did Henry hate you after the accident? You know, what scares me most is Tim."

"Henry really was compassionate during the days that followed. He was also frightened. After all, his wife's actions reflected on him. I don't think he really believed I would go through the pain of joining AA, but once I did, he was proud of me. It was, in a sense, a victory for him. He could stand in front of people and think, 'See what I was able to get her to do.'"

"I wonder if Tim will be like that."

"Everyone is different. Maybe I can help Tim understand. Henry actually stopped drinking in front of me. To this day . . . no, I take that back–until this day he never drank in front of me."

"This day?" China asked quickly. "Did he drink in front of you after the tennis game they played together?"

"Yes," Jo said slowly.

"Something must have happened in that game, Jo. I know because Tim was so awful to me. He sent out for a whore."

"He did what?" Jo's voice went up an octave.

"Don't be so shocked. My husband is like my father; they only use pros. Your husband probably gets involved; he's a romantic. My husband and my father don't have to think of anybody but themselves."

"China, do you want to keep your marriage together?"

"Yes. I love Tim even though he hurts me. I don't think he wants another woman, not a real woman. What about your marriage?"

"Well, if Henry wanted one special woman, I guess that would kill everything for me. I don't know if I could keep him if he truly loved another woman. As long as he has all these little secretarial romances, we're all right."

"Are you sure?"

"No," she said. "That's why I'm staying sober."

"How do I join AA, Jo?"

"Well, it's easier to get into than the River Club. I'll make a few calls from The Gates of Paradise and see what we can do for you fast. Meanwhile, stay away from the booze. It's poison for you and me. We'll go back and get dressed and go to tonight's dinner. Stay close to me. I'll be your friend."

China smiled. "I never had a real friend before."

Jo started the car and turned down the highway toward town. "When we get back to your car, I'll drop you off. There's a bar where we parked. Go in and call Tim. Tell him you had car trouble and are on your way back to The Gates of Paradise. Tell him you met me, and I am driving you back. I don't want you driving alone just now."

"Thank you," said China. She leaned over and kissed Jo. "But I want to drive back myself just to prove I can," she said. "I'll call Tim first, though."

"Are you sure you can walk into that bar and just make a phone call?"

"Yes," China said firmly.

Linda Sugarman picked up the Ace bandages from the drugstore counter and limped toward her car. Rotten tennis game. Miserable day. Nothing was going right. She looked up just in time to see China Edgar walking into the Long Lounge. Linda smiled. You just never knew when information like that might come in handy.

9

Chester Masterson had not changed from the dressing gown he was wearing when Barbara Anderson came to breakfast. Now at 3 P.M. he decided to shower, shave, and change. Ginger Mallory, the girl Tim told him about was coming at four. That would give him time. He put out a bottle of scotch, took two Gelusils, and went into the bathroom.

When Chester came out of the shower he put on a soft white shirt and navy slacks and went into the living room. He poured himself a drink and sat back. No. He wouldn't turn on television. He suddenly remembered. He went to the refrigerator and took out the Milky Ways and brought them into the living room. He sat back and sipped his scotch and reflected on his rules for sexual activity with unknown women. If he knew the whore, he would take her the standard way. Otherwise . . . he patted his box of Milky Ways . . . he would do it so he would not risk disease. A man as germ-conscious as Chester Masterson had to be careful what he did.

Ginger Mallory stopped at the ladies' room to put two shades of Kiss lipstick on her lips. Some of the girls she knew liked to talk about the men they made it with. Not Ginger. She always referred to Mr. A., the attorney, or Mr. B., the broker. She thought it was kind of cute to give them the same initial as their occupation. Get it? she would ask. She thought about what to call Mr. Masterson. Mr. C., the cosmetics. No. He'd probably think it meant something else. She giggled to herself. She wondered if he'd give her some cosmetics. Free. For the rest he'd have to pay. Oh no. That was right. That cute young guy, Tim, had said he'd take care of it. Right. Don't ask for money. She would have to remember that. Ginger wondered if Mr. Masterson had any hang-ups. God knows, when some of these guys got old they asked you to do weird things. Maybe he'd ask her to put eye make-up on her—oh no, that would probably be too corny for Mr. Masterson. He was one of those New York sophisticated people. She tugged at her skirt and wiggled her way toward Suite 1A.

Ginger Mallory was surprised by Chester Masterson's attitude toward her. He wasn't a bit gruff or nasty. He seemed kind of sweet. Judging from the talk around the bar he was a real bastard. That was true of a lot of men, though. They screwed everybody in business, but they were really nice about their screwing.

"Would you like a little late luncheon, my dear?" he asked.

She shook her head. "I don't like to eat before. You know, it's sort of like being an athlete. I don't do too good on a full stomach."

"Would you like to get a little more—uh, comfortable?"

Ginger nodded. She knew what that meant. She started the slow strip. Old guys usually liked the slow strip. Sometimes it took them a long time to get started, so a slow strip was good for taking up another thirty minutes. It helped them. She wondered whether she was getting paid by the hour or just for the job.

"You have a very nice body," Chester said gallantly. He was ready for her, but why tell her? He liked looking at women's bodies. He liked this woman's body. Tim was right. He wondered if she ever used Kiss Body Bath. Her skin looked pretty good. He squinted. No, she didn't need the eye cream yet, but she ought to try the moisturizer. Slight drying of the skin. Probably caused by all that sunbathing. Check it, he reminded himself. Does she have bathing strap marks? If she did, he'd have to warn her about the harmful effects of the sun. No. Not a bathing suit mark.

"Is your skin really that dark," he asked, "or do you use some kind of body make-up?"

She was very proud of her tan, and the man had noticed. She dimpled and flushed prettily. "Oh golly, I sunbathe, Mr. Masterson, but I never wear a bathing suit, so I don't get those ugly strap marks."

Chester shrugged. He never thought strap marks were ugly. They were always a kind of turn-on for him. Oh well, with the size of her breasts and that big, full ass she didn't have to worry about whether she had bathing suit marks or not. Chester began to smile. She had one of the nicest bodies he had ever seen. "You are very pretty, Miss Mallory."

"Thank you, Mr. Masterson." She looked around the room. She had all her clothes off. She was thinking about what to do next.

"Would you like a drink?"

She smiled. "I don't drink." Suddenly she spied the box of Milky Ways. "Gosh, is that candy for me?"

"It's for both of us," he said.

"Oh good. When I was a kid I used to go to the movies every Saturday, and I would always get enough money for the show and for a Milky Way. Isn't that funny that I like Milky Ways best?"

"Me too," Chester said quickly.

"How do you like them?" she asked.

He flushed. Did she know? "How do I like them?"

"Yeah. Frozen or regular?"

He relaxed. No, she didn't know. He'd have the fun of teaching her. The same way his first wife, The Whore, had taught him. He'd made every whore since do it.

She took a bite of the Milky Way. Most rich men thought they had to give you champagne. This was really cute. Milky Ways. She loved him already. It would be fun doing it with him even if he was old and sort of paunchy. He was so nice he'd probably give her lipstick, too. And it would even be her shade. He would be the kind to notice something like that. She looked at him. He was still dressed. He hadn't even unbuttoned another button on the shirt.

"You know I'm a three-way girl?" she asked.

"Three-way?"

"Yes," she smiled as sweetly as if she were taking his order for light bulbs. "I take it any way you want it. There are not a lot of really good three-way girls here at The Gates of Paradise. In fact, if you won't think I'm bragging too much, they say I am the best."

"I want it the fourth way," he said.

"I don't understand." She crossed her legs, indicating her vexation.

He picked up a Milky Way and held it up. "I want this," he said, "in there." He pointed.

Her eyes widened. Oh my goodness. A candy freak. "Why?" she croaked.

"Because that's where I like to eat it," he said.

She nodded dutifully, walked to the bedroom, and seconds later called, "I'm ready."

Chester walked into the bedroom.

"Hey," she said, leaning on her elbows, "what do you want first?"

"Use your imagination," he said. "Just remember that I get the Milky Way."

Ginger Mallory thought she had seen everything, and what she had not seen her girlfriends had. She giggled. Boy, the way Mr. Masterson did it sure made sex fattening.

After Ginger dressed and was ready to leave she said, "I just have one question, Mr. Masterson. If you want to eat candy that way, why don't you use Oh Henry!? Didn't you ever notice? Oh Henry! is really the right shape."

Chester shook his head. "I hate nuts."

Linda's limp was slight when she left town, but it became more pronounced the nearer she came to The Gates of Paradise. By the time she reached the hotel she could barely walk. But she knew that she was capable of an instant cure. At the moment a limp served her purposes. She moved her face into what she assumed to be a brave, pained look and opened the door.

Ken was standing in front of the dresser putting the finishing touches on his outfit for the Kiss-o-rama, the second night barbecue under the stars. As usual, rain had been predicted. Linda was late, and he did not know where she had gone. He was beginning to wonder. Predictable Linda did not miss major Kiss events. Now he was dressed—or would be as soon as he finished tying this damned bandana around his neck. When he heard her key in the door, he felt a sense of relief. He turned around and said with concern, "Where have you been, Linda?"

The carefully set look of pain vanished the moment she saw him. "Can't you even tie a red bandana around your neck so it looks right?" she asked in an exasperated tone.

Her annoyance was familiar, a comfort. He decided to tease her a little. "Stop answering questions with questions. Somebody will think you're Jewish."

She ignored the attempted banter. "You look stupid in that shirt, and those jeans don't fit right. I should have cut them up, too." Disgust flavored each word.

"Linda, I am a vice-president. I am not a cowboy." He was trying to keep his tone light, but the hurt crept through. "All I'm trying to do is dress for a barbecue. Don't start the barbecue in here. I get enough roastings."

She laughed. "I bet you do. You are so far out of things, Ken, that I can't understand how you hold your job." Now she strode across the room, the hurt ankle forgotten, and she began to search for other shirts in his closet.

He stared at the floor. She was right. He was always the last to know office happenings. Linda, who was not even in the office, knew about every firing and promotion before he did. He knew that Linda was a believer in the secretarial grapevine. She always maintained her Kiss contacts, and she knew about events before the ink was dry. "I've always been like this, Linda," he said apologetically. "Why did you marry me? I was never best in anything, and you always want the best in everything."

"It's so easy to stay informed, Ken. You never know anything. You just don't relate to people. That's your problem."

"It's more than that," he said. Now he was trying to analyze himself. He walked over to the desk and sat down. He rubbed his eyes and then blinked slowly, sadly shook his head, and said, "Linda, I'm just not shrewd."

She smiled. Shrewd. That was her favorite word, the watchword of her family. Linda was born in 1939, just long enough after the Depression so that her forty-year-old parents felt they could afford another child. Her beautiful, brilliant sister was born in 1931. It seemed to Linda that she spent her entire childhood running, trying to catch up to the sister, who was not only born earlier but with more looks and more brains. When Linda was eight, she learned how to answer to her sister's talents. Each fall when she entered a new classroom, the teacher would look at her, read the name, and say in surprise, "Are you—" Before the teacher could say the name, Linda would say quickly, "Yes, I'm the younger sister. I'm not as beautiful. I'm not as smart. But I am shrewd." That threw the teachers off-balance. What Linda failed to add as she introduced herself was that she was as shrewd as Grandma Eisman. In 1891 Shondor and Rachel Eisman sailed into New York Harbor. They were among the huddled masses yearning to breathe free. For two years they breathed the air of the Lower East Side, and then one day Shondor came home and told Rachel they were going to become real Americans. With their children in their arms and their packs on their backs they were going to South Dakota. He might as well have said Hong Kong. Grandma wept. She wailed. But to no avail. Grandpa Eisman, a stouthearted twenty-four-year-old immigrant, was about to become Sam Eisman, frontiersman.

Grandpa opened a general store, and Grandma worked in the store. But since the Indians could not speak Yiddish, Grandma Eisman had to learn a second language. She did. The language was Sioux. A year after they moved to Dakota, Grandpa developed a mysterious fever and never worked again. There were four family pictures of Grandpa Eisman, and in each he wore a toupee that was slightly askew. His eyes were glazed with the weariness of a noncombatant. Only Grandma Eisman had the ferocious look of an Indian killer, a horse trader, and a protective Jewish mother. In her life she was all three. And Linda was following in her footsteps. Standing in a hotel room at The Gates of Paradise, Linda smiled. No matter what happened she was Rachel Eisman's granddaughter.

"You're right, Ken. I am shrewd. And I am shrewd enough to get you the presidency of Kiss."

"I don't think I want it," he said in a half-whisper.

"Oh yes you do." She walked to the chair and stared down at him. "You want that job, and you are going to start to get it tonight because I have the formula for it right here." She tapped her head.

"No, Linda. I don't want it." He felt as if he were going to cry.

"Ken, some people have greatness thrust upon them. I am about to thrust greatness upon you."

"I don't want to be great."

"Of course you do. And the timing is right."

"No, it isn't."

"Listen, Ken. I'm going to tell you something you don't even know. Henry is leaving Kiss."

Ken's head snapped up. "No," he said in disbelief.

"Yes," she answered with her usual authority.

"How do you know?" He realized it was a foolish question. She knew because her friend, Rhoda, was Henry's secretary.

"Rhoda . . ." she began. Then she stopped. The look on Ken's face told her that he believed her.

"When?" he asked dully.

"When this convention ends. Nobody knows yet."

"Except you, of course."

"Except me."

"Tim will get the job," Ken said. "I'm positive it will be Tim. Chester can't overlook him."

"Chester Miserable can overlook anyone," Linda answered. "He can overlook his own daughter. He can overlook his wives. There is only one thing he can't overlook, and that's talent. That, Ken, is what is in your favor."

He shook his head. "It has to be Tim."

"Can't be," Linda said quickly. "You know how I can tell?"

"How?"

"He doesn't talk to Tim."

"What does that mean?"

"At conventions things happen because of the people chairmen talk to, not to the people they don't. This is a rule, Ken," she said seriously. "Always watch the people Chester doesn't talk to. They are destined for oblivion."

"But he doesn't talk to me, Linda."

Her forehead furrowed. "Engage him in conversation. It has to be you or Tim, and the faster you talk the more likely it is to be you. However, even if you don't talk, I know how to get the presidency for you."

"You do?"

"I just figured it out as I was driving back from town."

"What are you going to do?"

"I think I better start now. Hand me that phone."

When Sharon Kennedy heard the urgency in Linda's voice she figured it would be better to be late to the Kiss-o-rama than to miss the opportunity for a big story. "I'll wait here in my room for you," she promised.

Linda threw a raincoat over her tennis dress. "You stay here, and don't leave until I get back." She snapped on the television set. "Here, you can watch this. Remember. Don't leave. Don't answer the phone. Just hang in here, and I'll come back with the presidency on a silver platter."

Ken unknotted the bandana around his neck and moved his chair in front of the television set.

Linda, her ankle now completely healed, ran out the door. She was on her way to become a star. Well, Ken would become a star, and everyone knew that without Linda Ken was just another vice-president. As Linda's mother always said, "What's the difference what she's the star of as long as she's a star?"

From the time Linda could walk she took dancing lessons. Her mother would sit in the back of the rehearsal room, tap her foot in time to the music, and reassure her daughter that she was beautiful. Linda's mirror told her she was not beautiful, but she didn't want to hurt Mamma, so she nodded when she was told she was beautiful, and she knew that by hook or crook she had better be beautiful. She had her teeth straightened at twelve and her nose straightened at fourteen. By the time she was sixteen if she wasn't beautiful she was at least passable. Her sister, Joan Loretta (named for Joan Crawford and Loretta Young), was older and since she had both beauty and brilliance she had long ago sidestepped their mother. Joan Loretta was not going to be pushed around by a woman who didn't know Monet from Manet.

Linda (named for Linda Christian, whom her mother had once seen in a restaurant with Tyrone Power) was destined for stardom, however. The only thing that stopped Linda was talent, but Mamma never noticed. She sat with Linda in casting offices for films and television commercials. The fact that Linda never got a job did not bother Mamma. After all, it was California, and girls could still be discovered at Schwab's Drugstore the way

Lana Turner was. Mamma always remembered Lana Turner. Lana Turner and Grandma Eisman were proof that anything could happen in America.

Linda's father moved through her life like a Hollywood extra. He was a kind of good-natured nebbish who let Linda's mother run the world, and as long as he could sit in front of his TV set and watch the news and the football games, how bad could things be? By the time Linda was ready for college her sister had already been graduated *summa cum laude* and had married a boy from a rich Bel Air family. The competition was suffocating. So Linda went to her mother and said, "I'm not going to college." Her mother recovered in time to ask what she was going to do. Records? Movies? Television? Linda shook her head. "I'm going to New York and get a job." "Listen," her mamma said, "don't be a dummy. If you can't be talent, then hire talent."

Full of Mamma's ambition, Linda went to New York and got a job as an assistant producer for a film company that made television commercials. She did some casting, and she found that Mamma was right again. Linda loved the talent part of business. One day when she was casting a commercial for Kiss, Inc., Henry Burns, a product manager, asked her if she would like to work for the cosmetics company. He thought they ought to have their own casting director. Henry, in later years, was never really sure that the job was his idea. All he knew for certain was that one day Linda showed up for work at Kiss, and she reported to him. She made Henry Burns her man. It was no romance, just a good solid office relationship. Henry was not her type. It did not matter that Henry showed no signs of romantic interest in her; all that mattered to Linda was what Mamma had taught her: Linda mattered. Linda starred. Everybody else played second fiddle. In New York it was easier to feel like a star. Joan Loretta was twenty-five hundred miles away. For the first time Linda was totally herself or whatever it was Mamma had fashioned into a Linda Malamud. Linda was at Kiss two years when Ken Sugarman came to work there. He was a Californian, like Linda, and he was fresh out of graduate school at Stanford. Ken Sugarman had the intense look of a scholarship student (which he was), and he had the everyday nice looks of a Jewish middle-class boy (which he was).

Linda, who was privy to all office politics, marked Ken as a comer. And she also marked Ken for herself. She knew that Ken would be a salaried man forever unless she took him in hand and made something of him the way Mamma had made something of her. She took him to Paul Stuart and showed him what kind of suits to buy. She took him to Gucci and showed him what kind of briefcase to buy. And then she took him to Tiffany and showed him what kind of wedding ring to buy. When he found the ring she wanted, she took him to West Forty-seventh Street and showed him how to buy the same ring wholesale. Ken thought Linda was the smartest, shrewdest, cleverest person he had ever met. He was right. Ken was finally in good hands. After a haphazard growing-up period Ken knew where he was going. And in case he forgot, Linda reminded him each day. Before they were to announce their engagement, Linda decided to give Ken one small push to a big break. She went to see Henry. "Henry," she said sweetly, "I hate to talk about things going on in the office because now that you are a vice-president you don't have time for lots of little things. But I do know, Henry, that you believe nothing is more important than people, and so I feel I must tell you about one of your people." Henry looked up and smiled because Linda was wearing a demure Geoffrey Beene dress that looked like a little girl's jumper. "What do you want to tell me, Linda?" "Just that one of our employees, Ken Sugarman, has been offered a fantastic job at Revlon, and I think he may take it. He'd really rather stay here, but he doesn't even have a private office and a secretary." The next week Ken Sugarman, who didn't even know where the Revlon offices were, received a private office, a secretary, a new title, and a raise from Kiss, Inc. Overwhelmed and grateful, Ken believed good work certainly was rewarded at Kiss. He promptly decided to devote his career to such fine, understanding people. He made a decision to spend his life at Kiss, but he never told Linda. He knew it would not sound ambitious enough for her.

Linda left Kiss when she was pregnant with their first child. But Ken and she knew that she had never really left Kiss.

Now as she walked toward Sharon's room she was back at Kiss fully. She felt vital, needed. She was not only a part of Kiss. She was Kiss. She was about to change the course of events at Kiss,

Inc. She paused in front of the gift shop. Should she take Sharon a small present? No. That would seem like bribery. Better to act as if she were doing Sharon a favor.

Sharon stood in the doorway of her room. She was wearing her usual blue jeans. "Come on in, Linda. You sounded as if this were something urgent."

"It is," Linda said brusquely. "I'm here about a story."

Sharon was used to digging for stories. Anything that came too easily was not to be trusted. "Let's have a drink first. I think we both ought to relax before running off to tonight's multimillion-dollar extravaganza, the Kiss-o-rama. Sit down. Relax. I have some Fresca in my fridge." Sharon wanted time to think. She did not want to be steamrollered by this woman.

Linda smiled. Okay. She got the message. Cool it. "Fresca is not what Kiss people usually mean when they invite you for a drink."

"Come on. I'm not a Kiss person. I'm a reporter."

"And since you're here to cover our convention, what are you learning about us?"

"I'm glad you asked. I'm sort of asking that question myself. She tossed a can to Linda. "Sit down. Come on. Don't look so shocked. You can open a can of Fresca by yourself and drink it straight. Honestly, your mother is not watching. You don't need a glass."

"I guess I'm a victim of my upbringing."

"Not in my room."

"So what are you finding out about us?"

"Well, I can see that Chester is a real cutie. He has everybody walking a tightrope, and he never appears. Oh, once in a while he waves from the balcony like Mussolini, but he's not among you. He doesn't hang out with the peasants."

Linda smiled. "If people saw too much of him, they'd know what he's like."

"Do you know what he's like?"

"I used to work at Kiss."

"You look like you still do."

"If you mean that I worry about my husband—"

"Oh, let's not talk about your husband. Let's talk about Chester. Tell me some good Chester stories. I need them."

"Well, there's a great story about Chester when he was married to Gladyce, his third wife. They went to a party. Oh, you know, one of those big parties that *Women's Wear Daily* covers all the time, and Chester wouldn't eat a thing. Gladyce, who always sort of hovered, kept begging him to try some of the Iranian caviar and other goodies, but he kept saying no, no, no. Finally he said that the only thing that could tempt him was a bacon, lettuce, and tomato sandwich on white toast with a chocolate milk shake. So sure enough, the hostess sent out and the sandwich shop on the corner came up with his sandwich and shake."

"It must take a lot of confidence to do that," Sharon said. "He doesn't sound so bad to me."

"He has a terrible reputation, but I guess he's only awful to product managers and those above. When I worked there, he was always courteous to me. I mean that he didn't yell at me."

"Did he ever do anything nice for you? You know what I mean. Did he ever send your sick mother flowers . . . ?"

"My mother was never sick."

"Don't be so literal, Linda. I mean what positive thing did Chester ever do for you or anybody else? Did he send some kid through college or bake cookies for the PTA?"

Linda began to search her mind for remembered kindnesses. "I suppose you can say that he made it possible for a lot of people to have career opportunities they would not have had if he hadn't founded Kiss."

"We all know that, Linda. I want to know about Chester outside the mainstream."

Linda laughed. "There is no Chester outside the mainstream. His idea of the mainstream is the front page of the New York *Times*. And the rest of life is contained in gossip columns."

"In other words he doesn't take his eye off the ball."

"No. Of course you're aware that the big story here is finding the successor to Henry."

Sharon put the can of Fresca on the floor. She looked at Linda carefully. She realized Linda was setting the stage for whatever it was she wanted to say. "Why does Kiss need someone to replace Henry?"

"Henry is leaving Kiss." Damn. Linda had not meant to reveal this.

"You didn't really come here to tell me Henry was leaving, did you? It's really the big story of the convention; you're right about that. But what did you come here to tell me?"

"All right," Linda said. "You have the first part of the story. Now here's the rest. Chester is going to make a decision about the presidency in the next few days, and he doesn't even know it."

"You mean Chester doesn't know Henry is leaving the company?"

"Right. So he is going to have to do something fast. He will have to choose . . ."

"Your husband or Tim," Sharon finished, "and you are going to give me some background on both of them."

Linda's eyes widened. What made Sharon so perceptive?

Sharon smiled at Linda. Just because she wore blue jeans and said shit, was she supposed to be an insensitive, unaware person? She wondered if Linda realized that she had interviewed the secretary of state, had been to Russia, and once accompanied the President of the United States to China. No. Linda would think Sharon was assigned to marijuana busts.

"All right, Linda. Now we know that I know the score. First, let's talk about your husband."

"He's brilliant," Linda said quickly.

"Of course. And Tim?"

"A dullard. Oh," and now she looked slightly uncomfortable, "and then there is poor China."

"Poor? I thought she had enough money to bring back the French Revolution."

"Well, she's rich . . . if," Linda added significantly, "if you call having money being rich."

"It is one definition I have always found useful."

"China does have a problem, though," Linda said with sadness.

"Does that make her different?"

"Yes. This is no ordinary problem. China is an alcoholic."

"Oh, that," Sharon said lightly. "I've known that since I came here. She told me. So I guess that's no news."

Linda sat back. "But you don't understand. She is really an alcoholic. I saw her this afternoon going into the bar in town. She was alone. Anybody who drinks alone—"

"—doesn't have someone to drink with," Sharon concluded quickly. "Look, Linda, let me tell you something. I think you have more ambition than brains although I do not underestimate your intelligence. But I have more character than drive. I don't want to write a sordid story about a nice kid who has had a tough life. I did not come here to do an exposé of Chester and his family. I came here to write about the kinds of people who go to conventions. I came here to find out what makes American business tick. I do not want to uncover dirty things and hurt a lot of people. Some reporters do want that, and I guess you just picked the wrong one. I am not going to be a part of your stinking plot. I like China, and at the moment I like her a lot better than I like you. Now go back to your husband, and get set for the next act."

Linda looked over her shoulder on her way out of the room. "From the minute I met you I knew you were no reporter."

"And, Linda, I knew you were no lady."

Linda limped into the room.

Ken was still in front of the television set.

The contempt she felt for him was so strong she could taste it. Why couldn't he fight his own battles? Why did she have to demean herself in front of a filthy-talking reporter? She was angry. She would show Ken.

"Hey, come on," Ken said. "It's getting late."

"I am not going to the Kiss-o-rama." Until she said the words she did not know she wasn't going. But once the words were said she felt relief. Now she had an event, as well as people, she could ignore.

"Why aren't you going?"

"I hurt my ankle playing tennis today."

"You never even told me."

"I make it a habit not to tell you everything, Ken."

"Well, I don't want to go without you."

She wanted him out of the room. She wanted to be alone. She wanted to commune with Grandma Eisman. She wanted to get out of this rotten place.

"Just leave me alone, Ken," she said tensely.
"I can't face all those people without you," he said.
"Try, Ken. Just once in your life, try."
He nodded. "Whatever you say, Linda."

Ken spotted Henry making small talk with somebody's wife. He knew Henry would not mind being rescued.

"Well, if it isn't Cowboy Ken," Henry said, lifting his glass in a small salute.

"Amazed you could recognize me," Ken laughed.

"You know Corinne . . ."

"It's Maureen," the redhead said quickly, "and I am Sam Prentice's wife."

Ken's face lighted. "Sam Prentice? I can't tell you how much I think of your husband. We had a problem with the Shiny Stuff Lipline. Something was missing in that formula, and the tube kept breaking. No one could figure the reason, but your husband just stayed with the job and got to the bottom of the problem. And it's a good thing that he did because it's our best-selling lipstick now."

She beamed with pride. She couldn't wait to find Sam to tell him what this nice man had said. "And you are?" she asked timidly.

"Ken Sugarman, vice-president in charge of cosmetics and toiletries. But I wouldn't be without the good lab guys like Sam."

Once again she smiled the smile of wives and mothers who have just had good news from the front. "I'm going to tell Sam I met you," she said as she turned to leave. Over her shoulder she called out, "You are a darling man."

Henry watched her retreating figure. "That was nice, Ken. I couldn't remember her name or her husband's."

"But I'm no good with people," Ken replied. He was addressing the absent Linda.

Henry absent-mindedly patted Ken's shoulder. "Right. Right. Let's drink to the success of the convention." Henry's eyes darted around the crowd. Was he missing someone more interesting than Ken?

Ken took a big gulp of his drink, then blurted, "Henry, are you leaving Kiss?"

Henry had difficulty swallowing. How did anyone guess? Would Jo have said anything? No, of course not. But who knew? No one but Jo. And Rhoda. That was it. Rhoda. Rhoda and Linda. Linda and Ken. Ken and Henry.

Life wasn't so mysterious when you had a road map, but still people disappointed you. Why couldn't Rhoda keep quiet? "Ken," Henry said quietly, "it's true. Nobody knows for sure except you. I have not told Chester. I suggest that you not tell Chester. Nor should you have Linda say anything. Obviously you are in line for the presidency. There is you, and there is Tim. You do not have to be a certified genius to know I'd rather have you than Tim succeed me. I will do everything I can. I don't know what Chester will think about a manufacturing person rather than a sales type as head of the company. After all, Tim not only has the advantage of being Chester's son-in-law; he has the advantage of a sales background. But you are my first choice."

Ken swallowed. "I don't know if I'm good enough."

"You are," Henry said. "And I am saying it. That's even better than Linda telling you."

Ken blushed. So everybody knew how Linda pushed.

"Just keep this news from Linda."

"She knows," Ken said miserably.

"Of course she knows I am leaving. But she doesn't know that even without her prodding I am supporting you. Don't tell her. That's vital. Now mingle with the guests, Ken. I don't want rumors starting tonight."

Henry turned to the bartender. "Make it a double," he said quickly. He wondered whether Barbara had heard the rumors. No. Barbara was in Los Angeles today, so Linda had not reached her. He knew he had to see Barbara quickly. He called her room. There was no answer. She must be on her way down to the party.

Barbara was scheduled to be John Kingsley's dinner partner. That was Henry's doing. Each night of the convention Henry invited the guest of honor to sit at his table, and if the guest were interesting enough, Barbara was made his dinner partner. Obviously John Kingsley, the news commentator, was interesting enough.

Barbara searched the cocktail crowd around the pool for John Kingsley. Yes. There he was. The one in the business suit. Evidently he had just arrived and did not know this was a casual affair. Barbara adjusted her smile as she walked toward him. Before she reached him, however, Henry hurried to her and grabbed her arm.

"Barb, I must see you."

"More tennis?"

"I have better ideas." Now he loosened his grip. "Let's get together around midnight."

"And where will the first Mrs. Burns be?"

"We'll meet in your room."

"With everyone else so near? That doesn't sound like you, Henry. It's too dangerous."

"It's important."

Carol Morris and Dr. Schulz walked past.

"Furthermore," Henry said in an unnaturally loud voice, "I think it is vital that I see the new things before they go to Chester, so let me call you later."

Barbara nodded. It was unusual for Henry to take any risk. It must mean that he really did want to see the things photographed in Los Angeles earlier in the day. "It's been a tough day, Henry," she said in a small voice. "I do want you to see the things. I'm scared about tomorrow. There is so much riding on that presentation. You really went out on a limb for me in the early days of the project, and I just can't let you down."

He shook her hand. "If we were alone, baby, that isn't what I'd shake."

She nodded unhappily. Why did men always try to comfort you with sex?

John Kingsley had proof positive that he was the guest of honor when he saw the two women seated next to him: Jennifer Johnson (dare he tell her he used to listen to her sing when he was in high school?) and Barbara Anderson (was she somebody's girlfriend or could he make a pitch?).

John Kingsley's eyes took in all of Jennifer. He slid his chair closer to her. She did not move away—a promising beginning.

"Miss Johnson . . ."

"It's Jennifer."

"I was hoping you'd say that. Jennifer, you look fantastic."

"You like what I'm wearing?"

"I do. I just have one question. Is that an outfit or three coats of paint?"

"You're adorable," she said in her old imitation Marilyn Monroe voice.

"You sound more like a copywriter than a newscaster to me," said Barbara.

"Sorry about that," John Kingsley said as he turned to Barbara. Funny how pretty girls responded if they thought they were being ignored. He smiled at her. "What is it about this company that attracts all you beautiful women?"

Jennifer turned away when John Kingsley began to talk to Barbara. She had long ago learned that stars do not listen; stars must star.

Barbara sighed. Another guy. Another line. "I am so smart, Mr. Kingsley, that I am going to tell you right now that Jennifer is the one for you to pursue. Forget me."

"How could I ever forget you, Miss uh, uh . . ."

"Jennifer will shower you with Kiss hospitality."

"Careful. The fangs are showing."

"No, Mr. Kingsley, you're wrong. You are seated between us, and I am telling you the differences between us. She is kiss and I am tell."

"Clever, clever."

"Okay, so I'm corny, but at least I try."

"I don't need you to try for anything. Relax, Miss Big Business. It's more fun to talk to a smart woman than to go to bed with a dumb one."

"I didn't say Jennifer was dumb," Barbara said defensively.

"And I didn't say I was going to bed with her."

"I guess I'm uptight. These conventions always unnerve me."

"Why?"

"I hate being on display this way."

"I am on display all the time, and it doesn't bother me."

"That's different. I don't mind being on display in the line of duty, but I hate this pseudo stuff, this husband-wife pretending and the strain of doing business with men who are trying to keep their marriages afloat with a trip to a convention."

"Do you really think that's happening here?"

"Think?" Barbara laughed. "That man over there is having an affair with my secretary. They both think I don't know, but I do, and meanwhile he's here holding tight to his wife. The woman standing near the bar once had an affair with the president of the company. Her name is Carol Morris, and she doesn't think I know, and he doesn't think I know, but I do."

"And you are now having an affair with the president of the company?"

She looked at him in surprise. "Of course not."

"Then why didn't you tell me the name of the man who is having an affair with your secretary but make certain to tell me the name of the woman who once had an affair with the president?"

"I don't follow your logic," she said primly.

"Aren't you having an affair?" he asked.

"I am having an affair, Mr. Kingsley . . ."

"John . . ."

"Yes. John. I am having an affair with business. I am in love with my job, and if you don't believe it, you can ask my fiancé because he thinks I am passionate about business."

"Is he right?"

"Yes."

"Does business keep your feet warm on winter nights? Or does your married lover?"

"What are you trying to say?"

"I'm saying that I have figured out that you have a married lover, and so I know you have no one to keep your feet warm on winter nights. Because if you are having an affair with a married man, my dear, all you have is a man with cold feet."

She smiled ruefully at his perceptiveness. "How do you know so much?"

"I am on television. I am a twentieth-century oracle."

"I think you're a married man who is having an affair."

"Not just one. I am island hopping."

"Don't you love anybody?"

"That's heavy talk before dinner. Save it for later."

"I won't be talking to you later."

"Then save it for someone else. Look, I am going to turn the other way for a little while and have a conversation with Jennifer. I've liked her movies ever since I was old enough to eat popcorn in the picture show."

"What are you going to talk to her about?"

"Oh, I think I'll tell her that my mommy used to hold me on her lap to see Jennifer Johnson movies."

"That's not the way to get to her bed."

"Want to bet?" John Kingsley turned his back, and Barbara turned to her right to talk to Dr. Schulz.

"How vas your photo session?" he asked.

"Perfect. Well, I hope it was perfect. I'm getting the pictures later tonight. They're being flown in so I can be sure to have them at the meeting."

"Vell, since you vill get them tonight Henry vill see vot you haff brought back."

"How do you know he'll see them?"

"I heard him tell you he vanted to see the pictures, and later he said to me he vould haff a chance to see . . ."

"Never mind," she said shaking her head. Good old Henry. He did cover and recover his tracks.

The Kiss-o-rama was always an expensive evening, yet it was nothing more than a barbecue. There was a roast pig with an apple in its mouth and a groaning buffet filled with costly but bland-tasting food.

"Do you want to go and get in line for food?" John Kingsley asked Jennifer.

"If I get up, honey, I think the paint may peel."

So she remembered his comment. That was a good sign. This was the time to close the deal. "I want to see you stand in line, Jennifer, because I don't want to see just Jennifer from the waist up sitting here. I want to see what all of you is like. I want to see if . . ."

"Yeah. I know what you want to see. Honey, you don't have to just see it. You can touch it." She reached under the table, and he felt her hand on the inside of his leg.

"Now I can't leave the table," he said. "You'll have to get food for me."

"I'll get everything for you."

He nodded somewhat dazed. And he had been worried that he might not be able to make her?

When Jennifer stood up to go to the buffet, Henry came over and took her seat. "Is anyone getting dinner for you, John?"

"Jennifer kindly offered."

"Good. Good." Henry was playing president now, Barbara decided as she watched him. He was wearing his president smile along with his jeans. He was a sorcerer.

"We always have a wonderful time at our conventions," Henry said sincerely. "The purpose is to bring the men and women of Kiss together with their husbands and wives . . ."

"You don't have to explain," John said quickly.

Jennifer returned with two heaping platters, and Henry gladly gave up his seat. John Kingsley seemed like a know-it-all, and Henry no longer had to play up to people like that because they were Kiss guests. He leaned over Barbara as he walked back to his seat on the other side of the table. "Taking good care of our guest?" he asked.

"I think Jennifer is handling him. Literally," she smiled.

He patted her with the absent-minded pat of a man who is doing what is expected. Then he leaned over quickly and said in a voice loud enough to carry across the table to his wife, "Call me the minute the stuff comes in from Los Angeles. I'll look at it with you, and then we'll take it to Chester."

"Chester?" she asked, half-frozen.

"Sure," he smiled. "We wouldn't want to present something tomorrow that he had not seen tonight. We'll get to his room by 3 A.M."

Sharon looked around the table of twelve Kiss people with whom she had been seated. During dinner she had listened to complaints about a Midwest department store, a list of the best restaurants in New York, and an account of a bout with hepatitis. By nine-thirty she was yawning.

"Does this bore you?" asked Donald Bush, the salesman sitting next to her.

"It isn't exactly dinner with the Shah," Sharon said.
"It would be if Chester Masterson were here."
"Do you know Mr. Masterson well?" she asked.
"I don't know him at all, and I am trying to keep it that way. I'm afraid if he knows me he will summon me one day, and I will stand there just pawing the oriental rug and whinnying, and the next day I will be calling Avon for a job."
"Why is everyone so afraid of Mr. Masterson?"
"Because he is such a perfectionist. Most people will settle for second or third best or eighth best. Not Chester. And if he doesn't get what he wants, he yells and insults people."
"Since you know that much without knowing him, do you have any good Chester stories? I need specific anecdotes to round out my coverage of the convention."
"All I can tell you is that the unemployment lines are filled with people Chester admired—until he hired them. Everyone working somewhere else has great mystique, but once he hires people, he slaps them around, ignores them, and insults them. It is as if he always admires those things just beyond his grasp."
"And that's why you try to stay away from him?"
"Right. But I would like to get closer to you."
"You would?"
"I think you're cute."
"I'm twelve pounds overweight, and I am an intellectual. That makes me a lousy candidate for romance."
"Not in my book," he said.
"You're stuck forty miles from town, and all you have is what the company provided. And I guess in blue jeans we are all equal."
"No. You're more interesting to me. I like talking to people."
"So do I. And that's what I am missing here. I am not getting enough time to talk to the people at this convention. *Newsweek* sent me here to get the over-all atmosphere of a convention, you know, business people in a play spot. I've talked to some of the women, but I haven't really had a chance to know what people like you are about."
"I'm giving you the chance," Donald Bush said.
"Okay, Donald, if you really like talking to people, talk to me. Cut the romantic shit. Let's just talk."

"You know," he said reflectively, "sometimes it's a relief when a girl says no. Yeah, it would be nice just to talk."

"Okay. Let me ask you something. How do you as a salesman feel about conventions like this?"

"I think they are a nice way to improve your tennis game, and if you play with the right people it can improve your business life. Most of all, a convention like this gives me a chance to talk to somebody like Tim Edgar. Tim is really my boss, but we cannot ever talk casually. I can get to know Tim at a convention, and he can get to know me, and when an opening comes along, he'll remember the guy he talked to at the convention at The Gates of Paradise, and somebody will recommend me, and the next thing you know I will be promoted."

"Do you think all business works that way?"

"Any business that depends on personalities."

"And," Sharon asked, "do you think that all those people standing around the bar are talking to each other about advancing their careers?"

"One way or another. Look, if you really want to listen, pretend that I'm your date. We'll go over there. Don't talk to me. You listen on one side; I'll listen on the other, and then we can compare notes."

An hour later Sharon signaled Donald Bush. "I think I have everything I need for this."

"Come sit at the table, and I'll look at my notes."

"Your notes?"

"All written on a cocktail napkin."

"Let's see."

She made a great ceremony of spreading the napkin, and then she read, "Next pres. Manager, southwest. Discounts. Local advertising. Approaches one, two, three, four."

"I understand the first part," said Donald, "but what are approaches one, two, three, and four?"

"The things boys and girls say to each other in between that other stuff."

"Describe them."

"All right. Approach Number One. Boy goes up to girl and says, 'I love you.' Girl looks amazed but obviously believes what boy is saying. After several more stabs at conversation they presumably go off into the bushes or bedroom together because it is now all right for girl to go to bed with boy. He has said he loves her.

"Approach Number Two. Boy says he has no blankets on his bed. Asks girl for one. Girl says she has blankets. Boy says he knew he could ask her because in the office she always has everything like stationery and extra pens and stamps and he knew she would have blankets, too. Boy and girl are now intently involved in conversation.

"Approach Number Three. Girl says to boy that she has been trying to get into his department for months. Boy is so flattered he practically cries in his Margarita. They are now having a third drink discovering that they both like jazz and old movies and hate singles bars. I predict she will wind up in his department as well as apartment.

"Approach Number Four. Boy says to girl that he has seen her in several meetings and has always thought she was very smart. He is now sitting at the bar getting to know her better. I predict he will not get to know her better because she really is smart and vulnerable, and I guess she will go to bed early and alone."

"Whew," gasped Donald Bush, "I bet I know the names for all those stories."

"It is not important to know the names," Sharon said. "What matters is that they are a lot of people who are huddling together for business security. I am beginning to realize that people in the same business who share everyday problems find it easier and faster to share sex."

"Or love," answered Donald Bush. "You see, my wife was a demonstrator for Kiss at Dayton's in Minneapolis."

"And you made a pass at me even though you are married?"

"I didn't make a serious pass. I made a courtesy pass. I thought maybe I would be a good host and ask. But obviously you aren't looking for a man. I did think you needed a friend though, and I was willing to help."

"Thanks, Donald Bush, friend."

"You're welcome, Sharon. And if you ever get to Minneapolis, come and see the wife and me."

"Of course I will," she answered, knowing that she would

never look up Donald Bush, but that was one kind of social lie all civilized people practice.

Barbara walked by just as Sharon was folding her napkin notes. "Learning all about us?" Barbara asked as she sat down with Sharon.

"Nooooo," Sharon said slowly, "but I am learning some things."

"For instance?"

"Well, I'm not sure if this is true of all business or just Kiss, but as I walked around tonight overhearing conversations I was aware that every time I came across two or three women talking, the subject was business. Men here seem to talk about everything else. They talk about sports and girls and money, but they don't talk about the business. Why is that? For women small talk is business talk."

Barbara thought for a moment. "I guess because for most of us the preoccupation with business is newer and more exciting than it is for men. We women are like first-generation Americans compared to *Mayflower* descendants. We are still excited by the New World, and—wait." Barbara stopped talking. The public address system sputtered and shrieked.

"I was just paged," she said nervously. "That means the photographs and layouts from Los Angeles have been delivered. I have to go now. I can't wait to see them." She rose so quickly that her chair fell back on the stone patio. Near the edge of the crowd was Henry. She ran toward him, whispered to him that the package had arrived, and hurried toward her room.

"What's that whispering about?" Jo asked briskly.

"Barbara is going back to her room to wait for the ad materials," Henry said matter-of-factly.

"I thought she would go back only when they were delivered."

Henry wondered why he didn't want Jo to know that the package had been delivered. After making everyone aware publicly, why did he not follow the script? He squeezed his glass. "She will go back when she wants to go back. Stop prying."

"I didn't think I was prying," Jo replied haughtily. "I thought I was just showing some interest, and I had always heard that a little interest was a good thing."

"Leave me alone," Henry said sharply, and put the highball glass on the bar with so much force that it shattered.

"Is that some kind of symbolic act?" his wife asked sharply.

Henry did not answer. He turned and walked toward Barbara's room.

Although Henry left Jo quickly, he walked slowly toward Barbara's room. He had not yet decided precisely the way he was going to tell her that he was leaving Kiss. Should he tell her now before tomorrow's meeting or should he wait until the pressure of thc meeting was over? He was still uncertain when he knocked at her door.

"Henry." Her eyes were shining when she saw him.

He thought to himself, That's love.

"Henry, the ads are spectacular. Chester was right. The girl makes it brilliant."

So there was another reason for her sparkling eyes, a reason that had nothing to do with Henry. At least not now. But wait. Just wait. He would get to her. He would take away that business glow. He'd prove that he could affect her emotions more than anyone or anything.

"Henry. Say something. Come in. Don't just stand there." She took his arm and pulled him through the door. "Have a drink. Have an ad."

"Have an ex-president of Kiss," he said taking off his jacket.

"What are you talking about? Did Chester make you chairman?"

"No."

"Then what are you saying?"

"Can't you guess?"

She shook her head.

"Smart lady like you who can change on a dime whenever Chester blows the whistle must have figured this one out. Don't tell me a silly fellow like me could do something you wouldn't figure out in advance."

"I don't know what you are talking about. Sit down and tell me what is going on." The sparkle was out of her eyes. Instead there was a look of concern. He was right. He could replace that sparkle in seconds.

"You seem to be the genius who knows how to call shots with

the chairman," Henry said. "Maybe you ought to tell me what's going on."

"Henry, I understand and love you more than anyone in the whole world. I don't know why you are angry, but you are."

"Why am I angry? Simply, my dear, because I walked in here just to see you. I was thinking, of course, that you would be happy to see me. But is it me you want? No. It's the president of Kiss. You want to show off again. You want to shout, 'Look at me. Look at what I did.'"

"That's not true, Henry, and you know it. Whatever I am at Kiss, Inc., is the result of what you taught me."

"I don't think you need me to teach you anything."

Barbara stood silent for a minute. Then she put one arm around Henry's waist. With her other hand she began to unbutton her cotton shirt slowly. Henry felt the anger rising in himself. What right did she have to take the initiative? Was she usurping his manhood, too? He grabbed her arm from around him, pushed her against the wall, and held her still as he ripped the shirt from her. He untied the blue denim skirt, and it fell to the floor. Then he picked her up and walked over to the bed, dropped her on it, and took her with a ferocity she had never known. She felt as if all the breath had been pumped from her.

Minutes later he rolled off her onto his back. He did not speak. Hurt and bewildered, Barbara turned toward the wall.

When she turned again toward Henry, she was weeping. "Henry, you are the most gentle man in the world. You've been so tender and so perfect with me, and this . . . this whatever that we just had . . . was violent. I didn't know you tonight."

"Maybe you never have. I didn't know me tonight, Barbara."

"Do you want to cry, too, Henry?"

She put her arms around him and felt sobs shake his body. Later, still holding each other, they fell asleep. Barbara awakened first. She knew it was not morning, and when she looked at her clock, she was surprised to find that it was only midnight.

Henry awakened a few moments later. He leaned toward her. "I really do want to talk to you."

"In bed?"

"In some ways yes, but really no. I want to talk to you with both of us dressed and sitting in chairs like grownups."

"All right."

With a drink in his hand and his open plaid shirt Henry felt comfortable, at ease for the first time that night. "I wish this were the start of our evening together," he said. "I feel more like talking now."

"What was bothering you before?"

"Fear and jealousy. Very bad twins."

"How can you be afraid or jealous of me?"

"I don't know. I don't really want to explore that now, Barbie." He knew she loved him to call her Barbie.

"What were you trying to tell me when you came here?"

"Something I should have told you a month ago, but something I wanted to carry inside me and only me. I really didn't want to share the news because I didn't want your advice. I was afraid of it. Barbie, Oxxon has offered me their presidency."

"And you want it?"

"Of course I want it. It's everything I want. It's a multinational, a chance to run my own show."

"We'll never get that here."

He put his arm around her. "My girl. Only you would understand that."

"Does that mean Jo doesn't?"

"What makes you so smart?"

"The same thing that makes you so transparent. Love."

"Will you love me even if I leave?"

"What does that have to do with it?"

"Well, if I'm the president of Oxxon . . ."

"I will be a vice-president or product manager or something."

Henry blanched. "You can't go with me," he said quickly.

"You don't want me?" she asked in a shocked tone.

"You can't move to Switzerland."

"Why? You can."

"That's different. I can take my home and family."

She shook her head. "This is my chance to be your home and family. Now's the time to leave Jo, Henry. This is the time to make the break. New job. New country. New life."

"But I have already told Jo she is going."

"Untell her."

"Look, being the president of Oxxon is a social as well as a business thing. It means running a house. You can't work and run a house."

"Sure I can. I've done it all my life. That's all I've ever done. I'll take care of you, darling. I'll take the best care of you in all the world."

"Barbara, I am already in a marriage. I'm not ready to make new commitments to a woman. I am just deciding to make a new commitment to a job."

"This is going to be the best thing that ever happened to us. We are going to be the best business partnership the world has ever seen."

"I don't want a business partner."

"Since when?"

"I don't want a partner. I want a chance to go it alone. That's what I've always wanted."

"But Henry, I always think of us as a team. We do everything together in business, and I don't make decisions without you . . ."

". . . of course you make decisions alone. You wouldn't be much of an executive if you didn't."

"But I want to be a part of your life."

"Barbie, what I admire most about you is that you are not a part of my life. I mean you have a life without me. You don't cling. You don't make demands. It's wonderful having a relationship with you."

"And that's all we are, a relationship?"

"How many people ever know a relationship?"

"I think most people do."

"No. Most people go through life locked in legal or illegal arrangements that have none of the joys of a relationship like ours."

"But Henry, outside of bed, what are the joys? I can't let anyone know about us. I have to be careful not to touch you. I can't ever reach out for you. You never exchange a look or a small squeeze or a tender word without looking first from side to side because 'Chester will find out' or 'Tim will figure it' or 'Ken will tell Linda, and she will tell everyone.' I've lived this strange, secret life with you for years. I want to be open, and this is our chance."

"Barbara, I do not want anyone clinging to my career."

"Stop using that word. I am not going to cling to your career. I am going to make it shine."

"One Linda Sugarman is enough in this world."

"Okay, Henry, I give up. I understand what you are saying. You are going to be the president of Oxxon, and maybe you'll send me a Christmas card with a little note appended. I always liked those little personal touches, remember? Let's see. On my card you can say something like, 'Dear Barbie, I have gone to Switzerland. Have a good life. Love, Henry Burns.' Be sure to sign your full name, Henry, because I plan to forget you very fast."

"We will never forget each other, Barbara."

"Right. One day you'll be in the lab, and somebody will say, 'Why don't we call this by the code name Product Q?' and you will say, 'That sounds quite familiar.'"

"Barbara, I don't think you're being realistic."

"Henry, I don't think you're being romantic."

"It's funny that a woman who is as strong in business as you are is still a romantic."

"Yeah, very funny. When the plane landed in Los Angeles today, I was driving to the photographer's studio, and I saw a billboard. I stopped for a light and copied the message on the back of an envelope because I wanted to tell you about it." She reached for her handbag and fumbled for the envelope. "It says, 'Helen, marry me soon already. I love you.'"

"I'd never put up a billboard like that, Barbie."

"No, but I might."

"Barbara, even though I will be working in Switzerland I'll still come to the United States, and I'd like to see you and spend time with you."

"Henry, let me tell you something. You just closed a chapter of my life. Once upon a time I was a little girl who came to Kiss, and I didn't know anything. Oh, I knew what they had taught me in college, which is about as close to real life as Hansel and Gretel are to you and me."

"They were brother and sister," he smiled.

"When I'm finished that's what we'll be, too," she said grimly. "Now you listen. You were the big man at Kiss, the big man in my life. I didn't know how to write a presentation except the kind that gets A's from professors who don't know about companies like Kiss. In college nobody teaches you that you don't have to be academically perfect when you work for somebody. You just have to do it their way. Well, baby, you taught me how to do it Chester's way. You taught me when to speak up in a meeting and when to turn a pale marble shade so I could fade into those cold marble boardroom walls. And I learned. I learned because I am still a good student. I learned how to do product introductions so that Chester thought they were his, and I learned how to look at colors and know a blue red from a yellow red in lipsticks. Oh, I learned. I learned so well that tomorrow I can get into that meeting in front of all those people, and I will turn everybody green. Everybody. They'll all wish they had been given the new product assignment. But you, Henry dear, you gave it to me, and the fact that you like sleeping with me had nothing to do with it. You gave it to me because you knew that I would do the best job. Well, I have. I have given you the hottest presentation the cosmetics business has ever seen. And I have also given you the only good love you will ever know. You're a taker, Henry. You took from Jo when she was young. You're taking from me now. And fortunately you are stopping the merry-go-round right this day. I think it just may be the best thing that ever happened to me. I think maybe you don't fit in my life anymore."

"But I still fit, Barbie. There's room for me if you're willing . . ."

"You don't get the message, Henry. I'm not willing. I want to be a combination of things in a man's life. I want to be a business friend and a real friend, and I want to be a lover. But I don't want to be any of those things if I have to exclude any of the others."

"I know we can work out something."

"We can't. But even though you are leaving Kiss, I still have my eye on the clock and the man in Suite 1A. I am going to show you the ads . . ."

"Barbara, remember the time we went to Rome and . . ."

". . . then you tell me if you want any changes made. Now don't give me impossible changes . . ."

". . . remember when you came into my office and said, 'I don't know how to tell you this, but I can't read a p & l . . ."

". . . and then if you approve the things we'll go right to Chester's room because I must get some sleep before the meeting tomorrow."

She thrust the ads in front of him and made him look at them. "They are terrific, Barbara," he said. He put his arms around her. "You are a professional."

"A professional fool," she said softly.

Barbara flipped the layouts on the coffee table in Chester's living room. "The new photos work. You were right again. I guess you are smarter than we are," she said almost apologetically.

Chester managed to fix his mouth into a crooked half-smile. "I'm always right. Only the dummies argue."

"I guess Barbara has proven she's no dummy," Henry said quickly.

Chester looked up slowly at Henry. "Yes," he said, "but have you?"

Henry began to speak, thought better of it, and said nothing.

"Well, where's your answer, Mr. Smartass?" Chester asked.

"No answers. It's too late in the evening for me," Henry said.

"Well, it's not too late for me," said Chester. "See that phone? It is going to ring in ten minutes. The call will be for me, but I won't take it."

Henry had worked for Chester long enough to know that if he asked no questions Chester would eventually be unable to withhold his secret. If he asked questions, Chester would clamp up perversely.

"Let's talk about Product Q," said Henry.

"I went to Los Angeles today," Barbara reported, "and I worked with a photographer and West Coast representatives from our advertising agency. They flew the material here just a short while ago, and, as I said, you were right. Putting a woman in the pictures makes the whole thing come alive."

"Just because you have a scientific discovery you do not have to be dull," Chester said. "Trouble with everybody is that they are afraid that we are such Puritans that if we promise pleasure, people won't buy the product. Just the opposite is true. The more you make people believe they will like something, the better the sales."

"Hey," Henry interrupted, "that's fancy language for you."

"It's the goddamned . . . excuse me, Barbara . . . it's the truth," said Chester.

Barbara opened her briefcase to review the copy. "Don't read me a thing right now," Chester said brusquely. "The telephone is going to ring."

On cue the telephone rang. Chester roared with laughter. "That miserable Hugo Baron is so nervous he is calling me at 4 A.M. New York time. Now let it ring."

"I thought Hugo Baron was one of your good friends," Henry said in a puzzled tone.

"He won't be when I answer the phone. Seven rings, and still I won't answer," Chester smiled. "Here's what's happening, and you can listen, too, Miss Product Q. Last week, Friday to be exact, I had lunch in New York with Hugo. Hugo and I always talk about business in a confidential way, so I asked him what he was doing. He told me he was about to become one of our suppliers. He was going to buy Principia, the glass mold company. Now you have to understand, Barbara, that glass costs are one of our biggest manufacturing costs, and I will do anything, absolutely anything, to hold prices on glass so I have more money for ingredients. So here my old friend Hugo was announcing he was about to become a supplier.

"But he didn't just say he'd be one of our suppliers. Oh no. Not Hugo. He said he was going to raise prices; he'd make me squirm. Then he laughed. Imagine that. That little creep Hugo Baron laughed at Chester Masterson. In business you learn not to show any emotion if a man has something that you want. Doesn't matter what it is. A woman. A formula. If he has it, and you want it, don't pant in public.

"So when Hugo stuck it to me about prices, I didn't yell. You can't believe that, can you? You don't think I can be a gentleman? Well, for money I can. I just sat back and ordered my usual tuna fish and tea, and nobody knew I was about to upset

Mr. Hugo Baron. I even smoked a cigar, and I hate cigars, but Hugo offered me a Cuban cigar, and I knew enough not to turn it down. So we sat back and smoked and relaxed, and I asked some questions. One thing you learn about rich men who buy and sell is that they love to talk about what they buy and sell. They like it even better when they tell another rich man. So Hugo told me this story. He told me all the details of the acquisition. He said he offered eighteen million for the company, and Principia would close Monday morning at 9 A.M.

"'Why don't you close today?' I asked Hugo, because I know a hot deal gets cold when it sits. Oh, said Hugo, he had to go to Nassau for the weekend with his girlfriend. Ha. I knew I had him by the—well, I knew I had him then. Any man who waits to close a business deal so he can get out of town on Friday afternoon deserves to lose the deal. One whore is as good as another. After we said good-by, I went to the office. And Hugo went to Nassau.

"I called my attorney and told him that at 5:01 that afternoon as Hugo was flying off to Nassau, I wanted him to call Principia and tell them he could better Hugo's deal. I wanted him to say that he had a buyer who would pay eighteen million two hundred thousand provided there were no topping privileges for Hugo, and the name of the new buyer would not be disclosed. I also said that if you don't close today, you buy the deal."

"What happened?" asked Henry.

"They closed. When Hugo called Monday about the closing, Principia told him there was a delay. No one told him what happened. You know why he's calling now?"

Barbara and Henry shook their heads.

"He just read tomorrow's *Times*, and the deal is announced on the financial pages. He wants to scream at me, and I won't take his calls," Chester said. "I'm telling you this story because there's something to be learned from it."

"What's that?" asked Barbara.

"Never mix business with friendship," said Chester.

"You have to admit," said Henry as they walked toward Barbara's room, "life with Chester is never dull."

She shook her finger. "Never mix business with friendship."

"Well," he said, taking her hand, but first looking to make certain no one was watching, "I'd like to discuss business with you, and you are my best friend."

She unlinked her hand from his. It had been a hard day, an exhausting night, and she wanted more than hand-holding.

There was a false cheerfulness in Henry's voice. "I think you are on the way to a major triumph."

"Only seven hours before the presentation, and I have a great triumph," she said sadly.

"At least I can feel that I am leaving you in a very good position at Kiss. Chester won't bite. I think you have him defanged."

"Henry, why are you leaving? Honestly, why are you leaving?"

"I told you. I want a chance to run my own show."

"That's not it. It doesn't matter who you are or where you work. You never run your own show. Even Chester doesn't. He just plays at being Chester Masterson."

"That's not true. I have watched him for years now. I think he once played at being Chester Masterson, but now after eighteen years of observing him I know he must *be* Chester Masterson."

"And you want to *be* Henry Burns?"

"Not the way Chester is. That's not my style. I'm not going to give my wife a birthday present of a tin can filled with $30,000 as Chester did with his second wife. And I am not going to indulge in sex orgies. And I am not going to offer a restaurateur $10,000 or $50,000 or a million dollars to stay open beyond closing hours so I can drink another cup of coffee."

"Are you leaving because you are running away from me?"

"Of course not."

"I think you are. I think you are feeling the noose. I think that maybe for the first time you did what you never expected to do. I'm different from Carol Morris or any of those other women in your life. I am not just another secretary, and you don't know where to file me. I think I really got to you, Henry. And I think you're running away."

"I'm confused."

She shook her head. "Every time I walk into your office I see the neatest, most organized desk top at Kiss. There is harmony on your desk and disorder within. If you stay at Kiss, you are going to become dissatisfied with your marriage, and you can't afford to do that. You cannot afford to disrupt your life."

"I don't think I love Jo. I did once, but it all got lost somewhere."

"Henry, it got lost in the relationship you created with me. You and I tried to build something that could stand apart from our legal and formal relationships. I gave you more than I ever gave any man. You gave me more than you gave Jo. You gave me love, and you hadn't given that for a long time."

"I don't think I ever gave it before. I was awed by Jo when I was young, and now that I'm older I am comforted by her. She tries to keep my life on an even keel. She doesn't know there have been other women."

"But I know. I know there were affairs, and some of them were at the office, and some were not. But that's all they were: affairs."

"This was a love affair, Barbara."

"You used the right tense, Henry. *Was.* It was a real love affair. But you're free now. Free to be yourself. Isn't that what you said you wanted? But you know whom you really freed with this? You freed me."

"Let me go to your room with you now and love you the way I really mean to love you."

She shook her head. "No, I told you I'm free. I am so free of you now, Henry, that for the first time since we first made love I can say 'no' and mean it."

"Barbara, we can't separate like this. We still have a lot of pleasure to give each other. Why cause ourselves pain?"

"This is the only way we can separate. You'll get over the pain of loving, and so will I. It won't be easy, but in the long run, it is easier than not living one's life fully. You will go back to your job, and I'll go back to mine. And who knows? Maybe I'll begin to like my fiancé more. I think I may work on that."

"But you don't have to give him up. I don't mind if he stays in your life."

"You know why you are a good executive, Henry? You never even hear the objections of another person. You just pluck the words you like and go ahead and do what you want. But not this time." She walked into her room and closed the door softly behind her.

Tuesday

John Kingsley smiled. All the brass was in the audience. Even Chester Masterson came out of hibernation to hear him.

Jo, her executive wife smile fixed neatly on her face, sat with hands folded. Next to her China's little doll-like face was raised expectantly. Barbara was chewing her lips nervously. Jennifer, slightly tired from the physical effort of pleasing John Kingsley six different ways the previous night, knew her mind would wander during the speech. Linda stared dully at the floor. Sharon sat with open notebook.

Meeting Room A was filled to capacity. The Kiss executives stood at the back. The exception was Chester, who sat in the first row. He was dressed neatly in a navy-blue suit with purple shirt and navy tie. It was Chester's standard office uniform. Like a general, he never varied his dress. The shirts, made for him by Turnbull & Asser in London, were ordered in groups of 365. Once a year they were sent back to London for laundering. The office joke was, "What does Chester wear leap year?"

Chester reached in his pocket for two Gelusils. He found them. Now the meeting could begin.

Henry introduced John Kingsley with a couple of small good-natured jokes. John Kingsley knew the audience was up for him. He felt slightly heady. So many faces, and they all adored John Kingsley. He reached in his breast pocket, took out his carefully prepared speech, and flashed his 7 P.M. network news smile. The audience recognized and loved it.

"He ought to sit down now," Sharon whispered to Donald Bush, who was seated next to her. "He'll never be better than this."

But John Kingsley did not sit down. Instead he said, "You are real people. This is what America is all about." He caressed the words as he spoke.

"What's that supposed to mean?" Sharon asked in annoyance.

Linda applauded vigorously.

"Why are you applauding?" Ken asked.

"Because Chester is," Linda whispered. "Come on, dummy, applaud."

Ken applauded.

"Kingsley's brilliant," Jo said to China. At that point Kingsley had spoken exactly eleven words.

John Kingsley responded to the applause by raising his arms like a victorious candidate.

"One more time with those arms, and Chester will make him president of Kiss," Tim said to Henry.

"Today," continued John Kingsley, "I am going to discuss 'The Need for Television in a Dynamic Society.'"

Now Linda turned to Ken in surprise. "That's a real four-yawn speech. I'll bet he never told his wife what he was going to do."

"This will be a hard-hitting speech for people with social conscience," John Kingsley said emphatically. It was the last thing he said that people heard. For the next eighteen minutes he droned. On and on and on. One cliché followed by another.

"I don't believe this," Sharon whispered to Donald Bush.

He did not answer. He was sleeping.

"John Kingsley promised to be an unusual speaker," Jennifer whispered to Jo, "but he sure as hell isn't. He's as boring as all the others who come here."

Barbara continued to chew her lips. "If he doesn't stop soon," Carol Morris whispered, "you'll be so maimed you won't be able to speak."

"I can't follow this," Barbara moaned. "I can't speak next."

"Wrong," said Carol. "It's the only kind of speech to follow. I talk to women's groups all the time, and the only trouble I have is following dynamite speakers. After this guy you have no place to go but up."

There was a smattering of applause when John Kingsley finished.

"Why was he so bad?" Linda asked Jennifer.

"Because he is like all those rip-and-read guys," said Jennifer. "They don't know how to talk for more than three minutes without commercial interruption. Listen to them, and you realize that people aren't interesting just because they're on TV. They must have some ideas to express, too."

“Hey, look,” Linda hissed. “I think Chester is about to express an idea.”

Chester rose slowly. He was shaking his head. The movement was negative. Little by little the postspeech audience buzzing died down. The audience held its collective breath. Chester insulted his own people as regularly as he dined. But how would he handle an outsider?

John Kingsley was frozen at the podium. The short applause had ended. Masterson was facing him. Should he thank him? No, that head shaking meant that Chester Masterson did not want John Kingsley's thanks.

“Mr. Kingsley,” said Chester in a voice that dripped dangerously of milk and honey. “Mr. Kingsley, it's really something that a big name newscaster like you would honor a simple little cosmetics company like us by coming to this meeting.”

Henry sank into his chair. He had been in enough marble-paneled boardroom meetings to know what was coming next.

Kingsley breathed a sigh of relief. Chester liked him after all.

“But Mr. Kingsley,” Chester continued, “you didn't keep your part of the bargain. We did what we were supposed to do. We paid you a hell of a lot of money, and we filled the chairs. But you, Mr. Kingsley, did not deliver. If you were a supplier, I'd cut you off. If you were a store, I wouldn't sell you. Because, Mr. Kingsley, you are nothing. Zero. Naught. You stink.”

Then Chester turned and strode out of the room. Not a sound could be heard.

John Kingsley reached for a glass of water, took two sips, smiled, and said, “I only had to hear that once. I'm leaving. But, gentlemen and ladies, he's your boss. So if you're staying, good luck. You'll need it.”

Then John Kingsley turned sharply and left the room.

There was not a sound to be heard. The audience was stunned. It had all happened so quickly.

Henry had guessed what Chester might do, but the scene startled him, nevertheless. Someday, he thought, I will be tough like that, too. I'll be tough like Chester and say what I think, and I'll be tough like Kingsley and not take anything from anybody. But not today. No not today. Today I'm still at Kiss. But when I get to Oxxon, I'll scare my guys by—

A tug at his jacket sleeve brought Henry back to the present. "What are we going to do?" whispered Tim.

"About what?"

"Chester left before the Product Q presentation," Tim said.

"We can get him back during the coffee break," Henry said, now firmly back in the Kiss meeting. "You know, Tim, we won't even have to go out to get him. Chester will come back on his own. Chester will want to see the reception Product Q gets. Don't worry. He'll be back for his applause."

"You know him better than anybody else knows him, don't you?" Tim asked.

"I have made it my business to know him."

"Then who is the next president?"

Henry smiled. "I know who it isn't."

"Who?" asked Tim.

"Me," said Henry. "I can't take the president number much longer." Then Henry said nothing. Plant the seed. Okay, smart kid. Now figure it out. Do I mean I'm leaving? Or do I mean I'm about to be chairman?

Tim wanted to ask more questions, but he decided not to. After all, Tim was family. He should know more than Henry, shouldn't he?

At the sound of the arriving coffee wagons, the meeting broke. In relief people ran for refreshments.

"Now what?" Sharon asked Jo.

Jo leaned over. "Now we have coffee and then a new product introduction by Barbara Anderson."

"Do you know what the product is?" Sharon asked.

"Nooo-oo," Jo said slowly, "and since it's secret maybe you should not either."

"Secret?" laughed Sharon. "What do you think this is? The CIA?"

"In some ways, yes," Jo answered, her smile fading with each word. "Yes, in some ways we have to be highly secretive."

"Oh shit," said Sharon, "you don't think a cosmetics company is *that* important?"

"You're young," Jo said, "and I suppose you think anything below the Pentagon Papers isn't worth stealing, and anyone other than public officials don't get involved in intrigue. But you're wrong. The perfidy in business is circular; it has no beginning and no ending. It just goes on and on. That's why we have so many precautions. We don't let anyone know the way we make our products. The plants are under heavy guard. No one can get in or out without a pass. All our products have code names so people can talk freely in offices and send memos without every secretary calling a friend on Wall Street to tell them what's going to happen next at Kiss."

Sharon shrugged. "I think business is boring."

"Sharon," said Jo tersely, "no one here cares if you find business boring. If John Kingsley is an example of what the media is dishing up, I find communications pompous and dull."

"Touché, madame," Sharon said with a mock bow from the waist.

China ran up to the two women and in her normally breathless voice whispered, "I've been looking for you, Jo. Oh," she said, her eyes growing bigger, "it's Sharon, too. How wonderful. Now I can sit with both of you."

Jo refixed her president's wife smile as carefully as if it were her lipstick. Why did I get angry at Sharon just now? Jo asked herself. Was that really my way of expressing the resentment I feel toward women who share Henry's life?

"Come on," China urged, pulling both of them back to Meeting Room A.

"Jo doesn't know if I should hear about the secret product," said Sharon.

"We'll ask Tim," said China, confident of her husband's opinion. Moments later she returned. "I couldn't find Tim and sort of ran across Father coming back to the meeting," she said in amazement, "and he wants Sharon to listen to Barbara. He wants Sharon's comments."

Sharon shrugged. "I guess he wants to hear about beauty from the great unwashed."

Barbara came out of her room armed only with a large emptiness and a small notebook. Already on the podium for her presentation were the layouts, slides, and product samples that she was convinced would change the life of women around the world.

As she mounted the few steps to the podium she checked the

audience. Yes. They were all there. The few who wanted her to succeed and the masses who were waiting to see Barbara commit corporate hara-kiri. She ticked off names and faces. Who would be voting for her?

Carol Morris. A friend, but not a real friend. It had nothing to do with who had loved Henry first. No, it was purely business. If Barbara were to slip one notch today, Carol would move up two. Carol had to be voting no.

Tim Edgar. Half-friend. Ambivalent because he needed Product Q in order to have a big sales success, but at the same time he would probably prefer a lightweight for her job. Tim abstained.

Ken Sugarman. Yes. A friend. A real friend. Too industrious to be a conniver. He was honestly rooting for her.

Henry? She could not look at Henry. Instead she looked at Chester. Chester was looking at her with a "show me" look on his face. All right, Chester, she said, I'll show you. She made a circle with her thumb and forefinger. Henry gasped. That was always their signal. Why was she giving it to Chester?

Barbara smiled at the audience, took a deep breath, and began the presentation.

Sharon entered the Bathhouse and smiled. "Hi," she said. The female attendant in her white uniform nodded and began to help Sharon remove her robe. "I want to go into the sauna."

"I think you'll find someone from your convention," the attendant responded.

The dry heat enveloped Sharon as she opened the sauna door. "Barbara," she said in surprise as she saw the figure seated on the first row of wooden seats.

Barbara looked up, her hair tied back, her face streaming with perspiration—or was it tears?

"Barbara," Sharon said enthusiastically, "congratulations. You were fantastic."

"Then why do I feel like the pits?" Barbara asked in a little voice.

Sharon sank beside her. "I can't believe it. You just had the wildest success. Even I, a true business dummy, know that you had a fabulous reception from those people. I mean when Jennifer got off her ass to applaud, and when the salesman next to me who slept through the John Kingsley report said, 'She's not too bad,' and six other men fell in love with you on the spot—"

"And don't leave out Chester," Barbara reminded her. "Chester kissed me."

"I didn't know Chester knew how to kiss," Sharon said. "I figured he was the kind of man who fucked you or ignored you. Nothing in between."

"Maybe I'd feel better if he had ignored me," Barbara said.

"Or fucked you," Sharon added matter-of-factly.

"Oh, Sharon," Barbara said, "I need to talk to somebody, and I can't talk to any of these people because I'll get two demerits if I do. Talk to me, will you?"

"Sure," Sharon promised, "but do you want to stay in this sweatbox?"

Barbara looked around. "Yes. Let's stay here," she said, "because I think it's the most private place."

"Also," added Sharon, "it's a hell of a lot easier to talk naked."

"When I made that presentation this morning," Barbara said, "I was so nervous. I had worked so long and hard on it, and I believe in Product Q."

"You really think it can work?" Sharon asked.

"Yes, but promise me one thing," Barbara said, "we're talking as friends now. Please don't break the story yet. I'll give you all the information a week before we make the general announcement. News of this would hype our stock, and we could all be in trouble with the SEC."

"That's a noble reason," Sharon answered. "Why should a dummy like me who maintains a balance of seventy-one cents in her checking account be responsible for changing the economic future of the world?"

"Don't make fun of me," Barbara said. "It's true. If anyone learns that Kiss has a product that makes face lifts unnecessary, it will be a sensation."

"Particularly for plastic surgeons," said Sharon.

"We won't be putting them out of business," said Barbara, "but we will replace some of their business with a facial treatment, Product Q."

"Do you have any name besides Product Q?"

"Not yet."

"This morning you said there were four steps. What are they?"

"I can't tell you. All you can know for now is that we do have four steps, and we sell the package for $150 at retail. We will guarantee the results for six months."

"And then?"

"And then," Barbara smiled, "we hook the customer once more for her sagging whatever."

"You sure it will go?" Sharon asked skeptically.

Barbara looked at her quizzically. "Sure? Who's sure of anything? I'm still not sure of me."

"You look like the coolest, most controlled person in the world," Sharon said. As she spoke she looked in Barbara's eyes. This time there was no mistaking the tears that rolled down her face.

"This is some nutty reaction," Barbara sobbed. "I have worked all these years to bring myself to this day, and now that I am here I'm miserable, and I don't know what to do."

"Well, you just go out and get your product on the market," Sharon said.

"You don't understand," Barbara answered. "I don't want to get the product on the market."

"What do you want?"

"I don't know." Barbara was still crying.

"Look," Sharon said, reaching to pat Barbara's hand, "why don't you go back a few chapters, and maybe if I know more I can be more helpful."

"I've worked all my life," Barbara said, "and I haven't minded. Honestly I haven't. After all, you and I have grown up at a time when the best thing to be is a woman with a career. But let me ask you something, Sharon. Are you happy with your fascinating career?"

"I wasn't until I started living with Tom," Sharon answered.

"Then I'm not the only one," Barbara said in relief. "I thought that work was really my salvation, the salvation for a lot of the women in my generation. We were going to do it like men. You know, we'd get ulcers and have heart attacks and push people around, and we'd be just like men. But I don't want to be like a man. I want to be a woman. I want to sleep with a man."

"That shouldn't be so tough for a pretty woman like you," Sharon said.

"I can sleep with salesmen for a few nights here and there, but I can't sleep forever with the only man in the world I want."

"Is that your fiancé?" Sharon asked.

Barbara shook her head. "Hardly. The man I want is married, and he's going to move out of the country, and when I asked Henry to take me with him, he said no. And I have a great big hole where everything inside me used to be."

"You mean work doesn't fill it and success on a podium isn't as good as cuddling in bed?"

"You got it," Barbara answered. Then she shook her head. "Do you believe it? I'm beginning to talk like you."

Sharon smiled. "No, you're still Barbara. Now let me understand this. You have a fiancé you don't want and a married man named Henry that you do."

Barbara nodded.

"Why don't you want the fiancé?"

"His name is Paul, and I don't know why I don't want him."

"Is it because you can have him?" asked Sharon.

"No," said Barbara. "I know I should be grateful. I wasn't born stupid or ugly or handicapped, but even somebody who knows she has had advantages can feel her life is—well, pointless. It's really only in the last year that business has become so easy. Until now I used to work hard and wait for answers, and I was afraid most of the time. Oh, I don't mean stage fright like today. I mean the everyday frights. But now that I have stopped planning every step, now that I can roll with the punches and be more relaxed, the whole business thing comes a lot easier. But my personal life is nothing. It's like the inside of my old Raggedy Ann doll. All sawdust."

"Let me tell you something," Sharon said. "I thought that if I got a job on a news magazine it would be the best thing that ever happened to me, and in some ways I guess it is. But seeing every Off-Broadway play with other women and going to dinner with people who work late—because you work late—isn't what life is all about. When I met Tom, things really changed. It's not that it's always so wonderful between us. Really, most of the time it isn't. We're not alike at all. He's introverted and I'm extroverted, but he sleeps with me all the time. And that's what all us liberated women are afraid to say. We still want to sleep with a man."

"But," Barbara added, "not just any man."

"And," Sharon continued, "we don't want any of that sappy romanticism of the 1950s. We want love."

"Do you know what love is?" Barbara asked.

Sharon smiled. "I answered that question for Tom once. It took me a long time to come up with the right answer, but I think I have it now. Love is trust. It means trusting somebody enough to share your life with him. Anything else is just fooling around. And love goes when the trust goes."

"I really can't trust Henry with my life," Barbara said. "He won't take care of me."

"Then you can't afford to love him," Sharon said. "How about Paul?"

"I don't know if I can trust him or not," Barbara answered. "I have never really given him a chance. But I'm going to skip the banquet tonight and meet him instead. Maybe I'll get some answers."

"Come on," said Sharon, "we've been in this sauna so long I'm beginning to feel like a stewed tomato. Let's take a shower."

Barbara rose and followed Sharon through the wooden door.

And on the top level in the adjacent sauna Jo Burns tried to get up. She was dizzy. Oh, she was so dizzy. She tried to pull her body up from the wooden slab. What was making her so dizzy? Was it the heat that rose to the highest reaches of the sauna? Or was it the news that had just come steaming to her through the thin walls? So it was Henry and Barbara. Barbara and Henry. It wasn't a succession of secretaries. No, the late nights had been a succession of meetings with Barbara. The one thing she had always feared—his concentration on just one woman. She groaned. She was so weak. She hurt so much. Barbara had hurt, so she told Sharon. Who was there for Jo to tell? Who would comfort Jo? No one. Jo, the earth mother, was there for everyone else. For her husband. For her friends. For her children. Even for China. She had almost forgotten China was waiting for her. Yes. She had to move. Somebody needed her. China was waiting. With a desperate effort Jo pulled herself up off the wooden slab and walked down the levels inching her way cautiously to the door. She opened it, felt the cool air, and shivered. She leaned against the outside wall, counted to one hundred, took her robe from the hook, and walked toward her room, steadying her body with each step. No one was going to know that Jo was frightened.

"Hi," Jennifer called to Sharon and Barbara as they left the sauna.

"What are you doing?" Sharon asked.

"Getting an herbal wrap," Jennifer answered.

"What's that?" Sharon inquired.

"The best thing since men," Jennifer told her.

"I think I'm going to leave and go back to my room now," Barbara said.

"Are you all right?" Sharon asked.

"Ask me tomorrow at breakfast," Barbara said with a smile.

"What's wrong with her?" Jennifer asked Sharon.

"Nothing," Sharon shrugged, "just postpartum blues. She gave birth to a new product this morning, and you know how businesswomen are. They get so wrapped up in their jobs that they're sad when it's over."

"Not me," said Jennifer. "I'm getting wrapped up in this. Look. You can have one, too. Just lie here, and the lovely girls keep bringing you hot towels soaked in herbs, and they wrap you in them, and the next thing you know all your aches and pains disappear."

"I think I'll sit this one out," Sharon said.

"Don't you like getting beautiful?" Jennifer asked.

"Oh, I like some of the things they do here. I think massage is good, and I love the sauna."

"Do you like massage for relaxation or stimulation?" Jennifer asked.

"Is there a difference?"

"You don't know anything," Jennifer said, not in criticism but in surprise. "Massage can have a profound effect. If you have a masseuse who gets deeply into the muscle tissue, it can make you relax, lengthen out and narrow down."

"Jennifer, it all seems to have kept you in good shape. Women are willing to do anything to look young, aren't they?"

"Aaaah," Jennifer sighed as the herbal wraps were applied, "we will go to all lengths. Just think how much it hurts to pluck your eyebrows . . ."

"I don't pluck my eyebrows," said Sharon.

"Of course," Jennifer sighed. "But I do. I have had a face lift, too."

"But you can't tell by looking."

"I manage to hide the nips and tucks, and of course, I had the best man in New York. When your business is your face, you have to be sure you're good-looking enough to get and hold jobs."

"And men," continued Sharon, thinking of her conversation with Barbara.

"No, I don't think face lifts hold men," Jennifer said. "Men never even know the difference. It's women who notice wrinkles, not men. Men notice other things. I've been in Hollywood a long time now. About twenty years ago an actress friend of mine went to Biarritz, and she met a young man at the hotel. Was he a waiter? Concierge? No one knows to this day, but he was beautiful. That we all knew. My actress friend was then in her forties, and she brought home this beautiful twenty-four-year-old man. He was like a house pet. Such elegant manners. Such a handsome face. My friend kept him at her home, and while he was there he took wonderful care of her. They made marvelous love, of course, and he made my skinny friend begin to eat more, and soon her body became full and round. I tell you, there never was a more beautiful woman in Hollywood.

"After a while the actress told the boy they must be married. And so they were wed. She was, if anything, even more beautiful after the marriage. But two years later they were divorced, just as everyone had predicted. By then I knew the young Frenchman well, and I asked him if he divorced his wife because she looked too old for him. 'No,' he said, 'did you ever see anyone more beautiful than she? Of course I did not divorce her because she was too old. After all, I am a Frenchman, and in France we know the value of older women. No,' he said, 'I divorced her because she was trying to run my life. She was too bossy. I couldn't stand it.'"

Sharon smiled. "You're telling me then that what's inside is still more important than what's outside."

"It sounds like a funny thing for an actress to say," Jennifer continued, "but your wrinkles mean less than you think they do. The extra pounds—not fifty or sixty extra pounds—but the seven or eight extra pounds are not the difference between love and pfffft."

"But still," said Sharon, "you go through all this stuff, and you have even had your face lifted."

"For women, darling, for women. Because my face looks good, Kiss hires me, and women look at me, and I have a few securities now for my old age. It wasn't the movies that made me independently wealthy; it was television commercials. So if Kiss wants me to look younger than you and squeeze my body into steam or soap bubbles or bathtubs of cod liver oil, I'll do it."

"And your body is your insurance policy?"

"I wish it weren't," said Jennifer. "I want somebody to take care of me. I've been married, you know. Seventeen years is a long time to be married. And that's how long it was for me. Now I can't stand not having a man."

"Lonely?"

"Sure I'm lonely," said Jennifer. "I want somebody there to pick up the pieces when I fall apart. I want somebody to take care of me, not necessarily support me."

"And do you want to take care of a man, too?"

Jennifer smiled. "Of course not. This next marriage is going to be for Jennifer. I've been the love route already. It doesn't work."

Sharon looked at her sadly. "I hope you're wrong."

"Sit in that pool over there," Jennifer said pointing to the Jacuzzi, "meditate for a while, and then let me know if you still think love is so terrific."

Sharon walked slowly to the Jacuzzi.

"Hello, Sharon." It was Linda at the other end of the pool.

Sharon slid into the water. "Linda, I think I came on too strong with you. Honestly, I didn't mean to sound like Miss Goody Two Shoes. I'm just not good at understanding all this business intrigue."

"Oh sure. Forget it."

Sharon breathed a small sigh of relief. "Okay then. Let's bury the hatchet or drown the oars. Or whatever."

Linda shrugged.

Sharon looked at her. Linda was the first woman she had met in years who was not easily offended.

"Getting good stuff for your story?" asked Linda.

"On some of the filler stuff I can use your help," Sharon said.

Linda smiled. So Sharon had finally figured out that Little Linda had brains.

"You can begin, Linda, by telling me why I got that Christmas present from Kiss today."

"Oh, you mean the gift pack that was delivered to your room?"

"Gift pack? It looks like my birthday and Christmas wrapped into one."

"At every convention," explained Linda, "the president sends a personal gift to each of us attending. Of course it isn't really his personal gift. I mean, he doesn't buy it or anything like that. It's stuff he sort of assembles for us."

"Mine had a sewing kit," reported Sharon.

"Oh, look at the other side. You'll see that it's the gift of one of the women's magazines. You know, Kiss is big in the women's books, so we get little presents."

"Is that why magazines don't have any money for writers?"

"Don't take it personally. Without advertising, where would writers and magazines be?"

"All right. Now tell me about the rest of the presents," said Sharon. "First, where did Jennifer's book on beauty come from?"

"Publisher's gift. The publisher figured that if the people here read *The Jennifer Johnson Guide to Beauty* they'll talk about it. Publishers like word-of-mouth advertising."

"And who gave us the gift assortment of Kiss products? Was that from Chester?"

"Oh, Chester probably doesn't even know about the gift packages."

"And why a silver tray in that package?"

"So husbands who came here without their wives can give something from the convention to their wives."

"But who uses silver trays anymore?" asked Sharon.

"That's the point. Women never put these packages together. Men stand around and guess what women want. They never guess right, so I have a closet filled with silver pitchers, paperweights, and assorted junk. Someday I'm going to have the fanciest garage sale in Westchester."

"Thanks for the rundown," said Sharon. "You have a reporter's way of looking at things. You get to the heart of a story."

"Then you'll know what I mean, Sharon, when I tell you that Kiss, Inc., is not the story here."

"You have already told me what the story is. Remember? You told me about the presidency."

"No," Linda interrupted. "The presidency is the Kiss story, but Kiss is not the real story at The Gates of Paradise. The real story here *is* The Gates of Paradise."

"What do you mean? A feature story on spas? Everybody's done that. So The Gates of Paradise is another fancy resort that combines health and convention facilities. So what's the big news?"

Linda splashed her hand in disgust in the Jacuzzi. "You don't even know what I'm talking about." Then she waded next to Sharon and whispered, "See that woman who is walking toward the sauna?"

"The redhead with the silicone tits?"

"Yes. She just came out of the Ion Bath."

"Ion Bath. Where's that? On Mars? Did her UFO just land?"

"Don't be funny. The Ion Bath is a specialty here at The Gates of Paradise. It's modeled on a treatment at one of England's top health spas. The Gates of Paradise gives the Ion Bath just to people whose bodies are puffy, rough, or neglected. For instance, none of us would get it. But—"

"—but her body is puffy and how," Sharon said.

"Stop talking," Linda said in exasperation as the woman walked past them. The two women in the Jacuzzi remained silent and watched as the redhead walked past them.

"Now let me tell about the Ion Bath," continued Linda. "It is given in a box like a steam cabinet, and they use carbon dioxide and steam and positive and negative ions to open and cleanse the pores. Now do you want to know why that woman needs an Ion Bath?"

Sharon nodded.

"Because she is puffy from a beating."

"A beating?" Sharon's voice went up an octave.

"A beating. She has welts on her back. That woman is Brandy McCarthy."

"Brandy McCarthy?" Sharon asked in surprise. "I remember her. She used to do a children's show on television. What happened to her?"

"She grew up, honey. She really grew up. She's the girlfriend of Tony Franzi, one of the Mafiosi who own The Gates of Paradise."

"The Mafia owns The Gates of Paradise?"

"If you didn't know that," Linda said, "let me give you some other facts you are probably missing. Christmas is December twenty-fifth, and February usually has twenty-eight days."

"I heard the rumors, but I didn't believe there were Mafia connections here. It's so pretty," Sharon said lamely.

"You know that the Mafia has gone legit. Well, this is one of the places they own now. So while you and I sit around and let them draw all the impurities out of our skins, they are figuring ways to put them back in our lives. Anyway, Sharon, to be honest, I thought that's why your magazine sent you here. I figured you were an undercover agent."

"No," Sharon said, "I'm not even getting a very good convention story. And now you throw me a Mafia curve."

"It's not new. There have been stories in the media about Mafia involvement here," Linda said. "I've read some things myself."

"But none of that belongs in my story," said Sharon. "I am just doing a story on American business."

"Isn't that the Mafia?" asked Linda.

Sharon smiled. "I guess so, but now I'm waterlogged, so I'm going back to my room and rest up for the junior prom tonight."

Linda paddled to the stairway of the Jacuzzi as Sharon walked up the steps. "You mean you aren't going to do anything about it?"

"If you mean the Mafia, that's right," said Sharon. "I am not going to do anything about it."

"Why?"

"Because there is nothing I can do. It's too big. It's too much. I can't handle it."

"You really don't have any guts, Sharon."

"Oh yes, I do. And I don't want them spilled in The Gates of Paradise sauna."

Tim Edgar stretched his long body on the massage table, and Sam, the head masseur, took a careful look. "Hey, you got no fat. You in good shape, fella."

Tim smiled. Why shouldn't he be in good shape? Who except Tim had a right to have a body like this?

"Ya havin' a nice time?" Sam asked.

"I am thirty-one years old. I was born in Boston to a fine old family, and I am now part of a rotten new family. I assume that answers all your questions, and I can now get a first-rate massage with no conversation from you."

Sam shrugged. You got all kinds on the table. This was probably a kid who had too much all his life.

Tim sighed. He felt his body relaxing. His mind was at ease, too. The body and mind of Tim Edgar—whoever he was. Well, he knew the vital statistics. He was born in Boston after the Second World War. Pierce Edgar came back from the service to father him and then abruptly tell his young wife that he was going to return to Europe because a French girl and his baby were waiting for him. Tim's mother, Cynthia, had been Pierce Edgar's childhood sweetheart, and their union was blessed with the good wishes of both families. When Pierce made his decision to return to France, the proper Edgar family promptly disowned their black sheep son, and then, as if ignoring Tim and his mother would erase the whole memory of Pierce Edgar's transgression, the senior Edgars promptly removed Tim and Cynthia from their lives.

First memory, Tim thought. First memory. He went to Betsy Breckenridge's birthday party. Everybody's daddy came later and had martinis and birthday cake or whatever it was that daddies drank with birthday cake. No daddy came for Tim. He went into Mr. Breckenridge's study and curled up in the leather chair and pretended he was in his daddy's chair. Mr. Breckenridge found him there. "Hey, the little Edgar bastard is in my chair," Mr. Breckenridge shouted to the other fathers. Tim thought Mr. Breckenridge sounded like the daddy bear in Goldilocks. He felt frightened. He did not know what a bastard was, but he knew he didn't like the sound of it. The other fathers walked in the study when Betsy's father called to them. They looked at Tim and laughed and laughed. Timmy cried.

Fade. Cut to third grade. Beautiful Cynthia Edgar married again. This time her husband was a wealthy New Yorker. Timmy, his mommy, and new daddy moved to Manhattan, and Cynthia promptly enrolled him in an excellent school. Third grade was going to be fun. Now he would have a daddy. But Uncle Dan, his new daddy, did not want to go to school events. He was fifty-seven years old and had already had children and was damned if he would play PTA games again. He also did not want to adopt the little bastard. Timmy knew that because he heard him tell Cynthia one night. Uncle Dan thought it was enough that he paid for Tim's education and clothes and God-knows-what. Timmy wondered which of his possessions was a God-knows-what. Cynthia, who had more beauty than brains or compassion, was grateful for a nice roof and three meals at Voisin and the Colony, and she was not going to do anything that would send herself and her son back to Boston and a tiny flat. She smiled and pushed Timmy into the backs of rooms and into the back of her mind. It wasn't too difficult for Cynthia to forget Timmy because the year after she married Uncle Dan they had a baby. Uncle Dan seemed sort of angry about the new baby at first. He said Cynthia had tricked him in order to keep him, and he'd show her that what he wanted wasn't a cow but a beautiful woman. Timmy knew that from that time on Uncle Dan managed to meet a lot of beautiful women. Cynthia seemed sad, but she seemed sadder for the new baby than she did for Timmy. Timmy, at least, had a father who sent him Christmas cards, beautiful golden cards that said "Joyeux Noël."

By the time Timmy was old enough for prep school, there was not a prep school that wanted Timmy. He was characterized by his teachers in day school as mean, nasty, and a poor student. But he was an outstanding athlete.

He was proficient in all racket sports, and he found that girls seemed to like good-looking boys who wore their tennis sweaters tied casually about their necks. Racket in hand, he traveled from country club to country club, and a lot of young ladies before they reached their eighteenth birthdays had reached some kind of sexual union with Tim Edgar. Not bad for a public school kid, he thought. "I am going to be the best stud in East Hampton," he said one summer, "and then I am going to be the best stud in New York City," he said one winter. And that year was probably the first time in his life he ever lived up to his expectations for himself.

Uncle Dan was never very generous with Tim, and Cynthia was never very concerned. From the time he was fifteen Tim was determined that he would take his good looks and family tree to the bank.

Dissolve to California. Now on the amateur tennis circuit, Tim got invited to all the post-tennis parties. In Palm Springs at Natalie Wood's house he first saw Penny Palmer. "Is she rich?" he asked his doubles partner. "Hell yes," was the answer. "She is so ugly that you know she has to be the richest girl in the room." From that moment Tim pursued her. Puffing and panting, he pursued her. Up Palm Springs and down San Diego he pursued her. But Penny Palmer, who (it was rumored) was Elizabeth Arden's niece, said no. He couldn't believe it. What right did an ugly girl have to say no? "You're too dumb for me, Tim," said Penny. "I do not plan to love a beautiful body. I will love a beautiful mind." Shaken, Tim left her life. He was relieved three years later to hear that she had married a homosexual symphony conductor. It proved, he said, that she didn't know a baton from a baton.

The month after Penny Palmer tossed Tim, he landed China Masterson. China was made to order for Tim. She looked good; she didn't talk much; and she was very rich. As an added bonus she had a family business that could accommodate Tim. And he was getting a father.

All his life Tim had been in the kind of milieu where Chester Masterson was a favorite topic of conversation, but Tim didn't know Chester Masterson from Bat Masterson. Tim listened only when the conversation turned to girls or sports. He figured you didn't have to know anything about business in order to marry a rich girl.

Of course he had not counted on marrying the rich girl who was the daughter of Chester Masterson.

"My daddy wants to meet you," China said one day. So Tim went to meet his new father. After all, when you grow up fatherless and stepfatherless, it is kind of exciting to get a father-in-law.

"You got any money?" Chester Masterson barked.

"My family—"

"I didn't ask you about your family," Chester said crisply. He did not tell Tim that he had no curiosity about his family because he had already had them thoroughly investigated. Chester already knew Tim had no money, but he wanted to find out if Tim were honest. "I have just one question," Chester said, looking directly at Tim, "do you have any money?"

"No." Tim did not hesitate. He did not apologize.

All right, thought Chester, at least the kid is honest. "You will need a job," he said. Chester picked up his telephone. "Listen," he barked at his secretary, "get hold of Henry, and put um uh . . . what's your name?"

"Tim."

"Tim what?"

"Tim Edgar."

Chester smiled. Now he had cut the kid down to size. These family-rich, money-poor kids all needed that. "Right. Right. Henry, see who needs a man. Show me how good your personnel department is at fitting people to jobs. Put Tim Edgar to work. How do I know what he can do? He's tall. Let him reach for the high shelves."

Tim smiled, but Henry did not smile back. Tim sat and waited through the conversation; he waited for Chester to be kind and friendly and warm and say the things that TV fathers always said. It was the last time Tim ever waited for Chester to show kindness. By the end of the day he had learned that Chester never showed kindness, and Chester's daughter occupied no more of his thoughts than Tim did of his father's.

Tim went to see China that night. "We have something in common," he said. "We are Christmas card kids. I think your father probably sends you Christmas cards . . ."

". . . Oh no," she answered, "his secretary does."

Tim started at Kiss in the office, but when it became apparent that he didn't have the background to read profit and loss statements, he was moved to sales. Tim starred. He played the right amount of tennis and smiled at the right number of people.

When Henry told Chester that Tim was working out, Chester couldn't believe it. "He's good enough to get involved at a higher level; I want to move him up," Henry said. Chester was reluctant at first. "He won't get any special treatment from me," Chester promised Henry.

"That's good," said Henry. "I get very jealous. Remember, no kissing him on the forehead or patting his knee just because he's your kid."

Business was more fun than Tim expected. He liked the partying and the friendliness of the department store people. He liked planning promotions and seeing his ideas make sales. When he went home, he would tell China about things. She would smile and paint her nails. Somewhere along the way they had two children. Tim was not going to be like his father. Or his stepfather. But business was so interesting, and how much could you discuss with a two-year-old? He started staying away more and more. The one-day business trips became one-day, two-night trips, and weekends seemed to be such a good time to cement business relationships.

Tim had a totally complacent partner in China. China never complained. She thought it was nice to be married. If she were dissatisfied or felt some small, slight injury, she would just open another bottle and go to the refrigerator for ice cubes. Sometimes, Tim knew, she forgot the ice cubes.

"Hey," Sam the masseur called across the room, "look at this guy. He fell asleep. Well, that's what happens when you got nothin' but money."

Tim opened his eyes. He wasn't sleeping, just drifting. Drifting back and forth in his memory. He sat up and looked at Sam. "You don't know it, but you're right," Tim said. "I have nothing but money. Only it's my wife's money. So take that away, and I have nothing." He wrapped himself in a long white terry robe and walked back to his room. He sensed that the next twenty-four hours would be the critical time for Chester in choosing a new president. Henry would move up to chairman. After all, Chester couldn't be chairman forever, could he? He smiled as he asked himself that question. Chester could be anything forever. If only China weren't such a—he didn't even finish the sentence in his mind. China was China. He couldn't change that. He could just take a deep breath and accept it. He opened the door of the room and thought he'd rest for an hour before the big dinner. Instead of a quiet, uninhabited room he saw China and Jo seated in two deep chairs. With two glasses on the cocktail table, of course.

"What are you doing here?" Tim asked.

"Just having a friendly drink," Jo said.

"I could have guessed that," Tim said flatly.

"A friendly drink of tonic—no vodka. No gin. Just tonic," Jo said.

"Well, that's a real switch for both of you," Tim said.

"Oh, not for Jo," China answered quickly. "She has belonged to AA for a long time."

"AA?" asked Tim.

"Alcoholics Anonymous," Jo said. "I learned the hard way that I'm just not a good social drinker."

"And you trying to say China isn't either?" Tim asked defensively.

"That's right. She's not," Jo responded. "China cannot drink any more than I can."

Tim looked at Jo evenly. "China never killed anyone," he said.

"Tim," China cried out.

"No, let him say it," Jo said calmly. "We all know."

"But I didn't until you told me," said China.

"That's because you're illiterate," Tim said as he slowly and deliberately poured himself a gin on the rocks.

"Yes, I know," China said.

"Don't talk to China like this," Jo said to Tim. "China needs help. She doesn't need to be hurt another time."

"She doesn't need to be hurt?" Tim said. "What about the rest of us? Ask her what she says to me."

Jo took a deep breath. How did she get into this role of marriage counselor? "China dear," she said tenderly, "what have you said to Tim to make him so resentful?"

China looked blank and shrugged.

"Then let me tell you," said Tim. "From the day we were married she reminded me that it was her allowance that made it possible for us to have the big apartment in the city and later the house in Westchester. She counted out the money. She handed it to me like a child. Of course," he added with a small shrug, "if she didn't have enough fingers to add properly, she'd make a few mistakes."

"I can't help it if I'm rich," China said righteously.

"So here we are," Jo said. "Two deprived people thinking they can make a marriage."

"Oh, I'm not deprived," said China. "I'm very rich."

"See what I mean?" Tim asked.

"Tim, sit down," Jo instructed. "I have been through a great deal, and I have learned a lot. I want to talk to you both. When I went into AA after I—after my—oh hell, yes I can say it. When I went into AA after I killed another human being, I was full of guilt and self-hate. AA alone couldn't set me straight. It took some psychiatric help as well. I want to talk to you about some of the things I know now because I think they matter to both of you, too." She took a deep breath.

"But I'm not like you," China said, "so how can you help us?"

Tim looked at her in disgust. "China, shut up and listen."

"When I say you are deprived," Jo said, "I mean that you both came from underloved homes. I don't know a great deal about you, Tim, but I have picked up stories from time to time, and I've heard the way you refer to your family. China, of course, came from a family that could not have cared less about her as a person."

"My father likes my fingernails," China said proudly, extending her hands.

"China, I told you to shut up," Tim said harshly.

Jo started to chastise him, then thought better of it. "You each came to this marriage as very poor people. You were deprived of love and affection in your homes. How could you be expected to create it then in the home that you built together? Instead of trading endearments, the two of you trade accusations. You, China, accuse Tim of being financially inadequate . . ."

Tim smiled self-righteously.

" . . . and you, Tim, accuse China of being stupid."

Tim's smile disappeared. China said, "How could you know that when you don't even live in our house?"

"It's easy to see," Jo said. "We think we walk around in heavy protective layers and no one sees what's going on inside. In truth, most of us are walking through life dressed in Saran Wrap. Slightly protected, but highly visible."

"Do you dabble in psychiatry frequently?" Tim asked curtly.

"Only when necessary," Jo said. "And I think this is necessary. I cannot solve your problems. I can only point them out to you. You are going to have to find your answers."

"How?" asked China.

"You began today," Jo reminded her. "This afternoon we went to an AA meeting, and China learned some things she never knew before."

"You mean she learned how to drink boilermakers?" Tim asked snidely.

"Tim, drop it," Jo said. "For the last time I am telling you that you are damaging China by that attitude. You are willing her into drunkenness. You want her to be damaged. You want her to be the enemy, lose belief in herself and demonstrate that she is worthless as a woman. Somehow you think that makes you worth more as a man. It doesn't, Tim. It makes you worth less. You won't be president of Kiss by beating down China. You will have a chance if you give her support."

"Her father doesn't give a damn for her," Tim said quickly.

"All the more reason you must," said Jo. "And if you give her support you prove you have one of the qualities for leadership."

"Did your husband give you support?" Tim asked.

"When I desperately needed it, he did," she said.

"And now?" Tim probed.

"And now he gives it to me on occasion," Jo said softly as she recalled the conversation she had heard in the sauna.

"You mean when he's between girls?" Tim asked.

"I can handle that now," Jo said. "I couldn't handle it at another time in my life, so I drank to make it disappear. I was a drunk. Now I try to be a sober person who faces facts and makes decisions."

Tim nodded.

"Tim, you have so much anger that I really cannot deal with it, and I'm not emotionally involved with you. How can you expect China to handle it?" Jo asked.

"I found out," said China, "that I may not be as dumb as I think I am. If you drink a lot the memory can fail."

"There is a lot that doctors now agree on when it comes to alcoholism," said Jo. "For instance, the medical profession agrees that alcoholics suffer from a disease. Most people drink a little socially, and maybe occasionally get drunk. But an excessive drinker gets drunk frequently. Excessive drinking is an addiction, and we who drink—or drank—excessively really cannot give it up on our own. The only help for us is never to drink."

"I'm drinking plain tonic now," China reminded Tim.

"We went to a meeting of Alcoholics Anonymous today because I wanted China to see what it's really like," Jo said.

"And you found a bunch of do-gooders telling you about that old devil, alcohol?" Tim countered.

"Oh no," said China. "The people were all so—well, all so positive. They told what had happened to them."

"And," continued Jo, "nobody moralized. That's not what AA is about. AA is supportive, but nobody shakes his finger at the drinker. We try to give each other aid and comfort. China knows that when we return to New York she can go to AA. She also knows she can call me any time of the day or night that she thinks she has to have a drink, and I will come and be with her."

"I don't know that China has the willpower to do this," Tim said.

"Nor do I," said Jo.

"Nor do I," echoed China.

"China," Tim asked in his first direct conversation with her since they had started talking, "do you really want to stop drinking?"

She shrugged her shoulders. "I don't know."

"Let me ask you something instead," Jo said. "Do you want China to stop drinking, Tim?"

"I don't want her to turn into some kind of self-righteous crusader," he said.

"It's better than what she is now," Jo answered. "As it is China is not valuable to herself, to you, to your children or to society. She is nonfunctioning. The purpose of all this is to give her life some direction."

"She has direction," Tim said. "She goes in the direction of Saks Fifth Avenue, the boutiques—"

"Stop," Jo cautioned. "We want to give her life some direction in terms of her abilities to make decisions and face life as it is. You're not an easy man, Tim, and you are not going to be of any help to China until you first help yourself. I know enough to realize that you need some professional help. I think that when you return to New York you must both want to and agree to get some professional counseling."

"You mean you're not going to be our doctor?" Tim said with a malicious grin. "After all, you've done such a terrific job with your life."

"I am living my life the way I think I have to," Jo said, "but at least it's the way I think I have to. I made some decisions. I agreed to overlook the indiscretions in my husband's life, and I found the strength to do it. I used to drink problems into some kind of fuzzy oblivion. Now I can face them. I made the decision a long time ago not to divorce my husband. I love Henry. Can you understand that, Tim? Can you two love-starved people understand that there are some things we do in life just for love? And you know something else? In his own cockeyed way, Henry loves me, too. He becomes infatuated easily, and maybe that's one reason I love him. Maybe if he couldn't give his heart from time to time, he wouldn't have that underneath warmth that I know is there. I don't think I could be married to a cold man. And men who never can succumb to another woman can't have a lot of sexuality in their relationships with their wives either. Oh, I'm not saying that you have to go to bed with every girl who appeals to you. But I think that feeling something for another woman isn't all bad. It might be pretty good. Because when a man is aroused by another woman, he can come home and be aroused by his own wife. And," she said with a smile, "it can make for a lot of warm, happy nights."

"So what are the steps for us?" Tim asked.

"That," said Jo with a smile, "is a good question. A constructive question. Recovery begins with an honest desire for help. I think China really wants to be helped now."

"And especially because I know alcoholism is a sickness," China said.

"A sickness," Jo repeated, "but it's not a cold. It's not going to go away with two aspirin. But you do understand that your addiction can be arrested.

"There are people, you know, who believe in the addictive personality, that we who are alcoholics are addicts. And the only way to cure an addiction is to replace it with another. So to cure alcoholism we replace it with an addiction to nonalcoholism. That's what AA is in a way. It's an addiction, a way of life we force on ourselves. Of course, alcohol and drugs are not the only addictions. Excessive anything is an addiction. For instance, excessive eating is an addiction which can be replaced by another addiction: dieting."

China said, "But I don't eat much."

"We're not comparing eating and drinking except to say that in excess they are similar," Jo explained gently.

"I know the first thing I have to do is stop drinking," China said with almost a religious fervor.

"You may have to, but I don't," said Tim as he stood to make himself another drink.

"Wrong," said Jo. "What you have to do, Tim, is make a commitment to make China well. She isn't strong enough to do it alone. Nor was I. Henry did help me, and one of the reasons I will never leave Henry is that when I decided to straighten out my life, he stayed at my side. Now that he has strayed I'll wait and help him straighten out his life."

"I didn't marry China to be a guardian," Tim said.

"Why did you marry her?" Jo asked.

Tim was silent.

"If you can't come up with a pretty answer, why be surprised at what has happened to your lives. You still have a chance, Tim.

And if you have the strength for this, who knows? You just may have the strength to be the next president of Kiss."

"Let me think about it," Tim said.

"I will leave you alone and let you think about it," Jo answered. "After all we have the President's Ball tonight, and I want to be refreshed."

"Thank you, Jo," China said. She leaned over and kissed the older woman. "I love you."

Jo looked at China's face; her eyes were filled with tears. "When was the last time you said that?" Jo asked.

"I don't think I ever said it before," China answered.

"Then practice, my dear," said Jo. "Practice. You can start with your children, and who knows? It may get up to Tim."

"Where have you been?" Henry asked sharply. "You know I want to have some people come to our suite for drinks before the ball."

Jo walked over to Henry and slipped her arm through his. "Henry, I have had a very full day. I won't go into details, but I just came from Tim and China's room. Earlier I had a sauna. And . . . oh, darling, you're not really interested in all the little things that happened to me. But the one big thing that happened to me today is that when the whole day ended, I still loved you."

He looked at her quizzically. "I always knew that," he said.

"Oh yes," she smiled, "but I didn't."

Linda rubbed her body dry. Should she go over and talk to Brandy McCarthy or not? Then she reminded herself that she was Grandma Eisman's own flesh and blood. She approached the redhead. "Pardon me, but are you Brandy McCarthy?"

The woman gasped. "How did you know me?" she asked in a small, frightened voice.

"You were practically a fixture in my household ten years ago. My children watched you every Saturday morning. You had little puppets . . ."

"Marionettes," Brandy McCarthy interrupted. "I had marionettes." Her green eyes misted as if she were looking back for ten lost years. "Yes, it was ten years ago, wasn't it?" She sighed and shook her head sadly.

"But weren't those good times?" Linda asked.

"Mmmm, yes, I guess you'd say that." Brandy McCarthy's response was recited with the enthusiasm of a laundry list.

"Are you all right?" Linda asked with concern.

"No," she said quietly. "I'm not all right."

"Come sit here on this bench with me," Linda said. "I'll stay with you until you feel better."

When Linda left Brandy an hour later, Linda knew she had enough information to blow The Gates of Paradise to the gates of hell. There was only one thing she did not know. She did not know what she planned to do with her new-found knowledge.

Chester Masterson took off his shoes and looked at the pile of papers on the desk. Which should he read first? He pushed the financial reports to one side and picked up *Vogue*. Now there was an idea magazine. You didn't get ideas from financial reports or from financial pages that simply told about other people's successes and failures. No. You got new product ideas by thumbing through *Vogue* or the European beauty magazines. After all, how had Product Q been born? It wasn't Barbara's idea, and she knew it. It wasn't Henry's baby, even if he acted as if it were. Hadn't Barbara said today, right on stage in front of everyone, that if it weren't for Chester Masterson's insights women would still be slaves to cosmetic surgery? Hadn't Barbara promised that face lifts would be out of style two years from now?

Chester leaned back and smiled. He was going to change the face of America. Women were going to be able to erase telltale age lines overnight. He, Chester Masterson, would give America youth without surgery. Chester resisted the impulse to stand and cheer himself.

After all, who had dreamed the grand dream? He had. He first thought of the possibilities one night in his office. It had been late. He was working because the Gladys-Gladyce debacle was still fresh in his mind, and he did not like going home alone. So he stayed in the office late and instructed Henry to stay, too. He did not want to talk to Henry. Chester just wanted Henry there in case he thought of something to say. He had not thought of anything to say for almost an hour. Henry got up to go to the bathroom. Chester took a magazine break. He picked up an old copy of *Vogue* and began flipping idly through the pages. *Vogue* and all the other beauty magazines at Kiss always had paper clips marking cosmetics ads and editorial pages. Chester looked at the ads but didn't bother reading the rest of the magazine until later.

Now, because it was an old copy whose beauty ads had been memorized by Chester, he turned to the marked editorial pages. An article caught his eye. It was about skin care, a plastic surgeon explaining that one element in the aging process is the atrophy or sagging of muscles. The surgeon went on to say that plastic surgery does not literally correct this. Chester Masterson put the magazine down slowly. He was puzzled.

Henry walked back in the room. "Call Dr. Schulz," Chester commanded.

"It's 2 A.M.," Henry said.

"So what?"

"So can't it wait until morning?" asked Henry.

"No. If face lifts are not always the answer to removing wrinkles from the aging skin, what can be?"

"A new product for Kiss," Henry said sarcastically.

"That's right," said Chester.

Henry looked at Chester in disbelief. "Don't you think anything is impossible?" he asked.

"No," answered Chester firmly.

Henry dialed Dr. Wilhelm Schulz. The smiling scientist got out of bed, dressed, and drove from Westchester to the office. He arrived at 4 A.M. When he left, he was not smiling. "I have been given an impossible assignment by an impossible man," he said to Henry.

"I agree," an exhausted Henry answered.

Chester knew they all thought he was crazy, but after today who was crazy? Only the people who said it couldn't be done. Only the people who gave the reasons it would not work.

Yes, today had been quite a day. Product Q was going to change Kiss. It might even make the company a multinational. The wrinkle treatment could spawn a whole line of lesser priced spin-offs. It was mind-boggling. But not to Chester Masterson.

For Chester the solution to one problem was marked by the

recognition of another. If they had the product, then the next problem would be the name.

How would they name Product Q? He shook his head. He knew what "they" would do. They would follow their usual stupid procedures. "They" were the creative department of Kiss, Inc. They would call the advertising agency and come up with a list of dictionary words that sounded good. They'd take words like Soft. Or two words like New Faces or Young Again.

He chuckled to himself. Those idiots. Sometimes they would make up names. They'd sit around and ask each other what sounds like Kleenex or Kodak or Xerox. Then their stupid list would go to legal, and the lawyers would do what everyone expected them to do. The lawyers would say no. If the names were really good and had a competitive edge, the lawyers would say no because that name made too big a claim. Or else they would say that someone else had the name.

How could he get around the name dreamer-uppers and the lawyers?

He smiled. He could get around them by naming the product with a name no one could challenge.

Chester leaned back in his chair and closed his eyes.

Somewhere people were making love and eating caviar. Not Chester.

He was thinking about a good name for Product Q.

What would set it apart and make everybody know it was a breakthrough in science?

What would draw attention to their company?

What would give them the competitive edge that always set Kiss apart from everybody else?

He sat up and smiled.

He knew what the name would be.

He could see the packaging now. Very sophisticated. A kit. Maybe compartmented. Might even do one in real leather and charge five hundred bucks for it. Sock it to the women. That's the only way they believed you. Give 'em quality, but charge the hell out of them.

Especially for a product that was going to be called the Chester Masterson Lift.

*

"Look," said Sharon to Tim, "I did not grow up in Chopped Liver, U.S.A. I don't understand what this hors d'oeuvre table is all about."

"What makes you think I understand?" Tim asked.

"You're the bride's family," Sharon answered. "Come on, what's all the stuff out there?"

"First of all, there's no chopped liver," Tim reported.

"Then what's that big mound in the shape of your logo?"

"That's pâté."

"Pâté de foie gras?"

"I guess all your years of French paid off," Tim said.

"Explain this scene to me, please," Sharon asked. "I thought all corporations were always on economy binges and cutting back costs, and what I see here would rival Versailles on a good night."

"Well, this is the President's Ball," Tim explained, "and every year Henry has this as his private little party. First comes this cocktail party. Then at dinner we have round tables that each seat ten. There's a host at each one. Henry, of course, is superhost. It's kind of Henry's thank-you to everyone. We begin with an extravagant cocktail hour, build up to a typical convention dinner which is—"

"—creamed chicken," continued Sharon.

"Creamed chicken?" he said derisively. "That's for peasants. No, we have roast beef, new potatoes, and peas. One word of caution. Never eat the potatoes at a convention dinner."

"Why?" asked Sharon.

"Because I have a theory that since everyone is always dieting, no one at a convention dinner ever eats the potatoes. Therefore, they go back to the kitchen uneaten. And the next night they reappear at another convention. Therefore, one should never eat the potatoes. Who knows? They may be six or seven years old."

Sharon laughed, "Can I use that in the *Newsweek* story, Tim?"

"Sure," he said, "but if you really are going to use this in the story, don't forget the ice sculpture. Ice sculpture on the hors d'oeuvre table is to a convention what Santa Claus is to Christmas."

"Tell me about some of those other tidbits," Sharon said.

"To be honest, Sharon, I grew up with rich kids. All we ever served was white bread, ham, potato chips, and dip. People with money don't serve like this. Only parties that are expensed give you this kind of food."

"You mean if this weren't an expense account party we wouldn't be eating like this?"

"Come on," said Tim, "you have to be kidding. Of course you know that if it weren't for expense accounts half the restaurants in New York would be closed. Companies like ours really spend, too. We take each other to lunch at wonderful places like the Four Seasons and call that an expense. And we can take the people who buy from us. And that's an expense. If you have the right kind of job, you never have to eat at anything less than a three-star restaurant, and it doesn't come out of your take-home pay."

"Ah, Tim," she sighed, "life is so different on the editorial side. There are days I struggle to make it to the Sabrett stand."

"Then come to this table, and be my guest. Here's smoked salmon with capers. That's caviar . . . Iron Gate . . . the best."

"What are deviled eggs doing there?" she asked.

"Probably sneaked in from another convention," he answered.

"What's this talk about another convention?" Henry, handsome in a tuxedo, was his customary cool self. "Are you enjoying the cocktail hour, Sharon? Is our friend, Tim, taking good care of you?"

"Everybody is being very courteous," Sharon said. She wasn't going to tell him about Linda. And she wasn't going to tell him the rumor about his leaving. At least she wasn't going to ask now. Why was it so hard to ask a man protected by a tuxedo what was going on under that penguin outfit?

Henry smiled again, a kind of old-style Bachrach portrait smile, and went off to kiss a few wives and shake a few hands.

"What do you think of Henry?" Sharon asked Tim.

"He's been a good president for Chester," Tim answered. "Henry is no star, but you can't be a star and work for Chester. We've been through star-time executives. You know, you get an executive who thinks he's responsible for the increased sales, so he releases a story to the press. Next day he's released from Kiss.

Chester is a one-man band, and everybody else has to blow softly. Very softly."

"What happens if somebody like Henry decides he wants to take his tuba down the street so this band won't drown him out?"

"Chester says good-by without regrets," Tim said.

Sharon shook her head. "Even I can figure that out. I don't think Chester lets anyone leave him. I think Chester is probably good at firing people, but he can't stand rejection."

"That's pretty astute for just a couple of days," Tim said.

"I did my homework before I came here," Sharon told him. "I am a reporter, and I try to be a good one. I'm getting all the background I can because I have a date to interview Chester Masterson in his suite tomorrow morning."

"The convention will be over by then . . . except for Chester's traditional luncheon for the executives," said Tim.

"Will Chester be here at the party tonight?" asked Sharon.

"Of course not," said Tim. "Somebody might ask him to dance, and who knows? He might even be forced to remember the name of his daughter. Let's not tax the chairman too greatly."

"Henry is going to tax him greatly," Sharon said softly.

Tim looked puzzled.

"You mean you don't know?" she asked.

He shook his head. "I can't figure out what you're saying."

"The rumor around here is that Henry is leaving Kiss, and Chester is going to have to pick a president a lot faster than he thought he would."

"How do you know?" Tim asked.

"I'm a reporter," Sharon said. She was not going to tell him that Linda Sugarman was an even better reporter.

"I can't believe Henry would leave," Tim said. "Just this afternoon Jo and China and I were—we were talking," he concluded lamely.

"Well, this minute Henry and I were talking, but I still think he is leaving."

"Okay, then," said Tim, "since you seem to know everything, who is going to be the next president?"

"It could be you or it could be Ken Sugarman according to my inside sources. I also feel that if Henry were moved to chairman he'd have a voice in the picking of the next president, but if he leaves of his own accord, he will not have anything to say. I think Henry will have the power of a petunia if he quits. So I think all these people who are kissing—excuse the pun—around Henry are playing the wrong card. Chester, as usual, has all the trumps."

Tim whistled. "I wonder if Jo knows."

Sharon shrugged. "Doesn't matter if she does or doesn't. I wonder if Chester knows."

Tim smiled. "It seems to me he ought to know, Sharon, and who has a better right to tell him than a member of his own family?"

Sharon looked at Tim. "I have a sick feeling, Tim, that I just played into Linda Sugarman's hands."

"What do you mean by that?" Tim asked.

"I wish I knew. Where are you going?"

Tim laughed. "You of all people must have figured that out." He kissed her lightly on the cheek and then called back, "Incidentally, if China is looking for me, tell her I'm taking care of—uh—a few family matters. And give her a glass of ginger ale with my compliments."

At the other end of the bar Linda sipped her vodka and tonic slowly. Good. Sharon was talking to Tim. That meant Sharon was telling Tim. Nice kid, Sharon, but still naïve. Linda was happy for the first time since she had arrived at the Kiss convention. Henry, that rotten bastard, was about to get what he deserved. Henry had always had it in his power to go to Chester and recommend Ken for the presidency. But did he? Oh no. Too afraid. Too afraid to make a mistake. Henry was disgusting. All smiles and tap dancing on the surface. Underneath there was no character, no strength, no commitment. He never stood up for Jo during that whole drinking and murder mess. But look how she, Linda, had stood up for her husband. Always. Why didn't Henry fight for what he believed? Didn't he understand you had to fight for everything you wanted in life? But, of course, Henry wouldn't soil his hands. No, he was too busy going to the Union League Club for lunch. Chester didn't put Ken up for membership. No, he had Henry join. Well, they'd all pay for it. They'd pay for the snubs and the insults and the acting holier-than-thou. Just wait until Chester learned that dear Henry was about to double-cross him. Wasn't quitting the same as double-crossing in Chester's mind? And who would stand in front of Chester and tell him he'd been a stupid jerk, a business cuckold? None other than darling Tim, the son-in-law who had the future of an ice-cream cone. Oh, it was too delicious to imagine. Linda gulped her drink quickly. She watched Tim leave the room. She knew exactly where he was going. Linda wished with all her heart that she could be in Chester Masterson's suite the moment Tim walked in.

Chester took the remote control button for the television set and hit it. Again. And again. Then he threw it across the room. Television stinks. Business stinks. Everything stinks. Chester was bored. Now that he knew where he was taking Product Q, life was dull dull dull.

"Sir," came the voice behind him.

Oh no. The son-in-law. What's his name? China was probably going to have another baby, and he wanted to make sure about the trust fund. As long as Tim kept China he could have all the trust funds Chester could assemble. "Yeah? What is it?" Chester asked.

"I'd like to have a drink and sit down with you," said Tim.

"Why?" said Chester.

"Because I have something important to tell you."

"The last person who told me something important left me unimpressed. When people are breathless to tell you things, you soon find out that those things are important to them, not to you."

"This, sir, is important to you," Tim promised.

"Is it about you?" Chester asked.

"No, sir."

"In that case it may be important," said Chester. He turned in his chair to look at Tim. "Ha ha. Look at you in that funny suit. Where do you think you're going?"

"Tonight is the President's Ball, remember? We all wear tuxedos to Henry's party."

"Henry's party." Chester said the words like a curse. "And who pays for Henry's party?"

"I guess it's just a euphemism . . ."

". . . A what? Why don't you forget those Harvard words and talk English with me sometime?"

"Yes, sir."

"Sit down. Sit down. I can't keep looking up at you like this." Tim sat obediently, and faced Chester. Tim had a choice now, and he knew his future depended on which topic he chose to discuss with Chester. He could tell him about Henry. Or he could tell him that China was an alcoholic. He debated for a moment. In a way both reflected on Chester as a man. If he were a better boss, maybe Henry would have stayed. If he were a better father, maybe China wouldn't be going to AA. On which level was it better to talk to Chester Masterson if you wanted to be the next president of Kiss?

"Sir," said Tim, "I just learned something today that I think must be brought to your attention immediately."

"Well, for God's sake, what is it?" Chester asked impatiently.

It was Tim's last chance to change his mind. Which would he mention?

"Sir, Henry Burns is going to leave Kiss."

Chester leaned forward. "Why?"

"I don't know."

"As usual you don't know. Get out, dummy."

Tim rose to leave. "I-I-I-I just thought you'd like to know," he said feebly.

"What makes you think I didn't?" Chester snapped.

Tim left. He was going back to being a guest at the President's Ball. Somehow he thought that would be his role next year, too. Guest, not host.

The moment Tim left, Chester picked up the telephone. "Get me London," he barked. "I don't give a damn what time it is. Get me London. I've got some business to take care of."

Chester drummed his fingers on the table. Inside he was seething. Sure, they left you. They all left you. The wives, whores all of them. And the people you gave the big jobs. They were whores, too. And they left. They all left for the only thing that mattered. Money. He'd show them all. When it came to money, there was nothing he couldn't buy.

China was standing next to Jo. Tim walked over to China and kissed her. No wonder she was such a sad little girl. His heart went out to her. His heart went out to himself. They were the victims of Chester Masterson. He felt less than a man. Chester had never let her be a woman.

"China," whispered Tim, "I'd like to get away from here. What would you say if I left Kiss?"

"I want to stay here with Jo," China whispered. "Let's not ever leave Kiss."

Tim put his arm around her. She wasn't ever going to be anything but a little, helpless child. And he would have to decide whether he could live with that and her father's company forever.

Jo smiled her warm president's wife smile at Tim. She put her hand on his arm. "You are being a true supportive husband," she said.

He hated Jo with all his heart at that moment. What right did she have to interfere with his life and shake up China and him?

Tim smiled warmly at Jo.

Sharon walked past and waved.

Bitch, thought Tim. If he hadn't talked to her, he wouldn't have gone to Chester.

Sharon kept weaving through the crowd. She wanted to hear some Kiss gossip or rumors. Had the news about Henry spread through the ranks? It did not seem as if people knew. They were all deferential toward Henry. They laughed at his cocktail party jokes.

JOKE: A Polish man went to rob a bank. He put a stocking cap on his face, wore old clothes, disguised his appearance. But the teller laughed when he pointed the gun at her and said, "You must be Polish."

"How do you know? I'm wearing a mask," he said.

"Yes," she answered, "but you sawed off the wrong end of the shotgun."

Polite laughter. Sharon decided that if Henry were leaving nobody would bother to laugh at such a feeble joke.

"What are you doing, Sharon? Listening for the first robin?"

"Oh, Jennifer," Sharon said, "I didn't even see you. Wow, how could I miss you?"

"I am nothing that silicone and money can't buy," Jennifer shrugged.

"What do you figure is going on here tonight?" Sharon asked.

"I think we are watching the classic power plays. There's a rumor floating through the crowd that could change everyone's lives . . ."

Sharon smiled. Linda certainly had been a busy one. "Do you mean the story about Henry leaving the company?"

"How did you hear it?" Jennifer asked.

"Probably the same way you did."

"Linda?"

"Linda Know-it-all. How does she get her information?"

"It doesn't matter, but everybody at Kiss knows that Linda is on the telephone almost all day every day talking to people in the company. She knows everything. If Henry is leaving, and I have no proof that he is, then I would bet that Linda knows who is going to be the next president."

"Do you think it will be Ken?" Sharon asked.

"It could be," said Jennifer, "because I am not sure that Chester would trust the company to Tim. But if the story is inaccurate and Henry doesn't leave and becomes chairman then . . . oh hell, Sharon, I don't know. I'm only sure of one thing. It won't be you or me."

"I'll drink to that," Sharon said.

Linda elbowed her way toward the two women. "Careful, Eve, here comes the snake," said Sharon.

"Now what are you two whispering about?" asked Linda.

"Sharon, who is so fashion-conscious, wants to write some commentary on the clothes the women are wearing tonight." Linda ignored the obvious untruth.

"Why don't you start right here?" asked Linda. "Now I can tell that Jennifer's dress is so sexy that it must be an Oscar de la Renta. Right?" she asked with the enthusiasm of a child waiting for a gold star to be put on her forehead.

Jennifer smiled. "I never look at labels, darling. It's so middle class." She walked away quickly.

"Jennifer is basically very nasty," Linda said soberly.

The last thing Sharon wanted was to be forced to comment to Linda about another woman. She reached for a conversational ploy. "Um, did you have a nice relaxing time in the Bathhouse after I left you?"

"Let's say I had an interesting time. Let me ask you one more time, Sharon, and it's important that you level with me. Are you here looking for a Mafia story?"

Sharon shook her head.

"You're not giving me all that stuff about privileged information, are you? I mean you're not worried that I'd tell somebody?"

"A little cream puff like you? Oh come on, Linda, we know that you wouldn't tell anybody anything unless you wanted something in return."

"I have goals, but what's so wrong about wanting to be paid for good deeds?"

"Did you ever hear of just doing something for someone with no reward in sight?" asked Sharon.

"I've heard of it, but I don't believe in it. I told you I am out to get the presidency of Kiss for my husband. What's so terrible about that?"

"If he were a paraplegic, it would be nice for you to wave your arms and walk for him. But since he looks as if he has all his faculties, why not let him do the running himself?"

"Because he is a lousy runner," said Linda.

"And you?"

"I am great around the track. Here. Have another slug of caviar. The dinner is never as good as the hors d'oeuvres."

Sharon was curious. Linda never dropped information idly. "Why did you ask me again if I were doing a Mafia story?"

"Because you should be," said Linda.

"Why?"

"The place is crawling with the story."

"Oh, everything is a story here," said Sharon.

"Yes. And some are good stories, and some are not," Linda said.

"You know who's a good story? Barbara Anderson."

"Oh, you mean that stuff about the new career woman. You can't talk to Barbara tonight, though. She isn't here."

"Where is she?" asked Sharon.

"She skipped. She's meeting her fiancé at a motel down the road."

"What are you? Her travel agent?"

Linda smiled. "Oh, I just happen to pick up on things that are happening. I guess you could say it's just another one of my middle-class characteristics." She smiled knowingly at Sharon.

Paul Thurston watched New York disappear beneath the clouds. Good-by, Empire State Building. Good-by, United Nations. Good-by, East River. Hello, friendly skies of reunited. Forget New York, where Barbara was always on. Think about California, where she'd be off. Off from the Kiss people. Away from the Kiss office. Or would she? How much of her was in love with business, and how much of her energy was it taking to respond to her inner need for success? And had she finally been able to resolve whatever conflict or question kept her from saying yes to marriage today?

Paul closed his eyes. It felt good to float. Maybe he was floating back to the pink balloon of his dreams. That's what he called it: the Pink Balloon. It was the memory of Barbara and him in Puerto Rico. They had floated that weekend, that perfect first time. He wanted more perfect times, but he knew that even if the perfect time never came again he still wanted Barbara. He knew that the moment had finally come for Paul Thurston to marry. He sensed it in the same way he sensed things in the laboratory. It was step two following step one. Paul had never been a gay blade. His idea of a good time, his father once said, was to go to the public library and look at books. His father said it with contempt because he believed books were for girls. Secretly Paul's father wondered if his son weren't just a bit girlish. To reassure his father, Paul took out an occasional young woman. But Paul's passion was not women. Paul could not remember a time he did not dream of being a scientist. He loved his work. He was proud of what he did. He wanted to be proud of a wife and home. He knew Barbara would always make him proud. And somewhere within him, she was able to light a fire. Until Puerto Rico no one had ever reached that inner part of Paul.

He opened his eyes. "Dr. Thurston," the stewardess said, "do you want a pillow?"

He shook his head.

"Do you want something to drink?"

Again he shook his head.

"Are you all right?"

He nodded.

The stewardess sensed that she might be able to make the doctor more comfortable. She sat in the seat next to him. He was in his forties, she thought, but he had such a nice face, a boyish look. He definitely wasn't one of those make-it-with-every-stew men. "We have only four passengers in first class today, so that means I can sit a lot during this flight."

He smiled.

Even his smile is sweet, she thought. But he looks as if his mind is in a doctor's little black bag. He's looking at me, but he doesn't see me. "What kind of doctor are you?" she asked.

"I am a researcher," he said. His voice was firmer than she expected.

"Are you going to a medical convention?"

"I am going to meet my fiancée."

"Tell me about her."

"Oh, Barbara is—" He had a hard time continuing. "Barbara is a very unusual woman." He turned sideways in his seat and regarded the stewardess next to him for the first time. She was trying to make him enjoy his trip. He owed her his attention. "She resembles you. No. Maybe Barbara is a little slimmer. But she has long hair and pretty skin. Barbara is very regal-looking. It's surprising because she isn't old enough to have that much confidence, but she acquired it quickly with business success."

"What does she do?"

"She's an executive in . . ." No. Don't tell. It would sound as if he were bragging about Barbara. He didn't want the stewardess to feel put down. Let's see. What kinds of jobs could women have? "She is a buyer for a department store."

"Oh, that must be interesting. Tell me more."

"Do you really want to hear about her and me?" Paul asked.

The pretty stewardess put her hand on her chin. "Oh, I love to hear love stories," she said with a sigh.

Paul looked at her jacket. The name Joanne was printed on the tag. "Joanne," said Paul, "I am going to tell you about Barbara, but you know something? I've never talked about her to anyone." He knew the sensation of flying was making him giddy.

"Would you like a drink first?"

"Yes. That's a fine idea. I'm going to relax." And maybe, he thought idly, that would make it possible to be transported in the Pink Balloon, and have another Puerto Rico when he got to California and Barbara.

Once again she interrupted his reverie, this time to bring him a tray with two small bottles of scotch and water. He mixed his drink, moved the seat to a reclining position, and raised his glass in a small salute. "To the Pink Balloon," he said.

"Is that what you call the plane?" she asked.

"No," he smiled. "That's something I never said out loud to anyone before now."

"Not even to Barbara?"

"Not even to Barbara."

Joanne shrugged. "How did you meet Barbara?"

"I almost didn't meet her," Paul confided. "My friends were giving a party, and they said they had someone for me to meet. I didn't think it would be a woman because they know I'm shy about blind dates. I hate walking into a room knowing I'm supposed to fall madly in love with a woman my friends like. So I went to the party thinking it was another scientist I was meeting. Of course the thing that happened was that I was drawn to Barbara. It was a big party, and she was standing alone in the corner. I thought she was probably frightened. Later I learned she was only bored. I was the frightened one. But we left together, and we went to a little neighborhood restaurant and had dinner, and that night I talked to her just the way I'm talking to you. Sort of relaxed and warm conversation. I asked to see her again and again. She always seemed to be free on weekends so that's when we went out. One weekend I suggested we go to Puerto Rico. One of the doctors I work with had just been there, and it sounded like a good idea. She said yes, and on the plane coming back, I proposed, and she agreed to marry me." He took another sip of his drink. "That's my story," he said.

"And Barbara is waiting for you somewhere in California?"

He nodded. Then he realized how rude he had been. Thoughtful, kind Paul Thurston had gone on and on about himself. What about this nice girl? Did she have something she wanted to say? He thought for a moment. He didn't want to pry. He'd be cautious. "Do a lot of people talk to you like this?"

"Not the regular flyers, the businessmen who travel a couple of times a week. They just get on a plane and open their briefcases and go to work. The businessmen who fly occasionally talk to us. And women talk to us. So do people who are scared."

"Everybody's scared."

"Oh, I mean the kind who are afraid to fly."

"Barbara's not afraid to fly. I'm not either. I don't think that Barbara is afraid of anything except marrying me."

"Is she in love with another man?"

"Of course not," he said quickly. He did not tell Joanne, but those thoughts and fears had been with him ever since the plane ride back to New York from Puerto Rico.

"Do you think you could tell if she were in love with someone else?" Joanne asked.

Paul shook his head. If Barbara didn't want him to know, he knew he would not want to know. If only Barbara would agree to get married now and have a family and be a nice, normal American statistic.

Joanne smiled, but it was not a happy smile. "I'm asking you because I was married to one of our captains, and I know what it is all about. When we got married I grounded myself. I wanted to take care of him and be home for him. At first it was great, and he would tell me all about our friends who were still flying, and then pretty soon I didn't know all the names. I guess that's when I first felt the distance between us. At the beginning it wasn't much of a separation. Oh, maybe about Forty-second Street to Forty-third Street. But when it became Eighty-ninth Street I began to worry. It turned out I had good reason to be worried. There was another woman. I couldn't believe it. I couldn't do anything about it either. We're divorced now, and I started flying again."

"Are you married again?"

"I'm not going to get married for a long time."

"I wonder if Barbara is saying that, too," Paul said.

"Maybe she just likes things the way they are and is afraid that life won't be as good with you once you get married."

"No," Paul said slowly. "I think she's afraid it isn't good now." He thought of the love-making in New York, Barbara tense and unresponding while he reverted to the shyness and lack of demonstrativeness that had always been his hallmark. It was true that only in Puerto Rico in a world apart from the world they both knew had they ever really found each other. Well, this night would tell whether shedding their everyday world could give them the magic they needed.

"Is Barbara working in California?"

"Sort of."

"She must be really devoted to her work."

"I would say Barbara's real devotion is to the company she's with."

"She must have a wonderful boss."

Paul laughed. "She works for a certified megalomaniac, but her immediate superior, the president of the company, is different. He is bright and has helped her a lot, gone out of his way to help her grow up. When she went there, she was just a young woman with a good mind but no experience, and he befriended her and did . . ." His voice began to trail off. The faraway look came back into his eyes. He remembered the return flight to New York. Of course, Henry was in New York. She was going back to Henry. That's why she had been so unsure with him. Whenever Henry came into view, Paul faded into the background. Paul put his glass down on the armrest. He didn't want anymore to drink. He wanted to be alone and to think. "Please let me rest," he said. "I don't mean to be impolite, but I'm tired." He wanted to tell Joanne. He wanted to tell somebody. But how could you say to a perfect stranger that for the first time you really knew what it was that frightened you?

Barbara looked at the sign. "Minimum speed 40 MPH." Then she pressed harder on the accelerator. At the rate she was going she could be arrested for nonspeeding. Underdriving. That's what she was doing.

Going slowly.

Feeling her way.

Postponing decisions. A woman was supposed to be happy when she was on her way to meet the man she loved. Smile, Barbara. You're in love.

But . . . now she slowed her speed again . . . were you in love if you were driving to a decision? This meeting tonight would end up a live-or-die decision about Paul and herself. She remembered another time when she had made a decision, a life-or-death decision, about Henry. They had been working together for a few months. And she was aware of many things. She was aware of his long looks at her. She knew that he spoke to her just a little more often than necessary. Most of all, she sensed that his eyes were on her even when she wasn't around. Finally she realized that Henry Burns was stalking her. The sexual tension was there in every meeting. Barbara knew it didn't mean love; it meant only that he was a man aware of her femaleness.

One night she stayed at the office until after seven o'clock, and as she walked down the hall she passed Henry's office. She could have gone the short way and not made the swing past his door. But no. She took the long way. Henry called to her.

"I didn't know you were still here," she said.

"I'm not," he answered. "Only my body is filling this chair. I sent my head to the barbershop."

"Looks like they did a fine job."

"You look pretty fine to me," he answered. He looked at her, and she felt the way she did when she was thirteen and loved a boy named Chipper Brown and her horse, Fair Lady.

"Why don't you come in my office? You don't have to stand in the doorway. I've got a bottle and two glasses."

"And some etchings?" she laughed.

"No. Will layouts do?"

She laughed again. She liked Henry. She wanted to know him better. Henry could be an interesting game. So far the only game she had found at Kiss, Inc., was called money.

If she had not walked out of her way that night, would they have happened? Of course, Henry told her a thousand times in the succeeding years as he held her in his arms and promised her —what did he promise her?

Two years later she still did not know what Henry had promised her. Never a promotion. Certainly not marriage. What was it that held her, then? Was it only that snap-crackle sexual tension? Was it just physical? No. She couldn't afford to think that. No. Women like Barbara went to bed for love, not kicks. Why had she chosen life in Henry's office that night?

Why did she choose death last night for the Us that was Barbara and Henry?

And what would she choose with Paul?

She peered intently at the highway signs.

It never occurred to her to wonder what Paul would choose.

Henry ran his fingers under the collar of his shirt. Hot under the collar. Yes, that was a good description of him tonight. He wanted to get people seated. The cocktail party was going on too long. He looked around for Jeff Garfield, the public relations man. He'd know how to move the crowd. Henry felt a tug at his elbow and turned; it was Jeff. Henry smiled in relief. "What the hell do we have to do to get these people into the dining room?"

"I've arranged to have chimes in two minutes," Jeff said.

Henry made a face. "I hate chimes."

"Well, it gets worse," Jeff promised. "I put Mrs. Kamatchky at your table."

"Who is she?"

"Her husband is winning one of the President's Awards tonight. He is the fastest worker on the line in Altoona."

"She is not sitting next to me, is she?" Henry asked apprehensively.

Jeff nodded. "I thought you wanted to give the local folks a thrill."

"Let someone else thrill them," said Henry. "Put Jennifer on one side of me and the little girl from *Newsweek* on the other."

"Yes, sir."

"You have sixty seconds to change the place cards," Henry reminded him.

Jeff hurried off just as the chimes sounded.

The round tables were covered with bright pink tablecloths,

and in the center of each table was an arrangement of bright red roses. Red ribbons extended from the centerpiece, and in front of each woman's plate was a gift box attached to the ribbon.

"What's in the box?" Sharon asked Henry.

"Open it and see."

"Oh," she said, a trace of disappointment in her voice, "it's only a couple of lipsticks."

Jennifer laughed. "Sure, only a couple of lipsticks. Except that one is called Pink-a-ling and the other is called New China. Sharon baby, those are the two new hot Chinese lacquer shades Kiss, Inc., is going to introduce to a pale, lackluster America."

"Tomorrow the world," said Henry.

"Meaning you still think Kiss should be a multinational?" Jennifer asked.

"Of course," he said. "This can't go in the story, Sharon, but we can't ever get the kind of sales we must have to expand if we don't become a worldwide company."

"Is getting big what it's all about?" Sharon asked.

Henry nodded. "Yeah. It's what it's all about. I guess I've been looking for the right words to explain the actions in my own life, but there they are. Getting big is what it's all about."

Jennifer looked at him. "You said that with such desire, Henry, that it sounded as if you were talking about a woman, and all the time it was only business."

"Business is the sexiest thing going," Henry said.

"Henry," Jennifer said, pretending surprise, "and I thought you were such a romantic."

"Not me," he said. "I have a romantic potential somewhere between a turnip and a mushroom."

"That's the perfect thing to say to me," Jennifer shrugged. "Now you know I'll never chase you."

Henry made a funny little sound of disappointment.

Sharon said, "I think I may puke."

"Then change tables, will you?" asked Jennifer.

The dinner, as predicted, was dull. Dessert, however, was the first act of the evening. All the lights were dimmed, and the waiters walked in bearing a flaming baked Alaska for each table. The baked Alaska was applauded as warmly as if it were an act at the Palace.

"I don't think I'll ever get used to business," Sharon said to Jennifer.

"It's show business with suits," Jennifer whispered.

A small stage had been cleared in the center of the dining room. As the baked Alaskas were cut, Henry walked to the stage. "This has been a wonderful week for me," Henry said, flashing a big smile, "and it's only the beginning. It's the start of a new relationship with your company for each of you. We are first in research. We are first in product development. We are first in marketing and merchandising. And we are going to be first in sales."

A cheer interrupted him.

"And why are we first? Because of you. Each of you, the heart and soul . . ."

". . . and liver and kidneys," whispered Sharon to Jennifer.

". . . of this wonderful business," Henry continued.

"Cut the blah blah blah," Sharon whispered again to Jennifer.

"Tonight," Henry said in stentorian tones, "we are going to recognize those people who are receiving the President's Award for outstanding service during the year. These are the people who have performed above and beyond the call of duty to make this company what it is today. First, let me ask Stanley Kamatchky of Altoona to come forward. I want to say, first, that I only wish I could have spent more time with each of you this week, but I know that you will benefit just by associating with some of your fellow workers, people you might not have met otherwise. Stanley, you have done a splendid job . . ."

Sharon thought she must have dozed, and when she came back to consciousness, Henry was kissing someone named Rose Kamatchky on the cheek, and Rose's bosom was heaving mightily under her tight taffeta blouse.

Stanley grabbed the microphone from Henry's hand.

Jeff Garfield turned ashen. This was not scripted.

"I would like to say a few things," Stanley began. "First, I want to thank Chester Masterson for founding the company, and I wish he was here tonight so I could do it in person. Then I want to tell you that I love working for Kiss. See, here's how I think about my job. I make cosmetics, and women fall in love with them. They become a part of their lives. I am like the marriage broker. I bring the woman and the cosmetics together. Sometimes the marriages don't always work out, but what can you expect?"

The audience howled with delight. Stanley Kamatchky never heard anything like it in Altoona. Rose was so embarrassed she thought she would die. "Shut up, Stanley," she whispered under her breath. "Sit down already."

Stanley smiled to his audience. "I love you all," he said. Then he turned to Henry. "You may be the president of Kiss, but I am the emperor of the line in Altoona. And the emperor wouldn't change places with the president." Stanley bowed and walked back to his seat. Rose followed dutifully. The audience stood and cheered.

Henry was annoyed. Nobody ever made speeches except Henry at the President's Ball. Why did Jeff Garfield allow some hick from Altoona to upstage him? What if word got back to Chester Masterson? Chester would sock this to him every chance. Then Henry realized Chester's chances to goad him would soon end.

Henry looked at his watch. "Ladies and gentlemen," he said, calling the audience back to order, "in the interest of saving time because we have a great show for you tonight, I am going to name the other winners of the President's Award and ask each to stand at his table. Then we'll have one big round of applause for all our winners, and we wish each of you continued success with our company."

Jennifer said, "Sharon, poor Henry has no sense of show business. You have to play to other people. It doesn't matter if someone else gets the laughs. What matters is that you do not look like a jerk. Henry looks like a spoilsport. If they don't play his game, he picks up the ball and bat and goes home. First, of course, he changes the rules of the game."

The four other winners stood dutifully, blushed modestly, and sat down. Then Henry turned the show over to Jeff Garfield and the paid entertainment.

When Jennifer heard the first act announced, she groaned and whispered to Sharon, "Just hope the microphone goes dead. It's the only way that comic can be a success."

The microphone worked, and the comedian didn't.

The second act, two singers, knew the audience needed picking up. But they couldn't do it with an act Jeff Garfield had been promised was a safe one, a medley of Sigmund Romberg tunes.

Henry wished he were in New York.

The third act, the headliner, was Tiny Trotter, a comedienne whose jokes on childbirth and gynecologists were standard fare on late night variety shows.

Jo looked across the table to see how Henry was surviving. She knew it was going to be a long, unhappy night. It was going to be a Henry No-Talk night. When things went bad, Henry stopped talking. He went to bed and brooded. He tossed occasionally, and if she reached across the double bed to comfort him, he pulled away. Henry, in defeat, wanted no one.

She saw Jennifer turn to talk to him. Jo knew it was a mistake. There was no helping Henry at a time like this.

Chester Masterson picked up the telephone and said, "Don't tell me I can't get through to London. I can."

Minutes later the telephone wires hummed, and London was on the line.

"Something just happened in my company," said Chester, "and I am going to fire Henry Burns. The job can be Lord Edmondson's if he wants it."

"Mr. Masterson," said the London connection, "you can't get Lord Edmondson. He's the hottest man in international business today. He's going to be the next head of—"

"I don't care if he's going to be the King of England," Chester said. "I want Lord Edmondson."

Chester smiled at his own humor. This was what he loved, the old power surge, the decision-making. Damned if he'd ever let anyone think that Henry put one over on him. He'd move himself to executive chairman today. He'd get a chairman hired, have a president appointed before Henry even had a chance to quit. That would do it. Never let those bastards get one up on you. Whoever it was that hired Henry ought to know they were getting a reject. Henry was about to be tossed out of Kiss, Inc. And Chester Masterson personally was doing the tossing.

"What do we offer Lord Edmondson?" London repeated.

"Give him everything but Buckingham Palace and my stock," Chester said.

"Oh, all right," said London, "but it won't work."

Chester laughed. "Don't tell me it won't work. With me everything works." Chester slammed the receiver. He was trying to get a man. Meanwhile he wanted a woman. He was lonely. He was bored. He was nervous, too.

When Jennifer opened the note she was surprised. She tapped Henry on the arm. "Why do you think Chester wants to see me now?" she asked.

"How would I know?" Henry answered irritably. "Maybe he heard how lousy this show is, and he wants you to escape."

"Oh, I know what it is," she said smiling, but not with amusement. "He must think I have a red convertible up there."

"And he probably wants to test-drive it," Henry said bitterly.

"Hey, Henry," Jennifer said, "I can't help it if you're not a girl."

"You look very nice," Paul said stiffly.

"Thank you," Barbara answered in a Sunday voice.

They were standing in the middle of their room in the House of Blue Flowers Motel. The only blue flowers were painted on plastic bowls which sat in the middle of the double dresser.

Paul thought of his fantasies of the Pink Balloon. How could anything happen in this third-rate cardboard motel?

From the moment she drove into the place, Barbara knew she had made a mistake. The House of Blue Flowers was about as romantic as peanut butter. If she were going to make this thing work with Paul she'd need all the help she could get. A plastic motel. She smiled dolefully. The only thing missing was a jukebox.

How long had it been since she had seen Paul?

A week?

Four days?

She could not quite remember. So much had happened. She bit her lips. Nervous. She felt so nervous. Why couldn't she go forward and just embrace him? If it were Henry she would not have known who kissed first. With Paul she knew only that neither kissed. They stood in the middle of the room and greeted each other with about as much passion as a boy and girl whose date was arranged by their mothers.

Paul looked at her. Is she frightened? Is she as afraid as I am? Is she afraid we won't go up in the Pink Balloon? Or doesn't she even want to try anymore? She looked so remote. She must still be thinking about—well, about the people at Kiss. She was like another plastic flower in the House of Blue Flowers.

"How is the meeting going?" Paul asked.

"Fantastic." She smiled uncertainly. Now he had broken the ice. He had asked the first question. Should she go on? Yes, talk about business. That was safe. She could easily do seven minutes on "how's the meeting," pause for a station break, and then plan the rest of the conversation.

She launched into her monologue. ". . . and then when Chester called Henry and me to his room . . ."

"Does Chester know about you and Henry?" Paul asked in an unnaturally high voice. Paul did not know how the question came out. He did not know he was going to ask it just then. But it was the question in his mind and heart. He had to know. "Is Chester aware that Henry is in love with you?"

Barbara opened her mouth, but no sound came out. Finally she just shook her head.

He swallowed. "You seem to be in shock. I didn't mean to traumatize . . ."

The words made her snap to attention. Now she had something to be angry about. She hated Paul for knowing—or did he guess?—about Henry. But she could not reveal that anger. Now he gave her another outlet. Now she could rage in righteous indignation.

"Damn you and your medical words. You and your fancy language . . . Traumatize? What kind of way is that to talk to somebody you love? Her voice was shrill. "Damn you. Damn you. Damn you." She stabbed at him with her fists.

He pulled her arms down. He wanted to hold her close. He wanted to make the scent of flowers fill the room. But he could not say that. "Why didn't you tell me the truth?" he asked, his voice now back to normal tones. "Why didn't you tell me the real reason you keep putting off our marriage? Why didn't you tell me when the plane went back to New York?"

"Tell you what?" she asked angrily.

"Why didn't you tell me about you and Henry? Why did you just leave me to wonder what was wrong? Why didn't you give me any clues? How can we make things work if you don't tell me the truth?"

"Tell you the truth?" she asked bitterly. "Don't you realize that I don't want to know the truth."

"I can't fight shadows," Paul said softly. "You've never been honest with me."

Barbara's eyes filled with tears. She was going to cry. She didn't want to cry, but she wasn't going to try to stop. And she wasn't going to stop talking. "So who's been honest with me? The man I was sleeping with? Let me tell you something, Paul. Henry messed up my life. He got me to live two lives. He took the best of me and then rewarded me with leftovers. Until I met you I stayed home most of the time and ate my tuna fish while Henry ran up to the country for his charming little dinners. Couldn't you figure out why I was always free on weekends and not during the week? But what did Henry and I do at night? We stayed in his little apartment and made love. He couldn't take me to the theater. Someone might see us. He couldn't take me to good restaurants. What if I knew someone there? We couldn't do anything but lunch together. Nobody would get the picture if we lunched together. And if, occasionally, he'd touch my knee or give me a 'meet you at six at your place' look, who was to know? Not the department store buyer who was too busy eating his eighteen-dollar Kiss, Inc., expense account lunch to notice us."

"Do you still love him, Barbara?"

"I'll always love him."

"But . . . that's not love—that's—"

"Don't give me other names, Paul. I think it's love. But I am never going to see him again."

"Why?" he asked.

"Because he is leaving Kiss, Inc."

Paul's heart sank. So it wasn't her choice. It was Henry's.

"Henry is going to Switzerland," she said sadly.

"Maybe he will take you with him," Paul said.

"No, he won't."

"How do you know?"

"I asked him."

Paul sighed.

He sank on the edge of the bed. It was a double bed. A standard double bed in a room decorated in Latter Day Motel. There was the obligatory nightstand with a built-in red light to notify occupants of messages. A phone. A slightly soiled overstuffed chair. And, of course, dominating the room, a color television set.

Why hadn't he taken care of the reservations? Why hadn't he asked someone where to go the way he had before Puerto Rico? Why hadn't he asked for a suite in La Jolla? Henry would have done that. Henry had style. Henry probably would have ordered two suites. But would Henry still want Barbara if he knew there was another man? Probably not. That was the difference between Paul and Henry. Paul still wanted Barbara even if she might never be all his. For the first time Paul knew that he loved Barbara. He loved her more than the idea of marriage. He loved the woman he wanted to marry. She might be flawed. But so was he. He could not only accept a less than perfect person, he could love her as well. He smiled to himself. Score one for Paul.

"Barbara," he said slowly, picking and choosing his words. "It doesn't matter to me that Henry doesn't want you. I do."

"What do you want of me, Paul? Do you want a dear little wife who can preside at dinner parties and go to medical meetings?"

"No," he said thoughtfully. Then he looked up. She was standing there so hurt and angry, so alone. His heart went out to her. She really didn't have anyone except him at this moment. He wondered if she knew that. He was sure he could not tell her quickly. He might startle her. She was like a small, frightened rabbit. How could a woman five feet ten inches tall be small and frightened? When her heart was broken, he told himself. For the first time since they walked into the room, Paul wanted to act like the man Barbara would and could marry.

"Come here," he said quietly. He patted a place beside him on the bed. "I think you need someone to comfort you. I want to be that person."

"No, you don't," she said coldly, but she sat next to him. "You are looking for someone to play the role of wife in your life."

"You're right, you know. That's how it started. But that's not how I feel now." He put an arm around her. It was a small, tentative gesture, but when she did not resist, he increased the pressure on her shoulder.

"Paul, I'm a mess. I don't think you should want me."

"You are a mess right now, darling. So am I. Two messes. Maybe we deserve each other." He pulled her to him and kissed her. Did the scent of flowers suddenly fill the room? Were they on the Pink Balloon once more?

"I don't think we have anything that's real between us," she said. "I did have something very real with Henry." Crash.

"What? What real thing did you have?"

She looked at him. Her eyes were still wet.

"You don't have to tell me if you don't want to," he promised.

"It's just that I don't want to hurt you."

He already hurt so much that nothing could hurt more. "We've kept too much inside ourselves for too long. Let's let it out finally."

Barbara took a deep breath. Her voice was low but steady. "I had a very strong physical attraction to Henry, and I guess he did to me, too. He was my first lover, Paul."

Paul withdrew his arm and moved a few inches away. It was not easy to hear Barbara talk about Henry. "Then he was your only lover before me?"

"Yes," she said softly.

"Was it ever like Puerto Rico with him?" He had to know.

She smiled. She looked at Paul and knew how she must be hurting him despite his protestations. "When we went to Puerto Rico I was away from Henry and all thoughts of him. Who knows? Maybe if I had never seen him again, things would always have been that magic way with us. But I did see him again, and in some ridiculous way he had my loyalty, not you. So I decided that I couldn't be unfaithful to Henry by being faithful to you, the man I was intending to marry."

He nodded. "I wish I didn't understand, but I do."

She sighed deeply.

"Do you think your love for Henry came from gratitude because he did so much for your career?"

Barbara was silent. Finally she said, "No, I didn't go to bed to say thank you. Henry meant the thing I could not have. All my life I have chased illusions and looked for things that were beyond my grasp. I am your classic overachiever. I guess that Henry was a challenge, and I'm a great one for challenges. I knew I could not have him, so I wanted him all the more."

"Did he have qualities that you found necessary, maybe even irresistible?"

"I can't answer that," Barbara said, "but I liked to be with him. We always had so much to say to each other."

"We never talk to each other very much," he admitted.

"In some ways that is very peaceful."

"Would you like it if we talked more?"

"I think we should talk more about things that are really inside us, not just exchange information about 'how I spent my day.' It's a little like school children."

"Can I tell you something?" he asked shyly.

"Of course."

"I have a secret name for our Puerto Rico weekend."

"You do?"

"I call it the Pink Balloon."

"I didn't know you were such a romantic. Oh Paul dear . . ."

His heart sang. She called him dear. He didn't feel forty-one. He felt boyish . . . and, well, dear.

"The Pink Balloon?" she asked, clapping her hands in delight. "I wish I had thought of that. Of course it was the Pink Balloon."

"I thought you would think I was silly," he confessed.

She took his hand. "You are not silly, Paul. I think you are a very good man, and I don't think you've spent a lot of time using some of those good things you are. I don't think I've been as good to you as you have to me, and that worries me. I really think that now things can be different."

Paul wondered. Was it Henry that made the difference? Could she turn to him now that Henry was leaving? It did not matter.

"Do you still want to marry me knowing that I haven't been fair or honest?" she asked.

"Yes," he said. "But what about you? How do you feel?"

"For the first time since I have known you, Paul, I can honestly say that yes, with all my heart I do want to marry you."

"Is your job going to get in the way?" he asked.

"No more than yours," she answered.

Paul looked around the room and laughed out loud. "When I saw this room, I figured that nothing good could happen in a place like this."

"But it's not the place that makes it good."

"No," he said softly, "it's the people."

The telephone was ringing. So was the doorbell. Chester picked up the telephone. That movie star whore was probably at the door anyway. She could wait.

"Lord Edmondson will accept the chairmanship of Kiss, Inc.," the clipped British voice announced.

"I thought he couldn't be bought," Chester said.

"Evidently you had the magic numbers," London reported.

"I always do," Chester said matter-of-factly. "There is nothing I want that I cannot get when I want it." He thought of Jennifer standing on the other side of the door.

"Congratulations, sir," came the voice. "We will work out the details. We will be in touch with your attorneys. It's all happening so fast. It's a bit like your baseball bonus babies."

"Money buys you anything in the world you want," Chester announced.

He walked to the door. He felt triumphant. Now he was really ready for a woman.

He opened the door. No one was there.

Henry looked quizzically at Jennifer. "Why are you back at the party so soon? I thought you had an assignation with Mr. Sunshine."

"I rang his bell, but he didn't answer immediately, so I left," Jennifer said.

"That will cost you your job," Henry said. "How can you do a thing like that?"

"You wouldn't understand, Henry," she said, "but there are some days when the screwing I get isn't worth the screwing I get."

12

Wednesday

Chester Masterson put on his bathing suit and walked out of the cabana. It was the last day of the convention, time to relax and let the warm California sun melt everything except the ever-present icicles around his heart and mind. Despite the expletives and invectives, despite the frantic hirings and firings, Chester was cool. Cool emotions and a cool head were Chester's trademarks in business. Chester looked down at the pool from his second-level vantage point. He liked a cabana that was second deck. He loathed being near the wet bathers, the oily sun worshipers and the general hangers-on that were found at every pool.

There were a few starlet types sunning their bikinied bodies. Wasn't that Ginger Mallory over in the corner with a fat, bald man? What's the difference? Chester asked himself. For her the selling never stops. For him the buying never stopped. Buy people. Buy ideas. Money. The whole key was money. It always had been. When you had enough money, you could buy the best ideas. But still the biggest thrill was having the money to make your own ideas work.

Chester sat down and stared at his hands. He wanted something to do. He was tired of drinking orange juice and coffee. He was tired of watching television. He was marking time now, waiting for the proper moment to drop a few bombs. This time he was going to let everyone play into his hands. His hands. He rubbed them together in anticipation. What a day this would be. Even the sun was shining for him. He looked again at his hands. Oh. Now he knew what he could do. He went inside the cabana and opened a cardboard box. In it were twelve testers, sample tubes of lipstick shades. Chester pulled them out of the box one by one and applied the colors to the inside of his hand. He was proud that every Kiss product went on his body before it went into the stores. He stayed inside the cool cabana so that the lipsticks would not melt in the sun.

He loved the bold lines he drew with each tube. He held his hand away from him, as far as he could reach. Then he brought his hand in close. Pink-a-ling had too much yellow in it. New China was too blue. Leave those off-colors in the lab. He wanted fashion colors, colors that made women look good. You had to be careful when you went into the brown shades. He'd have to try that Brown Betty color again. See it on the other hand. Maybe his own pigmentation was interfering. But how could it be? When you applied lipstick on the palm of your hand, you were getting a true look at the color. But you always had to remember that no color would look the same on two women. That was the challenge of this business. That was the fun. Would the colors work? You never knew for sure. But nobody in the business had a better track record on guesses than Chester Masterson.

"Mr. Masterson. We have an appointment at eleven. And it's eleven."

Chester opened his eyes. He must have dozed. He blinked. He was stretched out on a chaise in front of the cabana. Hmmm. He was so comfortable. Oh yes. He had told the little girl from *Newsweek* she could interview him. But that was back in New York, about a hundred years ago.

"I'd reschedule it," Sharon said, "but since this is our last day, I figured we had better do our talking now."

"First thing you want to know is why I have lipstick on my hand. Right?" Chester was going to take command of the interview. No personal questions. No funny stuff.

"I figure you're testing shades," she answered.

He looked at her in surprise. "How did you know?"

"I read about you before I came here."

"What did you learn?"

"Not much. Oh, you're supposed to be a perfectionist. . ."

"Supposed to be?" Chester interrupted. "I'm not just supposed to be. I *am* a perfectionist. I want everything exactly right."

"Including the women in your life?"

"What kind of question is that?"

"Just one that will help me understand you. What I can gather is that your seeking of perfection is so encompassing that it floods your private life as well as your business life. For instance, China's nails . . ."

"What about China's nails?" he asked testily.

"Well, you have to admit they are a bit unusual."

He smiled and leaned back. "Oh that. They are the most unusual nails in the world, and she wears them because I am her father."

"You mean she doesn't like wearing her nails that way?"

"Of course she likes it. It makes her my daughter."

Sharon thought of the frightened girl with the private drinking problem. She wondered if that made her Chester's daughter, too.

"Let's talk about what you have seen here," Chester said. "What did you do each day?"

"I went to the meetings," she answered. "Most of the time you didn't show. Why was that?"

"I don't go to meetings unless I run them," he said.

"You could run the meetings here, couldn't you?"

"I can do anything I want," he said casually. "I can give raises, fire people, hire people. Anything."

"Then why don't you run these meetings?"

"Because this convention belongs to the sales department, and I don't want to get in their way."

"But you let Henry Burns run the meetings," Sharon protested, "and he's not a sales person."

"He isn't?" Chester laughed. "You don't know a hell of a lot . . . excuse me . . . you don't know much about companies. Henry is nothing but a sales head. We give him the title president so it will impress department store buyers. He has as much power when it comes to the future of Kiss as . . . as . . ." Chester was casting about for names.

"As I do?" she asked coyly.

He looked at her, and his eyes narrowed. "As you do. Hey . . . what's your name again?"

"Sharon. Sharon Kennedy."

"You a good writer, Sharon?"

"I was editor of my college paper."

"Don't give me that stuff. Are you a good writer?"

"Depends on what you call a good writer."

"Shakespeare, Jacqueline Susann," he said, naming the first two he could think of.

"I try to write more like Joan Didion," she said.

"Who?"

"She's a California writer I admire. Sort of a super journalist."

"I guess her stuff doesn't get printed in the New York papers much."

Sharon nodded. "Right."

"Are you as good as she is?"

"No. But maybe I will be someday."

"Write her name down before you leave, will you?" Chester asked. "You never know. She may be interested in a job."

No wonder he gets anybody he wants, Sharon thought. He's not afraid. He must be made of spare parts taken from the U. S. Marine Corps.

"Talking about jobs," Sharon said, "I want to ask if it's true that you pay executives more money than anyone else in the business."

"Of course it's true," Chester said.

"Why do you pay so much?"

"Because when you pay people a lot of money, more than they could get anyplace else, you own them. They can't afford to leave. They can't ever get another job like that. And money is a form of slavery."

"You want slaves?" she asked.

"Not slaves to me," he said, "slaves to their jobs. When people begin to make a lot of money, they raise their standard of living. And once they raise it, they can't go back to their old ways. So they get desperate about their jobs. They clutch them. They're willing to do anything just so you don't fire them."

"But you fire them anyway," she said.

"I fire them because it shows everybody else that when you don't toe the mark, I don't live up to my part of the bargain. I don't sign the checks."

"What do you think it takes to be a good executive?" Sharon asked.

"Wait a minute," Chester said. "What's that thing?"

"Oh, that's my tape recorder," she said. "I set it up while you were asleep. I figured that if I taped our talk then I wouldn't have to take notes. It makes it a lot easier for me."

Chester nodded. "Sure. That's what the whole world is about. Everybody is trying to make things easy. You just asked me what makes a good executive. I'll tell you. It's somebody who doesn't try to make things easy. It's somebody who just tries to make things good."

"We began by saying you were a perfectionist," she reminded him.

"I want to make the best cosmetics that were ever made. Tell me, Sharon, just tell me any company that was ever successful making shit."

"Fertilizer companies," she said quickly.

Chester threw his head back and laughed. Sure, it was an old joke, but it was his kind of humor. "You're okay."

Sharon felt pleased. She figured a "you're okay" in Chester's business was worth maybe a Pulitzer prize in her business.

"What are the hardest decisions you have had to make in business?" Sharon asked. The little machine whirred.

"Going into business wasn't a tough decision," Chester said, "but everything after it was. I didn't have any choice about going into my own business. I was out there as a salesman working for other people, and I knew I could not spend my life working for someone else. If I hadn't started Kiss, I would have started a food business or record company or movie studio."

"Would you have started an iron and steel business or been a real estate operator?"

"You are a smart kid. You know the difference," Chester said in admiration. "I only would have gone into a business that had a product that I could identify with. I can identify with something you can see or smell or taste or touch that makes you feel good or look good."

"But you don't like abstracts?"

"Right," he said. "I don't want to go out and look at a plot of ground and tell everybody that I own it."

"What are some of your other hard decisions?"

"You don't get off a subject, do you?" Chester asked.

"Not if it seems like a good one," she said.

"I'm making one of my hardest decisions right now."

"What's that?"

"I'm choosing a new president for Kiss."

"Why?"

"Come on. You're a reporter. You've been around here all week. You must have heard people talking about it."

"Yes, I have," Sharon admitted.

"So what are they saying?" Chester loved to listen to gossip, especially when he knew that it was gossip that he could influence. "What are they saying?" he asked again.

"That the candidates are your son-in-law Tim Edgar and Ken Sugarman."

"They are," Chester admitted. "Now let me ask you something, Miss Brains. Which of those two would you pick?"

Sharon choked. The closest she had ever been to influencing a power decision was the time she asked her father not to hit her little brother. She felt sorry for China. Who knew? Tim might leave China if he didn't get the presidency. On the other hand she hated Linda. It would serve Linda right not to get it. But wait. It wasn't Linda who was in the running. It was Ken. And he was a nice guy. A shnook where his wife was concerned but basically a nice person. Wow. She was glad she didn't have any power.

"I wish I knew which one to pick," Sharon said.

"But I have to pick someone," Chester reminded her.

"What's the most important thing the candidate must bring to the presidency?"

Chester rubbed his chin. "Respect for beauty," he said. "I don't want somebody who is tough and can sell. We have enough of those. I want someone who knows taste, who has taste."

"Does Tim?" she asked.

"I think so. But he's not smart. He doesn't have that sharp edge."

"You mean like Henry?"

"Henry?" Chester sneered. "I don't think that even Henry's razor has a sharp edge. Henry's had it."

So Henry was out? Sharon had to learn why. Or maybe he wasn't out, and Chester was just baiting her. The reporter in her signaled that she did not have the story. Yet. "Did you fire Henry?" she asked quickly.

"Ho ho, the little girl reporter is getting nosy," Chester said. "Well, turn up your tape, and let me tell you something. Chester Masterson will never let anyone or anything stand in the way of progress. And right now Henry Burns is standing in the way of progress."

"He seems to be all for progress," Sharon said in her best devil's advocate style.

"How's that?" Chester asked.

"He talks about Kiss being a multinational."

"Oh that," Chester sneered. "He doesn't know anything unless it's in a Harvard book."

Sharon had not been acquainted with Chester long enough to know that anything in a Harvard book or any reference to Harvard was an automatic put-down. Yet there was that condescending tone that told her Chester had decided Henry was kaput with Kiss. Yes, Henry was definitely no Kiss-y, no touch-y.

"Obviously you have other plans for becoming a multinational," Sharon said briskly.

"Right," said Chester. "We are going to do it with me as chairman of the executive committee and Lord Edmondson as chairman."

"Lord Edmondson? Is he related to the Queen or something?" Sharon asked.

"No," Chester said in a mocking tone, "he is not related to the Queen. For God's sake, he's bigger than the Queen. Lord Edmondson is more important than royalty. He's the head of Comfort Electronics in Europe."

"But what does that have to do with cosmetics?" Sharon asked.

"I know about cosmetics," Chester said. "We don't need another person to put color on the palm of his hand." He grinned. "That's my job. Comfort Electronics is one of the world's biggest companies. To go big throughout the world it takes someone who headed a company like that and can move in those international circles. You don't think someone like Henry Burns can do that, do you? The reason that Kiss hasn't become a multinational is not that we wouldn't. It was that we couldn't. Henry just wasn't the man for the job. He's all right to hold hands with Saks and Bergdorf. But for the big numbers, for Japan and the UK, it takes a big man."

"And that is Lord Edmondson?" Sharon asked.

"Yes."

"And when did you decide you were going to become a major multinational and really go after Lord Edmondson?" asked Sharon.

"Last night," Chester said. "I made up my mind last night. I got on the phone and decided to get him at any cost. So I gave him a deal he accepted."

"What's in the deal?"

"Houses, cars, stock, annuities, a yacht, a plane . . . and one more thing."

"What's that?" she asked.

"A clause that says I can take it all back if he doesn't perform."

"So you think he will?"

"I know he will," Chester said positively. "Money always does it. It's not so easy picking the president, though. My candidates already do what they do for money. It's a tough one."

"You need someone who will work intelligently with Lord Edmondson," Sharon said.

"Nobody works intelligently at Kiss," said Chester. "We work emotionally. I want somebody with fire and fury, somebody who doesn't need me to push him to greatness."

"Then you better keep looking," Sharon said. "It doesn't sound as if you've found your man."

Chester was getting tired. The little machine kept humming.

"You have nice skin," said Chester.

Sharon looked at him. Was he tired of being interviewed, uncomfortable? Or did he have a short attention span? She looked at him in a perplexed way.

"How come you have such nice skin?" he asked again.

She decided to give him her charm number. "Because, Mr. Masterson, I have used your products all my life."

"How would you like a job here?" he asked. "I can start you in public relations . . ."

"No way," she said. "I think business is the pits."

"What's that?"

"It's . . . oh hell . . . business to me is like acne to you."

"Oh, I see," he said slowly. "Do you want a job anyway?"

"No," she said. "You just met a person you can't buy."

"That's what they all say," Chester said. "We'll see. Now hand me that tape machine, will you?"

She took the machine, turned it off, and handed it to him. "First take out the tape," he said.

She removed the cartridge.

In one quick movement he took the cartridge from her hand. "You didn't think you were going out of here with my voice saying all those things, did you?" he asked.

She was bewildered. "Why did you do that?"

"So that when the story appears in *Newsweek*, I can deny everything. You can't prove a word of what I said."

"You don't play fair, Mr. Masterson," she said.

He laughed. "When you get older, you'll find out that winners never do."

Barbara checked her watch as she drove into The Gates of Paradise. Nine forty-five. Well, that wasn't too bad. Since today was departure day, there would be no morning meeting. She wondered if Chester realized she had been away. Probably not. At least she was back in time for whatever farewelling Chester might plan. To play it casually, she'd stop at the open air breakfast pavilion and have a cup of coffee with any Kiss people who might be there. She felt like a criminal. Why did she have to cover her tracks? Why couldn't she go away and go to bed with her very own fiancé just like other red-blooded healthy American women? She knew why. Because she still had sticky feelings about Henry. Because she was still overwhelmed at discovering that it was possible for her to have a sense of love and tenderness toward Paul. Was it really love? She didn't know. She would need the next few months to be sure.

She mounted the steps to the pavilion. She reached the serving level and saw just one person. Henry. Maybe there were other people there. She wasn't sure. Her heart stopped. It was Henry. The blood pounded in her temples. It was Henry. The old ache came back in her groin. It was Henry.

"Hello, Barbie," he said.

Oh, why did he have to use that endearing term? Why couldn't he be mean and rotten so she could hate him in peace? That was what she really wanted. She wanted to hate Henry, and instead she still felt this damned schoolgirl melting.

"Hello, Henry." Damn. She wanted to sound aloof, and she knew she sounded her same old dumb adoring self.

"Come on. Sit down, and I'll get you a cup of coffee with milk and one touch of real sugar," he said.

She sat down. If he told her to climb off the balcony she'd probably do that, too. Where was her resolve? Who stole her determination? When she had left Paul just ninety minutes before, she hadn't felt like that.

Wait a minute, she said to herself. Wait a minute. Of course she hadn't felt dopey dummy weak when she left Paul. His love gave her strength. Henry's love sapped her strength.

That was the difference, and in a twinkling, in one insightful flash, she had seen the light.

Paul made her strong.

Henry made her weak.

She took a deep breath. She climbed back from the imaginary balcony. She was on solid emotional ground again. Whew. That had been a close one.

"Barbie," he said as he set the coffee cup in front of her, "we can't be over, and you know it."

My, she felt strong. And she hadn't even drunk the coffee yet. This was going to be good. So this is what it was like when somebody wanted you, and you played hard to get. Whee. It was joy time.

"Henry," she said, now playing the game as if she were up for an Academy Award, "I wish that I could agree. But for me it is over."

Henry turned pale. This girl, this darling girl he had raised from her beginnings at Kiss, was now successful, and she was turning him down. She couldn't do that to Henry Burns. Nobody did that to Henry Burns. She couldn't walk out. No. He had made a mistake yesterday. He'd take her to Switzerland with him. If she were smart enough to work at Kiss, she'd make it at Oxxon, too. He put his hand on hers. "I have thought about us a great deal ever since I told you I am leaving Kiss, and I realize that I cannot leave here without you. You were right. I must take you with me. You must go to Switzerland. It will be perfect. We'll have Jo stay in New York, and you and I will get a house, a villa, an apartment . . . whatever you want . . . in Basel, and I'll commute."

"No, you won't." Her voice was firm.

"You just think I won't. Wait. You'll see. I will." Desperation was now creeping into his voice.

"No, Henry. You won't because I will not let you. I am not going to Switzerland with you. I am staying right here at Kiss. Remember? I am the mother of Product Q, and I'm going to take it to market. I have a very good business life here. And I also have a fiancé. No. Turn that around. First, I have a fiancé. And then I have a very good business life."

"But I want you, Barbie."

"No, you don't, Henry. You want what you can't have. And for the first time in my life I know what I want."

"What's that?" he asked.

"I want to come first with somebody. I want to be the one he can't afford to hurt. I want a man who will take care of me and who will let me take care of him."

"But what about us?" Henry was indignant. "What's to become of us?"

"Nothing," she said as she rose to leave. "And that's something I should have known long ago."

Henry walked back to his suite. He tried to digest the news of Barbara's new feelings toward her fiancé. She could not be leaving him for Paul Thurston. Impossible. Sex with Barbara was the best he had ever had, and he certainly knew enough to make expert comparisons. Barbara had had no other experience. She didn't know that an affair like theirs happened only once in a lifetime. He could not let her make a mistake and throw this away. Because it was more than sex. It was the involvement in the business, too. It had always been so easy to talk to her. She knew the people and the personalities. They could hold close, talk, and help each other's career. At least he had helped hers. He could help her again at Oxxon. But she said she wouldn't go to Oxxon. He would have to get her to change her mind. How would she get along in business without him?

Perhaps there was a way to save the relationship. To prove his love, he would have to make the supreme sacrifice. He would have to consider remaining at Kiss. First he'd have to broach the subject to Jo.

She was getting dressed when he walked into the bedroom. He sat down on the edge of the bed. "I've been thinking," he said abruptly, "and if moving to Switzerland is really going to upset you, maybe I should reconsider."

Jo put one foot into her pantyhose leg. So he decided he could not leave Barbara. Well, now he'd have to. She had crossed her emotional bridge. It happened in the sauna and the hours following that. She wasn't going back to the steam room.

"I'm resigned to the move," she said evenly. "It's all right with me. I can handle it."

"I don't think I have really been fair to you," he said. "Maybe New York is where we belong."

"The idea of Basel is appealing," she answered. "I hear the social life is marvelous, and so many of our friends ski in Switzerland that I'm sure I'll have a wonderful time."

"There is a language barrier," he reminded her.

"You forget. I'm smart, and I'm good at languages. I speak pretty fair French anyway."

"I think I should call the Oxxon people and tell them that my wife—"

"No, Henry. Don't call Oxxon. And most of all, don't lay it off on your wife. I'm strong. I'm ready. By the way, darling . . . are you?" She continued dressing.

Henry was confused. Who the hell could understand women?

No wonder Chester had nothing to do with them. Maybe he could finally appreciate Chester. Maybe all they needed was a good talk. He picked up the phone. Chester was out at the pool, but he'd see him in fifteen minutes at the cabana. Henry put on swim trunks. He didn't want to look out of place with Chester. Especially not today.

Chester smiled.

The sun was still shining. A good omen. This was going to be his day. He hadn't been this happy since Gladys-Gladyce had left. Funny how his last good time always seemed to coincide with the arrival or departure of a woman in his life.

"Hi, Chester."

It was Henry. This was the meeting Chester had anticipated since last night. This was the meeting he planned so carefully. So Henry thought that he could negotiate behind his back and then screw things up by resigning? Well, he was about to get a lesson in how to run a company. Chester regarded Henry carefully. Good-looking guy. But the trouble with good-looking guys was that they led from their looks instead of their brains. Chester shook his head. How had he ever made him president anyway? Now he wanted more than a handholder for department stores. He'd get a different kind of president this time. He already had a different kind of chairman.

"Sit down. Sit down," Chester said graciously. He'd fatten him for the kill. "How about a drink? Bloody Mary or . . ."

"Bloody Mary will be fine," Henry said. This was not like Chester. This was a new Chester. The old Chester would order a Bloody Mary for himself and let Henry watch him drink it.

Chester motioned to a waiter and gave him the order. "How do you think the meeting is going?" Chester asked.

"I think the morale is very high," Henry said. "The sessions have all been excellent."

"I don't think we are ever going to have outside speakers again," said Chester. "That newscaster, what-is-his-name, was an old . . ."

Henry interrupted. "I shouldn't listen to our public relations department. They don't know how to book a speaker. They don't have the brains they were born with."

Chester looked sidewise at Henry. "Careful," he said slowly. "You're beginning to sound like me, and one of me is enough around here."

"We could use a few more with your kind of insight," Henry said graciously.

"And what else do you think the company needs?" Oh, Chester loved this day. He was taking Henry right down the primrose path.

Henry cleared his throat. The old man had never been this warm. Maybe it was the sunshine. Maybe Ginger Mallory had pumped new life into the old guy. This certainly wasn't the same old New York bastard. "Chester," Henry said in his most confidential tone, "I still feel that we must become a multinational."

"Tell me why," said Chester. This was going to be even better than he had hoped.

"There is a fine cosmetics market in Japan. And I think we should sell our products there. Certainly opportunities still exist in Europe."

"How would you project sales the first year?" Chester asked.

"I would get our analysts to come in and review market potential," Henry answered quickly.

"But you haven't done that yet?" Chester asked.

"No, sir," Henry answered.

"I have." Boom. Chester dropped the first bomb.

Henry's eyes widened. "But you never discussed that with me."

"And why should I?" Chester asked innocently.

"Well, as the president . . ."

"As the president, Henry, you're out selling department stores and complaining about the way I run the company."

"No," said Henry quickly, "I never complain about the way you run the company. I think you do a superb job. Nobody has the color sense that you have."

"Cut the crap," Chester said sharply.

"I'm sorry." Henry felt sheepish. The moment he said, "I'm sorry," he knew he had lost Chester forever. It was Henry's insolence, his insouciance that had kept their relationship afloat. Now Chester had the upper hand, and they were through. Now Henry knew he could not stay at Kiss. He could not be president. He could not be chairman. Well, at least he had a good job to go to. He breathed deeply. Here was the moment he had waited for with joy. And now, sadly, it was here.

Henry stood up. "Chester, I want you to find a new president because I am resigning." He had expected to be thrilled when he said those words face-to-face with Chester. Somehow they gave him no satisfaction.

Chester yawned. "Hey, where the hell are our drinks?" he said.

Henry could not believe this. Chester could laugh at him. Chester could taunt him. But ignore him? And when he said the most important thing he had ever said? "Chester, I don't think you heard me."

"Yes. You said you are resigning. So what else is new?"

Henry sat down. "What kind of subhuman are you? Why don't you say something?"

"Obviously," said Chester, "because I don't think there is anything worth saying. You're a second-rate salesman, a nothing president, and I guess you realized that you were about to be fired."

"Fired?" Henry was smoldering inside. How could Chester be so cool? Of course he was not going to fire Henry. He just said that to irritate him. "Look, Chester, we both know you were not going to fire me—"

"Then why did I hire Lord Edmondson as chairman?"

"You did what?" Henry asked in disbelief.

"I hired the smartest corporate executive in the world to be chairman of Kiss," Chester said triumphantly.

"You're not telling me the truth."

"Yes, I am," Chester said. "You're so busy playing your little political games that you couldn't see the handwriting on the wall. You didn't even realize what you were doing. The only thing that mattered to you was the title. Long ago I learned I didn't have to pay people anything if I gave them titles. Why anyone would even want the title vice-president in this company is something I cannot understand. We have a vice-president for everything but toilet paper. You were like all the others. You wanted to be chairman. You never thought what it took to be chairman. You just wanted the right to use the jet and be saluted at "21." Well, that isn't what being chairman is. If you are the chairman, you run the company. You don't just sit back and dream of selling products all over the world. You figure out the ways to do it."

"But it's true," Henry protested. "I have the utmost respect for the quality standards . . ."

"Are you running for office?" Chester asked.

Henry smiled. He still had a chance, but he would have to move carefully. "No, Chester, I am not running for office, but we certainly have some candidates who are hot for my job."

Chester was all wide-eyed naïveté.

Henry was so absorbed in changing direction he did not notice the next trap being set.

"Who are the candidates for the presidency?" Chester asked.

"Tim."

"Who?" asked Chester.

Henry laughed. That Chester really could sock it to his family. "Tim Edgar, the not-too-bright son-in-law."

Chester smiled. "And you have already proven that you do not have to be too bright to be the president of Kiss."

Henry's laugh died like a candle in the wind.

Chester continued to smile. Squirm, bastard, he said to himself. You ain't seen nothin' yet.

"Of course," said Henry hastily, "there's Ken Sugarman, and he has brains."

"But his wife has all the balls in the family," Chester said.

"Ken's done a fine job for us," Henry persisted.

"Ken needs an American Express tour director to get to the men's room," Chester said.

"But it is important that we find a new president," said Henry.

"Why?" asked Chester.

"Because if you are determined to make us multinational . . ."

"I didn't say I was determined," Chester said quickly. "All I said was that I have reviewed the market potential."

"What did you find?" asked Henry.

"It took you long enough to ask that question," Chester said sharply.

Henry felt abashed. This was different from his other Chester meetings. For the first time he felt like a small boy in the principal's office. Usually he felt that he was a sparring with a temperamental bastard. Today he was put in the wrong, and Chester was situated in the right. When did these new roles come into being?

"I've made a lot of contributions to this company," Henry said weakly.

"So have I," retorted Chester, "but what does that have to do with the price of lipstick in France?"

Henry shook his head slowly. This was not the scene he had scripted in his dreams.

"You know what you're like, Henry? You're like a popular shade that women no longer demand. Your style of executive is not what we need next at Kiss. Personal salesmanship is dead. I need workers and thinkers. Our future is not in lipsticking the world. Our future depends on taking breakthrough products like the Chester Masterson Lift—"

"What?"

"Oh, I guess I didn't tell you. Product Q is going to be called the Chester Masterson Lift, and that is the product that is going to put us into the multinational group. We won't do it with a me-too product, and we won't do it with a me-too chairman. We need an outstanding executive team, one that can generate a lot of good financial press and good trade press. We need a really different kind of president. We need . . ." Chester smiled. He stopped talking. Now all the conversation was in his head. Of course. The perfect president. He had just named the perfect president in his mind. He'd get them all together for lunch. There was still time. He had to move fast. His conversation with Henry had already fled his mind.

"Henry, tell everybody to get here for lunch. Never mind about calling Tim and China. I'll call them myself."

Henry stood. "Yes, sir."

"Whatever happened to those Bloody Marys?" Chester asked.

"They were replaced by Bloody Henry," Henry said tersely.

It was not until Henry turned the key in his own suite that he realized he had never even told Chester where he was going. He felt tears sting his eyes. His whole world was being washed away. He looked for Jo. She stood, her usual cool and elegant self, in pale gray slacks and pale gray silk shirt with pearls. "Get undressed, and get into bed," he commanded. Quickly she took off her clothes and climbed into bed. Without being told she knew somehow someone had hurt Henry. This was no time for words.

Henry had already removed his bathing trunks. Hard and strong, he was waiting. The moment he felt her body next to him, he went limp. For the first time in his life.

Linda Sugarman took the call from Henry inviting her and Ken to lunch at Chester's cabana. What did the call mean? Linda did not know, but she was not going to speculate with Ken. In her heart she sensed Ken was not getting the presidency. If he were, would Henry make the call? No, it would be a call from the old man. She sighed. Ken's future was out of her hands. There came a time when you finally realized that you had done all you could. And the rest was in the hands of the gods. Or the demigods.

Linda sighed deeply. The time had finally come to do the thing she had wanted to do since she met Brandy McCarthy. She picked up the telephone and called Sharon. "Do you have a tape recorder?" she asked.

Sharon gulped. That nosy Linda knew everything. She probably saw Chester destroy the tape through her telescope. "Why?"

"I need it for an hour," Linda said brusquely.

"Come and get it," Sharon said. Silently she added, I hope it works better for you than it did for me.

When Brandy McCarthy came into the Bathhouse an hour later, Linda was waiting.

"Hi," said Linda.

"Why did you have to see me now?" asked Brandy.

"Oh, it's my last chance for a sauna before I go, and I thought maybe we could have another ten minutes together."

Brandy smiled wanly. "You want me to sit in that sauna with you?"

Linda nodded.

"Okay," said Brandy, "but the way I feel today I don't think it will do me much good."

"I think it will help me," smiled Linda.

Both women were right.

*

Paul watched Los Angeles disappear. He had certainly changed his life overnight. He felt a sense of anticipation. He wanted to push into the future. He thought about Barbara. She had so much to offer, and she had been offering it to the wrong man. Would he be the right man? He would try to be. He was not sure just why her career was so important to her. It was almost as if her career were both father and husband in her life. He knew he could not be both. Maybe the best thing he could be was a husband who would accommodate his life to her job and her need for love to his capacity to give it.

Barbara was so sad in so many ways. She had taken the responsibility for raising a family, but she had not had many rewards. Perhaps in their home freed of the pressures of an extramarital love, she might flower. Barbara was so tough on herself. Maybe she could learn to be less demanding. But then wasn't that one of the things that had attracted him in the first place? Didn't he like that seeking of perfection, that unwillingness to accept second best of herself?

Lean back, Paul, he said to himself as the plane climbed through the clouds. Wait for the Pink Balloon and let life happen. It would anyway.

Chester wondered if Henry was making all the calls. Yes, Henry operated from memory and habit. He would call everyone and sound as if he were running things. Chester could not remember whether he had told Henry to call Jennifer Johnson. Maybe he ought to call her. Just to be sure, of course. And if she happened to be free the hour before the luncheon . . . well, you just never knew what might happen if she stopped by early.

"Two nights with Jennifer Johnson. The guys at home would never believe this," Sid Fisher said. Sid was lying in Jennifer's bed watching as she carried a breakfast tray to him.

"And here is breakfast for the king of the jungle," she said solemnly.

"I can't believe it. You are the most incredible woman in the world."

"And I owe it all to my Kiss complexion," she said, parroting her own commercials.

"I'm going back to Indiana and sell this stuff like it has never been sold before. I've really seen what Kiss is all about at this convention."

"Oh come on, Sid," Jennifer said. "Kiss is not all screwing and screaming."

"You don't understand," said Sid Fisher, "when you work for a big company, and you're out in the hinterlands the way I am, you think that everything and everybody in New York is stupid. You think, if I were where those jerks are, I'd really show them how to run a company. But then you come to a convention, and when you see that there are plans for new products and you realize that these guys have to work every day for Chester Masterson . . . you're not as sure."

"Does Chester scare you?" Jennifer asked.

"Yeah. I shake when he walks into the room. God, I'll never forget the way he stood up and said to John Kingsley that he stinks. Imagine. Telling John Kingsley he stinks. That's like telling the Pope he should have been a Protestant."

"What most people do not understand," said Jennifer, "is that Chester operates solely on terror. He doesn't have polish. He doesn't have class. He has business genius. He has guts. He takes chances. Chester rolls the dice, and no matter the roll, Chester keeps going. There's nobody else in the world like him. Thank God."

"How do you know him so well?" Sid asked.

"When you've been to bed with as many guys as I have, and when you've had your confidence shattered and your heart broken, it's amazing what you learn. Come on. Drink your coffee and get dressed. I've got a plane to catch."

The telephone rang. "Want me to get it?" Sid asked.

"Not unless you want to say you're my hairdresser."

"You take it," he said.

Jennifer swept down on the telephone and said in her best movie voice, "Hello."

"Jennifer, it's Chester," said the voice.

She recognized the gravelly tones. The actress in her decided to play the scene for Sid Fisher. He was such a good audience. Too bad she had never done stock in Indiana. Evidently they would have loved her there. "Chester, darling, I've hardly seen you this week."

Sid Fisher sat upright in bed spilling the coffee on the white sheets. He was scared. What if Chester wanted to come over? No. Chester wouldn't come here. Sid decided he could relax and just enjoy knowing that for the first time in his life he was probably where Chester Masterson wanted to be.

"Chester, I can't get there that fast. I have to pack, and I have other little things to tidy up." She looked meaningfully at Sid. He knew he blushed, but he couldn't help it.

"No. No," she said firmly. "You cannot come here and help me pack. I have all the help I can use. Look, Chester, there are times when even a man like you has to understand that a woman has the right to say no."

Jennifer put the phone down. Damn. It was her chance to make Chester come to her. A perfect opportunity. It was practically career insurance, and she had blown it because some hotshot Hoosier was between her sheets. What the hell. You never did these things right.

Chester put the phone down. She really was a woman worth pursuing. The note last night hadn't worked. The call today didn't take. This was one you couldn't get just by whistling. That was kind of interesting. She probably had some guy in the sack with her. Well, he'd get her away from him. That was just the kind of challenge that excited Chester.

"Are you packed yet?" Tim asked.

"Just a few cosmetics to put away," China answered.

"Well, that's appropriate." There was more kindness than sarcasm in his voice.

When the telephone rang, China answered. "Hello," she said in her little girl voice.

"China," said the voice on the other end of the phone, "I want you to come here to lunch."

"Who is this?"

"Who is this?" the voice said in anger. "It's your father, that's who."

"My father?" she was bewildered. "I didn't recognize your

voice. I never heard it on the telephone. You never called me before."

"Of course I did," he said brusquely.

"No," she said without emotion. "I remember that you never called me on the telephone. You see, when I was at school I used to wait next to the telephone every birthday, but you never called."

"You got a present, didn't you?" he asked.

"Yes."

"Well, I was going to fire that goddamned Miss Winterhaven if she didn't get your presents to you."

"Yes, Father."

"Come to lunch in an hour at my cabana," Chester commanded.

"Yes, Father," she replied.

"What did your father want?" Tim asked.

"He just invited us to lunch," China said.

"Why?"

"He didn't say. Do you know, Tim, that was the first time I ever heard my father's voice on the telephone? I didn't recognize it." She made the statement in her usual surprised little girl voice.

"The bastard," Tim said.

"Why?" asked China. "I mean, why does that make him a bastard?" She was puzzled.

"Because he has been terrible to you."

China shook her head. "No, I just think he did what he thought fathers were supposed to do. It wasn't that he didn't care. He just didn't know. Look, he invited us to lunch today. Wasn't that nice?"

Tim stopped packing and looked at China. "Hey," he said, "I wonder if that means something. I wonder if he called and invited us because he is going to make the big announcement about the presidency."

"What announcement?" asked China.

Tim forgot that China in her fogged, alcoholic world did not know the palace struggle was nearing an end. And since her discovery of AA, she had not even thought of Kiss, Inc.

"Henry is leaving Kiss, so we need a new president," he said.

"What about Jo?" China asked with fear in her voice.

"He will take Jo with him."

"Will you still let me see her?" China asked.

"If you want."

"Don't let them take Jo away." China sounded frightened.

Tim didn't know what he could do about Jo's moving, but he decided not to tell China that the move meant Switzerland. No, it was better to let China think that Henry was going to another company in New York.

"Look, China," said Tim, "your father has to appoint a new president to replace Henry. And I think he is going to do it today. Maybe it means the job will be mine. You know, since he called you for the first time . . ."

"Do you really want it?" China asked.

"Yes."

"Then I hope you get it. I'll do anything to help you get it," she promised.

"Just be your own sweet self," he said with unaccustomed tenderness. Maybe this really could be the start of a good, new life for them. China off the sauce. Tim in the president's office. Yes, it could be a good, new life. "China," he called. "I have an idea. Why don't you put the new Pink-a-ling color on your nails before we go to lunch? I have a feeling it will please your dad."

"See?" she said. "It's a good thing I didn't pack my cosmetics." Dutifully she sat at the dressing table and one by one recolored her long, square nails, the nails that marked her as Chester Masterson's daughter.

13

Chester Masterson saw his daughter's nails before he noticed her. "Where did you get that sample batch of Pink-a-ling?" he asked.

"Tim gave it to me. He brought it from the office," China replied.

"It has too much yellow in it," Chester said in annoyance. "They better clean up that color before it goes on the market."

"Tell your president," said Tim. Then Tim sat back. He thought that was a rather good statement, a fine way to open the conversation among the three of them.

They were seated in Chester's cabana, the father, the daughter, and the son-in-law. Some trio, Tim decided. The father, maybe one of the brainiest and most daring executives in the country. The daughter, maybe one of the dumbest and most frightened women in the world. And the son-in-law trying to balance the dissimilarities and bring some harmony into their lives. I ought to get the presidency just for being here, Tim thought. Well, whatever was going to happen he would know soon.

"China," said Chester, this time in a gentle tone, "did Tim tell you that Henry Burns is leaving Kiss?"

China nodded.

"Do you know what that means?" he asked.

Her eyes filled. "It means Jo is leaving me."

"Jo? Jo who?" Chester asked.

Tim interrupted. China was struggling to explain Jo's role in her life. Tim could not bear to see her so confused. "Jo is Henry's wife, and China is very devoted to her."

"I didn't know that," Chester said.

What do you know of China? Tim thought. He said nothing. I am letting my wife stumble and fumble. She's flustered, but that's all right because I will pay any price for this presidency, he realized. Only the suspense is unbearable.

"We are going to restructure Kiss," Chester said.

"What?" asked China, her face blank.

"That means," said her father, "that we are going to have a new chairman . . ."

"What about you, sir?" Tim interrupted.

"What about me?" laughed Chester. "I am going to be the same thing I have always been, the impossible guy who runs things."

Tim smiled wanly. China continued to look puzzled.

Chester turned to Tim. At least Tim could follow the conversation. How could he be the father of a dimwit like China? Maybe he wasn't. What the hell. It was too late to think things like that. "Listen, Tim," Chester began, as if Tim were not listening with full attention. "We need some big organizational charts to make the bankers happy. So we'll reorganize. I don't care what title I get. The title doesn't matter. No matter what happens, I am still Chester Masterson, and I am Kiss. And as long as I live, that's the way it will be. The thing is that Wall Street is afraid I won't live forever, so they want some other people to get some of the titles. My new title is chairman of the executive committee.

"Congratulations," said Tim sarcastically. "Now who else is to be congratulated?"

"That's what I want to talk to China about," Chester said.

Tim sucked in his breath. Oh, it was going to happen. He smiled.

"The new chairman," said Chester, "is going to be Lord Edmondson."

"Brilliant," said Tim. He would love working for him, for Lord Edmondson was an acknowledged genius in international marketing.

"To bring him in, I have to give him stock, more stock than

you would imagine," said Chester. "In order to do that, I need some of your stock, China. You and your children have a lot that has been put in your names, and I want it back. You know, of course, that I am trustee of that stock and will be until you are thirty-five. So I'm selling your stock now. I just wanted to tell you. We'll pay book value, of course."

Book value? Tim reeled. Book value was about one tenth of the current market value. Chester was about to reduce China's fortune by ninety per cent. So this was the price they were to pay for the presidency. Tim smiled a small, crooked smile. "How much of the stock are you selling?"

"Hmmmm," said Chester slowly as he calculated the risk. If he could get all of China's stock, he would not have to give up any of his. Yes, that would be the best thing. But would they give it up without complaint? Chester hated ugly scenes. He'd have to continue to dangle the presidency. Tim, obviously, would do anything for the title including stripping his wife's fortune. "I think," said Chester, "I will sell it all."

"What if she wants to keep some?" asked Tim.

"Oh," said Chester offhandedly. "I don't think that would be too good an idea." Then he looked at Tim once more. Tim thought he could read an unspoken promise in Chester's eyes. Chester repeated, "You don't think keeping some stock would be a good idea, do you?"

"Not as long as there's stock left for the president," Tim said pointedly. With a little luck he might even change the balance of power in his household.

Chester loved cat-and-mouse games. Tim was better than Chester expected. "There will be stock left for the president," Chester promised. "Now it's agreed. Kiss, Inc., will buy China's stock at book value. And here are the papers to sign." Chester's lawyers appeared as if by magic, and when Tim nodded and smiled, China signed.

The meeting was over. Chester slapped his knees to indicate that he was finished. "Shall we go around the pool now and join our guests for lunch?" he asked.

Tim stood and extended his hand to Chester. "Isn't there something you want to say about the presidency, sir, before we go to lunch?"

Chester stood and ignored Tim's proffered hand. "Yes, I want to say one thing about the presidency. Tim, you're not getting it."

Chester walked down the steps of the cabana to the pool. The umbrella table looked so inviting with its beautifully set crystal service. Everyone stood as Chester descended. He smiled. There was nothing like power to remind you of your manhood. He looked at all of them.

Henry. Well, he had certainly given Henry his opportunities. He'd go on to some company thinking he had a chance to shape the world. Chester laughed to himself. Henry was going to find that he was nothing but a paid president. No matter what title Chester had or gave himself he was always the head man. The born president.

Jo. Henry's wife. Too bad she had that drinking problem. Nice-looking woman. First time he had ever noticed she had big tits. He wondered if she were any good in bed.

Ken. A hard worker who kept looking over both shoulders to make sure everyone knew how hard he was working. No style. But then Chester and Henry always had enough style so Ken didn't need any.

Linda. Ken's wife. No, it was the other way around. Ken was Linda's husband. She was a real four-baller.

Jennifer. Why couldn't he get in bed with her? She sure as hell wasn't protecting her virginity.

Sharon. He'd get her yet. No, not in bed. Fat asses in blue jeans were not for him. But he'd get her to work at Kiss. She looked smart.

Barbara. Too cold for him, but he wondered whether it was true that Henry was making out with her. She was too intellectual to be good in bed. But she sure as the devil was good in business.

"Sit down," Chester said gaily. "I want champagne. We are here to celebrate today." Chester debated saying that he had fired Henry. No, he'd let that story be circulated in the trade. It was better here to accept Henry's story. "Henry is leaving us," Chester announced. Then he could not refrain from adding, "I will not mention under what circumstances . . ." Chester laughed loudly at his own joke. No one else smiled. "Now you are probably wondering what will happen to Kiss, Inc., without Henry. Will we continue in business? Yes," he said emphatically. Then he pounded the table. "We will definitely continue in business." Still no one smiled.

"No, Henry is not going to put us out of business." Little beads of perspiration broke out on Henry's forehead. This was not Chester's usual cruel banter. This was supercruel. "We are going to have a new kind of management, a new kind of direction at Kiss," Chester promised, "because we are going to become a multinational and actively seek new markets, new products, and sophisticated marketing and management. Therefore, I am proud to announce that Lord Edmondson has accepted the chairmanship of Kiss, Inc. I know you are all wondering what will happen to me. Not much, but I will get a new title. I will be chairman of the executive committee."

He sat down. There was no sound.

Then Chester stood up again, an impish grin on his face. "Oh, one more thing that will probably interest you. The new president of Kiss will be Barbara Anderson."

Barbara gasped. All her hard-earned cool deserted her. "Who?" Her voice was hoarse.

There was polite, contained applause around the table followed by appreciative laughs at her question. It was the unspoken question of the other guests, too.

"Stand up, Barbara, you're the president," Chester commanded.

"I think you're putting me on," she said, rising slowly to her feet.

"I don't joke about things like that," Chester said. "Do you know why I am making you president?"

She shook her head.

"Because you are the only one here who can be my next president. I told you Kiss, Inc., is going multinational. You heard that, too, didn't you, Henry? Lord Edmondson is going to make us a big multinational, and the product to take us into the world market will not be a lipstick or nail enamel. No, it will be the thing that until today has been Product Q. From this day on it will be known by its trade name, the Chester Masterson Lift. You,

Barbara, are the one who believed in that product. You made it come to life. Now you'll have the chance to let it grow up and take its rightful place in the beauty world."

"I don't know what to say."

"Try saying very little," Chester said dryly. "I don't like people who talk all the time."

Barbara was not sure whether she ate lunch, just drank champagne, or did neither. She did not remember the congratulations of the people around the table. She did remember that Chester and his attorney took her up to the cabana, and the three of them sat around a table together.

"You're not afraid of the job?" asked Chester.

"A little. I'm overwhelmed. I never expected it," she admitted.

"You know when I decided to give it to you?" he asked.

She shook her head.

"When I realized my other possibilities. It's all right to bring in a chairman from the outside for a good reason, but how would it look if Kiss couldn't even find a president in its own organization? I couldn't hire both a chairman and a president from the outside. Tim couldn't have the job because he isn't smart enough. Ken couldn't have the job because his wife is too smart. If I'm going to have a woman run the company, it might as well be a woman who's already working here."

"I can't make this company my entire life the way you have," she said to Chester. "I want to be able to live a little, too."

"What does that mean?" he asked.

"It means I may be getting married within the next year," she said.

"It's all right with me," said Chester, "as long as Kiss is your lover."

She was pretty sure what he meant. She was anxious to get out and call Paul. It made her feel good to have someone to call, someone who cared. She wondered what Henry thought.

Should I broach the subject of Barbara's presidency? Jo asked herself. Well, why not? After all, it is a fact of life, Jo decided, and at my age I ought to be able to deal with the facts of life. "What do you think about Barbara's new job?" Jo asked Henry.

"What do you mean what do I think?" Henry was irritated.

They were packing for their trip back to New York.

"I mean would you have guessed it would be Barbara?" she asked.

"Why not?" The anger was beginning to edge his voice.

"After all," said Jo, "she was your protégée, and I would guess that you would be proud to have her recognized."

"She was not my protégée."

"But you taught her so much," Jo said.

"Where did you hear that?"

Jo was going to tell him she heard it in the sauna. No, she would not add to their problems. "Oh, just around, I guess."

"Well, it's not true. She did it on her own."

"Henry, my dear, none of us does anything on our own. For example, you have not built your career on your own. In fact, you built some of it on my own . . ."

"Oh, thank you. It's all you," he said sarcastically. "Then don't let me forget to thank you for getting me out of Kiss and into a foreign country just when Kiss is going multinational, and I could have had all my dreams. Thanks a lot."

"So that's it," she said quietly. "When it came right down to it, you didn't really want to leave. You were forced out."

"Not until the end," he said defensively.

"What if I had been more understanding in the beginning, a few days ago when you first said you wanted to leave? What if I had said then you ought to leave Kiss? Would that have made a difference?"

"Listen," said Henry, "my career is *my* career. Don't start interpreting it the way Linda does her husband's. I will still make the decisions."

"I understand."

"I cannot let you live my career. I want you in my home, but let's leave business out of it."

There was a small knife twisting inside her, but she knew now that he was hurting, too. And she knew the reasons. Yet she could not simply be a tool in his life. She must make one last effort. "Henry, I have had to do a lot of thinking about myself in the last few days. When I told China about myself, I think I opened a part of me that I had supposed was locked for good.

That was helpful. Strange, but in trying to comfort her, I helped myself. I know now that I can move with you, that I can face people knowing about me. I finally learned that I have the courage to accept myself for what I am. I do ask one thing, however. Please, my dear, let me be a part of your decisions. Don't take me by surprise again. Don't just burst in with news of a big, new change in our lives."

He shook his head. "You have to take me for what I am, Jo." To himself he said, If Barbara wouldn't take me for what I am, then you must. If you don't, how can I justify staying with you? She would not be the perfect mistress, so you must be the perfect wife.

"But will you share your life with me?" she asked. "Your business life?"

"No," he said firmly.

Jo was stunned. She had asked in tenderness and love, and she had been rebuffed. Henry had just told her that no price was too great for him to demand in order for her to remain his wife. Maybe in time things will . . . yet now, she knew that he must understand that she was hurt. "Henry," she said, "I'm not an indifferent woman. It will hurt me not to be a part of your major decisions."

"That," said Henry, "is the kind of hurt that goes with the territory."

"Your father," said Tim, "is the meanest man in the world."

China just sat and looked at her Pink-a-ling nails.

"Your father," said Tim, "is so rotten that I cannot believe he can live with so much meanness inside him."

China studied the square nails that she had colored just for her father.

"Listen, China," said Tim, "you are not a very rich little girl anymore. You have some cash, but you're not worth the millions you were when you woke up this morning."

China put her head down on her arms and began to cry.

"Don't cry," he said, putting an arm around her.

China lifted her tear-stained face. "Then you're leaving?"

"No," said Tim, "we're leaving. I'll never work at Kiss again.

It's funny, China, but I feel good. Your father may have done us a favor. He bought us two tickets out of Kiss."

China nodded. She stood up and kissed him on the cheek.

He held her close. She had been willing to do anything for him, anything he wanted to help his career. He felt such tenderness toward her. He was choked with emotion. "I love you, China," he said, "and I am going to take care of you."

China sighed. Her life certainly had changed this week. She had found a husband and a second mother. She had lost a father. But then she had never had one.

China kissed Tim gently, patted his cheek, and began to pack her things. On the sink in the bathroom were strewn the half-packed cosmetics she had left to attend luncheon with her father. She began to pack them slowly. Nail enamel. Into the bag. File. Into the bag. Manicure scissors. She eyed them for a few moments, and then instead of putting them into her bag, she did what she had wanted to do all her life. China cut each of her ten square, polished nails down to the quick.

When she finished, she looked at her hands. For the first time in her life she was not Chester Masterson's daughter.

She was Tim Edgar's wife.

"So you're still the chief flunky," Linda said to Ken.

"There are worse things in life," said Ken.

"I can't think of anything worse than owing your very existence to a madman."

"Oh, Chester's not a madman," said Ken.

"Then why did he stage that God-awful lunch? Why did he play that whole power number and embarrass each of us by making us watch him name Barbara the president?"

"He wanted to make Barbara feel important," said Ken.

"You are dumber than I thought," she said in exasperation.

Ken said nothing.

"Grandma Eisman wouldn't have stood by," said Linda.

"What would she have done?" asked Ken.

"She would have stood up and . . . and . . . and . . ."

"And what?"

"And walked out," said Linda, surprised by her own answer. "And that is what I am going to do."

"What?" asked Ken, bewildered.

"I am going to walk out. See this?" She held up a casette. "In here is a tape I made with Brandy McCarthy. It opens a whole can of worms. It has Mafia stuff that can fill all the jails in America. And it can do something else. It can buy my freedom."

"Buy your freedom?" Ken was puzzled.

"Ever since I got here, ever since I had breakfast with Jennifer, I knew that I would have to find my own way out. Jennifer told me I couldn't keep pushing you. I had to find my own way. When I saw Brandy McCarthy, I knew I had found the way. All I needed was to get her to spill some good stuff. So I worked on her. You know how good I am at asking questions. I got everything I needed. But then I had to have proof in case somebody put out a contract on her. So I grabbed her and took her into the steam room and borrowed Sharon's tape machine. Now I've got the story I need to get me a job on any magazine, newspaper or . . ."

"A job on a magazine? But you're a wife and mother," he protested.

"Wrong," she said. "I'm about to become an ex-wife and a working mother."

Sharon took out her one piece of scarred canvas luggage. She debated. Should she pack the free cosmetics they gave her? Might as well. Somebody at the magazine might want them.

She looked at the tape recorder. For all the good it did her, she should have left it in New York.

All around her people were picking up what was left of their lives and packing the pieces in fancy suitcases. She wondered what was left of her life. Time would tell about Tom. He was out finding himself. And she was . . . she was just out. She felt a great sadness. Was that because she saw business firsthand?

No, that luncheon had been nothing but a scene Chester staged. It had nothing to do with business. It was his personality, his way of doing things. She threw a shirt in the canvas bag. Maybe that's all business was anyway. Just men. And women. And their way of doing things.

*

Chester looked at the group on his plane as they took off from the small Gates of Paradise airstrip.

Barbara, now composed and over the first flush of surprise, was hard at work at the plane desk with Ken. Somebody said Linda was going back alone via Reno or Mexico.

Henry and Jo decided to fly commercial.

So did China and Tim.

Sharon was reading. Chester had decided to give her a ride back when Jennifer suggested it.

Jennifer. Yes, Jennifer suggested it after lunch when they went back to his room. Now she was playing gin rummy with him at the little table. It was a nice feeling to have a woman with him.

He looked from the cards to her face. "Why didn't you go to bed with me today?" he asked.

"I'm saving it, Chester."

"For what?" he asked.

"New York. Ever done it under a mirror?"

He felt the excitement creep from his collar to the roots of his hair.

"You will tonight," she said matter-of-factly.

"Just tonight?" he asked.

She cut the cards sharply. "Play your cards right, Chester, and then we'll see."

Epilogue

Chester rolled over and looked up at the ceiling. He'd never get used to that damned mirror Jennifer insisted on having over the bed.

"Awake?" he asked sleepily.

"Awake enough to start raising hell at another convention," she answered.

He looked at the long, sensual body next to him. Damn. The sight of her still excited him. And it had been a year. A whole year. This was the first time in his life he had ever had one good year with a woman.

"Who's going on the plane with us?" Jennifer asked.

"I don't know," said Chester. "Why don't you decide on the passenger list?"

"Chester," she teased, "don't tell me you're giving up some of your power."

"Well," said Chester, "if you can't give your wife the right to pick her own guest list, what can you give her?"

"Another thousand shares of Kiss stock," Jennifer said quickly.

"What are you doing?" Paul asked.

"Packing for the Kiss convention," Barbara answered.

"Hell," he said, "I forgot it was this weekend."

"I told you twice," she said sharply.

In three months of marriage Paul Thurston had learned that her sharp tone was a danger signal. It meant Barbara was hurting. He could not always find the source of the hurt, but he had learned how to start the healing process. "I'm going with you," he said.

"Oh, you'll probably hate it," she said in a voice that meant she expected him to corroborate her fears about his going.

"I'll take plenty of work with me so I'll not be underfoot," he promised.

She felt guilt pangs. Of course he had canceled patients to be with her. She did not want to offend Paul. It was time to make amends. "It's a nice marriage, isn't it?" she asked as she took his hand.

"When we both look up from our desks, it is," he answered.

"But it's been such a busy year," she sighed.

"Judging by hindsight," he said, "the Chester Masterson Lift is going to be your first big product success."

"Lord Edmondson is going to make it a worldwide smash," she said with delight.

"And you're managing to love the product, but not the man?" Paul asked, half joking. He had not mentioned the Pink Balloon in months.

"Don't tease," she said. "I'll always have scar tissue."

Barbara turned back to her packing. So this is what it was all about. This is what life was. You worked like hell in school and at a job. Finally you got the presidency and your picture on magazine covers. You got pensions and annuities, and they gave you gifts of stock. You knew you would never be poor or cold or hungry. And somewhere along the way you found a man who patted your hand and was acceptable to your friends. It was all summed up in a fortune cookie she read a few months ago, "You are doomed to a happy marriage."

If this was supposed to be the American dream, and she had it, why did she feel so let down?

Barbara Anderson Thurston sighed. She'd think about it again after the convention. She was really too busy now.

Linda Sugarman picked up the phone. "Me? Cover the Kiss convention? Charlie, you must be crazy.

"Look," she continued, "I guess you forgot that my ex-husband works for Kiss, and I went through all those political machinations last year. Now that I'm with *Newsweek,* I want to get away from that kind of assignment.

"Sure, sure, I know that the Brandy McCarthy tapes got me page-one stuff and TV coverage every night. Sure I know it got me my job with you and gave you your best Mafia story. And you know the Mafia doesn't scare me one bit. I'd go right back and do a story on them again.

"But you want to know what really scares the hell out of me?

"I'll tell you. Chester Masterson. Yes, Chester Masterson still scares me.

"I don't want to lose my job, Charlie, but please send somebody else to cover Kiss Plus One: The Year of the Woman President."

Ken Sugarman filled his briefcase with the papers he would need for his presentation at the Kiss convention.

Just a year ago he had dreaded the convention.

This year he could hardly wait for it to start.

Lord Edmondson was his kind of man. For the first time in his life Ken was supervising a project without advice from Linda. He was co-ordinating the Chester Masterson Lift for worldwide entry.

Brigit Swenson, Ken's bright assistant, poked her head in the office. "Anything I can do to help? Hey," she said, "you're wearing a new suit. You look terrific. A vest, too. You are distinguished."

"Distinguished enough to buy an associate a drink?" he asked.

"Me?" she queried.

"You," he answered.

"Me," she said.

"One more thing, Brigit."

"Yes, Ken."

"I think it might be a good idea if you went to the Kiss convention with me. It will mean a lot of work because I want to send memos, get some information from the men on the United Kingdom, and . . ."

"I'll go," she interrupted.

Ken took a deep breath and smiled. He stuffed the papers in his briefcase. He didn't have to study anymore. He didn't have to be nervous. The work was there. When you're good, you're good. And nobody has to tell you.

"Sharon, where is the group having dinner the first night of the convention?" Jeff Garfield, the head of Kiss public relations, asked.

"Shit, I forgot," Sharon said as she got up from behind the big walnut desk.

"What do you mean you forgot?" Jeff asked, annoyance emphasizing each word.

She walked over to the window overlooking Central Park. "I can't remember all those fancy things," she said.

"Try, baby, try."

She furrowed her brow. "Listen, it's enough I wear dresses now that I am associate vice-president of Kiss communications."

"How you got that fucking title is something I do not understand," said Jeff.

"I said no to Chester so many times that he realized he could not offer me a job. So he offered me a position. You see, Jennifer and I both know something you never learned, Jeff. We know that the only way to make Chester say yes is for you to say no."

China was sitting on the floor reading with the children and Mademoiselle when Tim came into the room. "And what are my babies doing?" he asked.

"Oh, Tim, we're all learning French together," China said, her pretty face animated.

"Now that we're in Switzerland, that is a very good idea," he said.

"We are going to stay, aren't we?" China asked in a concerned tone.

"Of course," he answered, bending to kiss the top of her head. "We are going to stay because Henry has given me a superb chance to work at Oxxon, and you can be near Jo. And we are going to show your father that we can survive without him."

She stood up and said, "I'm so happy, Tim." Then she cupped her hand to his ear, stood on her tiptoes, and whispered, "As soon as I learn to read French, I'm going to learn to read English."

*

Jo and Henry sat at the long, polished table, and the servants moved quietly between them.

"We do have excellent meals here, don't we?"

"You always find great cooks," Henry said.

"Yes, I believe that staffing a house is very important."

"Do you find it more difficult in Europe?"

"Mmmm, no," she said finally. "Of course after a year I have learned my way around."

"A year?" he asked. "A year since we are here?" He put his fork down and stared into space. A year since the Kiss convention. A year since Chester Masterson had turned Henry's life around. It had been some year. He had called Barbara a few times, but she never returned his calls. Had he not been so busy, he probably would have thought more about the unreturned calls. As it was he was trying to work with new people, new rules, and a whole new style of business. God knows these Swiss did not think like Americans. They were giving Henry his chance, his golden dream, his opportunity to be president of a multinational. But it was no bed of roses. The chairman, Heinrich Glassheim, had his own ideas about the way Oxxon should be run. And he did not want to Americanize the business according to Henry's beliefs. Each day was a challenge.

"Darling," said Jo, breaking his reverie, "the wine has been poured. Shall we toast?" Although she never drank, she always toasted.

Henry raised his wineglass. "To you, my dear, the lovely lady who runs my home. And," he added, "to Heinrich Glassheim, the son of a bitch who runs my life."